TWO MEN'S HONOR

The gun was pointed directly at the Texas Ranger's chest.

"This is for you, Silver Spurs," the cattle rustler said, his lips quirking into a smile as he flipped the gun around in his hand and presented it butt first to Cody.

Taking the weapon, Cody looked narrowly at Alvarez for a long moment. Then he slipped the Navy Colt behind his belt and said, "You could have gotten away. I was too busy to stop you."

"No, gringo, I could not. You forget. I gave you my word." He shook his head, adding, "I can see by the look of surprise on your face that you think I live outside the law, but it is just that my law is different from yours. And my word *is* my law. So I will go with you to Del Rio. But have no fear. We will meet again. Your gringo justice will not hold me for long."

Alvarez then guided his horse closer to the wagon and held his wrists against the saddle horn so they could be tied up again.

Cody hesitated for a moment, then kicked the brake lever to release the wheels of the wagon. "I don't reckon I need a rope, Alvarez. I've got your word. That'll do." Then the Texas Ranger slapped the reins against the backs of the horses and pointed them toward Del Rio, his prisoner riding proud and erect alongside him.

CODY'S LAW
Volume I

GUNMETAL JUSTICE

Matthew S. Hart

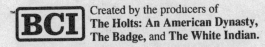

BCI™   Created by the producers of
The Holts: An American Dynasty,
The Badge, and **The White Indian.**

Book Creations Inc., Canaan, NY • Lyle Kenyon Engel, Founder

BANTAM BOOKS
NEW YORK · TORONTO · LONDON · SYDNEY · AUCKLAND

CODY'S LAW: GUNMETAL JUSTICE

*A Bantam Domain Book / published by arrangement with
Book Creations, Inc.*

Bantam edition / June 1991

*Produced by Book Creations, Inc.
Lyle Kenyon Engel, Founder*

*DOMAIN and the portrayal of a boxed "d" are trademarks of
Bantam Books, a division of Bantam Doubleday Dell Publishing
Group, Inc.*

ISBN 0-553-29030-4

Published simultaneously in the United States and Canada

Bantam Books are published by Bantam Books, a division of Bantam
Doubleday Dell Publishing Group, Inc. Its trademark, consisting of
the words "Bantam Books" and the portrayal of a rooster, is Regis-
tered in U.S. Patent and Trademark Office and in other countries.
Marca Registrada. Bantam Books, 666 Fifth Avenue, New York, New
York 10103.

PRINTED IN THE UNITED STATES OF AMERICA

RAD   0 9 8 7 6 5 4 3 2 1

For Livia, Shayna, and Joanna

"No man in the wrong can stand up against a man in the right who keeps on a-coming."

—Texas Ranger
Captain William "Wild Bill" McDonald

CHAPTER

||||||||||||||||||||||||| **1** |||||||||||||||||||||||||

A strong south breeze coming off the high central plains of Texas hit Cody in the face, bringing with it the smell of rain and a flurry of sounds. Must be a storm coming, he decided, giving a thoughtful tug on his reddish-brown mustache. He hoped he could get Alvarez to Del Rio before the weather turned.

Again the indistinct sounds drifted to the tall Texas Ranger's ears, and Cody pulled his bay gelding up short. One hand gripping the brim of his dark brown Stetson, he sat motionless in the saddle, listening intently. Behind him his prisoner wasn't making the task any easier.

"So now you are hearing things, eh, Silver Spurs?" Diego Alvarez hissed. "There is nothing out there. Only the lizards and these stinking treeless hills. And these ropes are too tight. My wrists are turning white like"—he spat in contempt—"like a damned gringo."

Cody paid no attention to the bandit. Alvarez had been muttering one complaint after another—the heat, his thirst, the rope bindings—for the past four days, ever since Cody had caught up to him in a San Antonio whorehouse. Alvarez had been about to take his pleasure with a girl when Cody had stepped into the room, clouted the Mexican's head with the butt of his Colt, then shoved him off the bed and onto the floor. The girl had screamed for a moment until Cody tipped his hat and smiled at her. Then she had started getting different ideas about the lean and muscular stranger who had so violently interrupted her business.

Unfortunately there had not been time for anything like that. Cody had gotten Alvarez's clothes back on him, tied him up, and put him on a horse. When the Mexican's senses had returned, Cody had officially arrested him in the name of the state of Texas for leading a band of cattle rustlers that had been plaguing the border area. Now, on the fourth day out of San Antonio, they were about an hour's ride from Ranger headquarters, where Alvarez would be held until the Val Verde County sheriff arranged to have him transported to El Paso to stand trial.

Alvarez had kept up his complaining the whole time, as if probing for a weakness in Cody's defenses, but he had never once betrayed any humiliation at being caught with his pants down by a gringo lawman and lashed to the saddle like a trussed-up turkey. He sat as proud and erect as any Indian chief or Spanish grandee, his short, stocky build confirming his Mexican-Cherokee parentage. His close-set brown eyes sat like dark bullet holes on either side of a hawkish beak of a nose, and his only facial hair was a straggly mustache that hung like twisted strands of wire from the corners of his mouth.

The rustler had given Cody the nickname Silver Spurs shortly after they had begun this trek through the southern foothills of the Blue Mountains. The first time he had used the name, he had nodded at Cody's spurs and said, "And so, Señor Silver Spurs, you are a gringo as vain as you are foolhardy. I might have been blinded by your shiny spurs once, but it is a long ride to Del Rio—and it will be a long time before your Ranger justice gets the best of Diego Alvarez."

The bandit's mocking words had left no doubt as to the disdain with which he viewed Cody and his fellow Texas Rangers. But each day saw yet another failed escape attempt, and Alvarez's tone became increasingly, though begrudgingly, respectful.

Cody kneed his horse toward the top of the hill

ahead, certain now that he *had* heard something. Alvarez, his hands tied securely to the saddle horn and his horse's reins lashed to Cody's mount, had no choice but to follow.

As the Ranger cautiously rode forward, he checked the cylinder of his long-barreled Frontier Colt. The hammer was resting on an empty chamber, but the other five were loaded. After returning the revolver to its holster, he lifted his Winchester '73 repeating rifle, levered a cartridge into it, and slipped it back in the saddle boot. With a final backward glance at his prisoner and an instinctive pat on the foot-long bowie knife sheathed on his belt, he rode over the rise and surveyed the panorama below.

A mesquite-dotted valley stretched far to the north into the Edwards Plateau. A ribbon of water meandered along the valley floor, easing its way to the Rio Grande, and on the near side of the stream, at the base of the hill on which Cody and his prisoner sat their horses, a rutted wagon road provided a passageway between the Rio Grande and the central plains of Texas.

Cody squinted as he tried to make out the objects rapidly approaching from the north along the narrow wagon trace. "Comanch'," he finally said under his breath, his horse already stirring restlessly under him.

"Yes, gringo, they are Comanche," Alvarez agreed, a hint of a smile playing across his mouth. "And I will slow you down, tied up like this." Indicating the bindings on his wrists, he suggested, "Let me loose, and you can ride like hell to your Rangers and bring them back before those heathens disappear again. And do not worry about me. I can get myself to El Paso." He laughed softly.

Cody felt the corners of his mouth twitching in a slight smile at the Mexican's audacity. But as he turned back to the scene in front of them, all trace of humor vanished. Before, his gaze had locked on the dozen or so Indians galloping through the valley, but now he could clearly discern that they were chasing something: a wagon with two riders, one of whom was struggling to keep the lunging pair of horses under control while the other fired a rifle at the braves quickly closing in.

Cody turned and looked uneasily at his prisoner. It was his responsibility to bring the cattle rustler to justice, but his first duty was to see to the safety of those two men below. His own guns might not be enough to turn away the Comanche attack, but his appearance so near Del Rio might convince the warriors that others were riding close behind. That left the question of whether to let Diego Alvarez go or leave him tied up here on the hill.

Alvarez seemed to read the Ranger's mind, and he nudged his mount forward alongside his captor's. Looking Cody in the eye, he declared, "If you untie me and return my pistol"—he nodded toward the holster that was draped over Cody's saddle horn—"I will ride with you against those accursed renegades." Accurately reading the dubious look that Cody gave him, he added, "It is true I am half-Cherokee, but I *spit* on the Comanche, who kill my people as quickly as they kill yours. And I will not try to escape. You have my word of honor—the word of Diego Alvarez."

Alvarez liked to hear himself talk, Cody thought, but there was something in the outlaw's tone that led the Ranger to believe he could trust the man. Besides, if he left Alvarez tied up, the outlaw would either manage to escape or be finished off by the Comanches—after they were through with Cody and the fleeing men. He could understand why Alvarez would not want to face that second possibility.

With no time to worry overmuch about it, Cody slid his bowie out of its sheath and leaned over to cut away the ropes around Alvarez's wrists. Then he lifted the holster from his saddle horn and handed it to the bandit, who quickly buckled it on.

"Let's go!" Cody shouted, and the two men spurred their mounts and raced down the hill toward the rapidly approaching Comanches.

* * *

As the wagon bounded along the hard-packed ground, Jeremiah Burgess, his white hair plastered with sweat, desperately fought the reins, trying to keep the horses in line. Although he could not see his young partner, who had climbed over the seat and was lying prone on the load of supplies, the reassuring sound of Rick Forman's Henry rifle told Burgess that his friend was still alive. But above the pounding of horses and wagon, Burgess could hear the shots and the high-pitched whoops of the Comanche war party as it narrowed the gap with its prey, and those Indians using bows were near enough now to send an occasional arrow whistling over Burgess's shoulder.

Suddenly, the Henry rifle fell silent. "Rick! You all right?" Burgess shouted over his shoulder.

He tried to convince himself that his friend was just reloading, but as the seconds passed and the shrill cries drew even closer, he forced himself to turn around on the seat. His eyes widened with shock at the grim truth.

Rick Forman was dead, half his face blown away and his body riddled with arrows. Now there was nothing between Jeremiah Burgess and the bloodthirsty Comanches but the lagging strength and spirit of two overworked horses.

Del Rio was at least an hour away, so there was little hope of rescue or assistance from that direction. For a moment, Burgess considered halting the wagon and taking a chance that the Indians would simply steal his supplies and leave him unharmed. But he had lived too long in Comanche country to believe there was a chance in hell of that happening. Forman had taken a few braves with him before dying, and with the Comanches wanting vengeance for that, Burgess's own death would be slow and tortured.

As he slapped the reins to get the last ounce of speed from his team, Burgess glanced down at the old Remington Army revolver in his holster and cursed himself for being too tightfisted to spend the twenty dollars it would have cost to convert it from a percussion model to one that used metallic cartridges. He had already used up four shots on the Indians before Forman had taken over with the Henry, which left him only a single round—certainly not enough to hold off his pursuers. And it would be next to impossible to reload a percussion gun while trying to control the galloping team.

But at least there was that one round—and one bullet was enough to end this thing before the Comanches caught up to him.

Taking the reins in his left hand and bracing his feet against the front of the wagon, Burgess lifted the revolver and pressed the muzzle up under his chin. With a final silent good-bye to his wife and a prayer to his God, he began to squeeze the old, stiff trigger.

An instant before the Remington fired, what felt like a burning poker slammed into Burgess's back just below the right shoulder blade. The impact sent the revolver spinning out of his hand, and it discharged as it struck the ground, then disappeared under the wagon. Knocked forward off the seat, Burgess automatically grabbed the side rail to keep from being thrown from the wagon. He knew what had hit him; during the Comanche uprisings of '58 and '59, he'd taken an arrow in the thigh.

Struggling back onto the seat, he steadied himself against the sickening sensation as he reached around with his left hand and felt the shaft protruding from his back. He did not know why there was so little pain . . . why he felt so strangely at peace . . . but it was as if the rough ground had leveled and softened, and the team of horses had become the mythical winged steeds of his childhood storybooks.

Seeing that the reins had fallen at his feet, Burgess cautiously bent forward and slipped them between his fingers. It seemed as though he were watching himself from a distance as he slapped the reins smartly and shouted, "Giddyap! Giddyap! *Faster!*"

And then the only thing he could see was a chariot being drawn into the clouds by two mighty steeds. Gone were the Comanches and their cries, the narrow Texas valley. Unseen as well were the two horsemen who had just appeared atop a nearby hill and were riding hell-bent for leather toward the rutted road below.

As Cody approached the careening wagon with Diego Alvarez at his side, he saw that their sudden appearance had caused the Comanches to slow down a bit. But Cody knew the Indians were just sizing up the situation and were not likely to give up the attack entirely. After all, the odds were still on their side. Cody could see that at least one of the men on the wagon—the young rifleman in back—had taken a slug and was out of action. And the white-haired driver had his hands full just keeping the horses under control.

That left the Ranger and his prisoner to face ten Comanche braves.

With a glance to the side to make sure Alvarez was still there, Cody raised his Winchester and squeezed off a shot, but the bullet missed its mark. No surprise there, Cody thought fleetingly; shooting from the back of a running horse was just about the trickiest proposition a man could attempt. He pulled his horse into a wide turn that brought him alongside the wagon, heading in the same direction, then motioned Alvarez to the other side. As they began to pull even with the vehicle, Cody turned and tried a second shot. This one was lucky and found one of the Indian mustangs, sending both horse and rider plunging to the ground.

Drawing closer to the wagon, Cody saw the arrow sticking out of the driver's back and marveled that the old man was managing to keep control of the team. Figuring the man could not keep going for long in that condition, Cody lifted his right leg over the saddle and urged his horse closer to the wagon. When the animal had matched the pace of the team, he tossed his rifle onto the wagon bed, then slipped his left foot out of the

stirrup and swung both legs over the side of the vehicle. Pushing off the saddle, he grabbed frantically at
the sideboards, then dropped down into the wagon
bed.

Cody snatched up his rifle and levered a cartridge
into place. Steadying himself against the bags and
crates, he took careful aim and fired again, and this
time the slug thudded into his target's naked chest and
spilled the Indian from his horse. Cody glanced at the
other side of the wagon and saw that Álvarez had just
downed a third brave.

With Alvarez covering him on horseback, Cody
crawled across the baggage to where the rifleman lay
sprawled. One glance at the lifeless form told him the
man was dead. Climbing over the seat, Cody dropped
down next to the older man, who seemed to be driving
the team in a trance, totally oblivious to what was
going on around him.

"You all right?" Cody shouted over the din of battle
as he shook the man's arm.

The wagoner slowly shifted on the seat and stared
uncertainly at the Ranger, as if he were seeing a ghost.
Then with a slight shake of the head, he pulled his arm
free of Cody's grip and turned back to the horses.

With a sharp, whistling *thunk,* an arrow pierced the
seat back an inch from Cody's shoulder. Spinning
around, he dropped to his knees in front of the seat,
then lifted his rifle over the backrest, searching for a
target. The remaining Comanches were riding in tight
formation close behind the wagon. Cody sighted on the
lead brave, then fired, missed, quickly levered the gun,
and fired again. The brave clutched at his chest as he
was knocked backward over the horse's rump. He
landed under the galloping hooves of the horse right
behind, causing it to stumble and throw its rider.

Alvarez followed with three quick shots from his
pistol, hitting yet another Indian. This brave managed
to stay on his horse, and he jerked the animal's mane
and turned it away from the chase. The other four war-

riors abruptly veered their horses as well, giving up the attack.

Cody lowered his rifle and watched as the Co- manches paused to pick up the braves who had been thrown from their horses. Moments later, the swiftly riding band disappeared into the hills to the northeast. Dropping his rifle to the floor of the wagon, Cody turned to the driver, who was still slapping the reins, as wild-eyed as he had been before.

"It's over," Cody told the driver in a loud voice. "Pull up, old-timer!" There was no response.

Grabbing the man's arms, Cody held on firmly, forc- ing the driver to turn and look at him. When the old man focused on the Ranger, his eyes took on a puzzled expression, and then his shoulders sagged and went limp. But his grip on the reins was as firm as ever, and Cody had to yank the man's wrists to rein in the lathered horses.

As the wagon rolled to a halt and Cody kicked on the brake, a startling transformation came over the driver. His trance seemed to break, and his body began to tremble—gently at first, then more and more violently. He pitched forward out of his seat, and just before he tumbled off the wagon, Cody caught hold of him and pulled him back onto the seat.

The man's body continued to shake uncontrollably, and he started to cough and wheeze. Cody touched the arrow in his back and tried to decide whether it would cause less damage to pull the shaft out than to force it through the other side. He glanced down at the arrow that had gone through the backrest of the buckboard seat. Its tip was protruding several inches. The ar- rowhead was narrow and long, with the base only slightly wider than the wooden shaft.

Hoping that the arrow in the old man's back was the same type, Cody decided to pull it out. He could tell it was not buried too deeply, and maybe the narrow base would cause only slightly more damage when it was removed.

Standing over the seat, Cody ripped away the wagoner's tattered shirt. He pressed his knee firmly against the small of the man's back, grasped the shaft in both hands, and pulled. As the driver screamed and started to lift up off the seat, Cody pressed harder with his knee and gave a sharp but steady upward pull. The arrow held in place for a second, then abruptly slid free, leaving a gaping hole that quickly filled with a rush of blood. The man's eyelids fluttered shut, and with a moaning sigh, he slipped into unconsciousness.

Cody tore a wide strip from the driver's shirt, wadded it into a ball, and pressed it firmly against the wound. Within seconds, it was soaked with blood, and he tossed it away and ripped another piece of cloth to replace it. The second wad did not saturate so quickly, and the third one seemed to stanch the flow of blood.

As he held this last wad of cloth in place against the wagoner's back, a voice called out from beside him, "Here, gringo, use this."

Cody looked up to see Diego Alvarez seated on his horse, holding out a long piece of cloth torn from his own shirt, which he was no longer wearing. Another strip of the shirt was tied roughly around the outlaw's upper left arm, and Cody could see the dark stain of blood on it.

"How bad is it?" Cody asked, gesturing toward the bandit's wound as he reached over and accepted the strip of cloth.

"It is of no consequence," Alvarez answered with a grin. "Just a graze. There's nothing like the taste of lead to quicken one's blood, eh?"

Nodding, Cody turned back to the wounded driver and started to wrap the cloth across the wadded bandage to hold it in place. Alvarez stepped from his horse into the wagon and helped Cody lift the unconscious man so that the makeshift bandage could be tied around his chest. When they were finished, they carefully lifted the old man over the wagon seat and made him as comfortable as possible among the supplies in back.

As Alvarez climbed off the wagon, Cody noticed that the wounded driver had opened his eyes slightly and was trying to speak. The Ranger bent over him and placed a reassuring hand on his shoulder. "We're only a few miles from Del Rio," Cody stated. "Don't try to move. We'll have you there in no time."

The man seemed to understand. He closed his eyes and almost appeared to be smiling.

Cody stepped back over the seat and picked up the reins. Beside the wagon, Alvarez was again seated on his horse, holding in one hand the reins of Cody's gelding. But it was the object in the outlaw's other hand that caught Cody's attention: the Navy Colt revolver that he had returned to Alvarez to use during the battle. The gun was pointed directly at the Texas Ranger's chest.

"This is for you, Silver Spurs," the cattle rustler said, his lips quirking into a smile as he flipped the gun around in his hand and presented it butt first to Cody.

Taking the weapon, Cody looked narrowly at Alvarez for a long moment. Then he slipped the Navy Colt behind his belt and said, "You could have gotten away. I was too busy to stop you."

"No, gringo, I could not. You forget. I gave you my word." He shook his head, adding, "I can see by the look of surprise on your face that you think I live outside the law, but it is just that my law is different from yours. And my word *is* my law. So I will go with you to Del Rio. But have no fear. We will meet again. Your gringo justice will not hold me for long."

Alvarez then guided his horse closer to the wagon and held his wrists against the saddle horn so they could be tied up again.

Cody hesitated for a moment, then kicked the brake lever to release the wheels of the wagon. "I don't reckon I need a rope, Alvarez. I've got your word. That'll do." Then the Texas Ranger slapped the reins against the backs of the horses and pointed them toward Del Rio, his prisoner riding proud and erect alongside him.

CHAPTER
2

His name was Samuel Clayton Woodbine Cody, but not many folks knew the first three parts of that long-winded moniker. With very few exceptions, to friends and enemies alike—and he had made plenty of both in his thirty-two years—he was just Cody.

He had been a lawman most of his adult life, first as a deputy sheriff in El Paso, then as a Texas Ranger since the force had been officially reactivated a year earlier in 1874. Cody's father had packed a badge, too, helping to organize the original Rangers in 1835 during the Texas Revolution. It was Adam Cody who had first worn the silver spurs—a gift from the Mexican land baron Alonso Morillo for having saved his life during the Comanche uprising in 1838.

Twenty-one years later, when young Sam Cody was sixteen, Adam—by then a successful rancher—was ambushed by a band of rustlers who had good reason to fear his skill with a gun. But in the years before his murder, the elder Cody had passed along that skill—along with his spurs—to the younger, who was equally handy with knife, lasso, tomahawk, and bow and arrow. Now Cody wore those silver spurs with a deep sense of pride—a symbol of the commitment to justice that Adam Cody had embodied and had instilled in his son.

Left with his mother and three older sisters to take care of, as well as a ranch, Cody had grown up in a hurry. Somehow he held the place together and kept it going, and two years later, when most of his friends left to join the Confederate Army at the outbreak of the Civil War, Cody stayed home. That ate at him, but he felt that his first responsibility was to his family. Plenty of his friends did not return from the war, and that hurt, too. Eventually, all three of his sisters married good Texas men, and Cody left the ranch in capable hands when he rode away to see if he could find the bandits who had bushwhacked his father.

He didn't like to think about that time in his life very often, for it had been full of blood and death, and the score had never been settled to his liking. But he had learned that even if he had been able to track down every member of the rustler gang and kill them, the deaths would not solve anything or bring his father back. It was that realization—and the heritage of Adam Cody—that had kept Cody from straying across the line into lawlessness himself. Too restless to return to the family ranch and a life of raising cattle, he had drifted into law work, thinking that maybe someday he'd go back home to stay, but not now. . . .

Not really handsome—his features were a bit too rugged and weather-beaten for that—Cody invariably clothed his tall, lean body in a black leather vest over a faded blue work shirt and denim pants tucked into high-topped boots, finished off with a dark brown, high-crowned Stetson. He could easily have been mistaken for a typical cow-country range rider—if not for the five-pointed star set in a silver circle pinned to his vest. Cody had carved the Ranger badge himself out of a Mexican ten-peso coin. His father's badge—which had also been handmade, and which Cody had hoped as a child to wear when he grew up—had been lost during one of the family's moves before they settled down on the ranch near Bandera.

He was a member of the Frontier Battalion, under the overall command of Major John B. Jones; his unit, Company C, was commanded by Captain Wallace Vickery and headquartered in Del Rio, halfway be-

tween Brownsville and El Paso, and it was through the
streets of that border town that Cody drove the wagon,
about an hour after the fight with the Comanches.

Men and women crowded along the boardwalks,
nodding and whispering among themselves. Store-
keepers, hearing the commotion, dropped their aprons
and hurried out to join the crowd, while children
scrambled out onto the dusty road, staring and pointing at the arrows that had turned the back of the buckboard into a pincushion.

"It's Alvarez!" one of the onlookers suddenly
shouted, and all movement stopped, except for one
mother bold enough to dash into the street and pull her
child to safety.

Cody paid little attention to the crowd as he drove
the wagon toward the far end of the street, where the
adobe structure housing Texas Ranger headquarters
stood beside the town jail. Rangers reported in at the
Company C building but were required to provide their
own food and lodgings. They used their own horses
and wore their own clothing, for there was no such
thing as a regulation Ranger uniform, and most of the
men wore the same denims and work shirts that nearly
everybody else in the West wore. Weapons and sometimes badges were the only things provided by the or-
ganization.

By the time Cody pulled the wagon up in front of
Company C headquarters, several Rangers had already gathered outside to see what the commotion was
about.

"Seth, Alan, there's a wounded man in the back,"
Cody called to a couple of his younger colleagues.
"Carry him to Doc's." As the two youthful lawmen
hurried over and began to lift the wounded driver from
the wagon, Cody climbed down and waited while his
prisoner dismounted.

Just then one of the other Rangers focused on the
shirtless Mexican stranger. Yanking his pistol from its
holster, the Ranger leaped down from the porch and
exclaimed, "Gawddamn, that there's Diego Alvarez!"

The Ranger reached out to grab hold of the prisoner, but Cody's fingers caught the man's wrist in an iron grasp. "Put that gun down," he said coolly. "No need for it here."

"But that's Alvarez! And he ain't even tied up."

"I know," Cody retorted.

The other man lowered his weapon in surprise, and when Cody let go of his wrist, the Ranger backed away and watched incredulously as Cody motioned toward the jail and said to Alvarez, "I have to turn you over to the sheriff. He'll take care of sending you on to El Paso."

Alvarez nodded and started past Cody, who stopped him with a hand on his arm. "I'd be glad to put in a word for you, tell the sheriff how you pitched in to help fight those Comanches today. Might do you some good when it comes time for sentencing."

Alvarez smirked at the other Rangers who were watching, then turned to Cody and said, "You are a brave man—a man of honor, Silver Spurs. But I do not think your testimony will be necessary in court. As I told you earlier, your gringo justice will not hold me for long. On that I again give you my word of honor."

Cody had to smile back at the bandit, then gave a small shake of his head and led the way over to the sheriff's office. Inside, he turned the Mexican over to Sheriff Christian Burke, an efficient, well-meaning, and unassuming hulk of a man in his late forties. Cody knew Burke often felt that he was working in the shadow of the Texas Rangers, whose presence in Del Rio guaranteed a reasonably quiet town. Even so, the pressures of trying to keep order on the Texas frontier had given his deep-set gray eyes a faint nervous tic, and his long, bulbous nose was beginning to show evidence of his growing reliance on the bottle for off-duty relaxation.

"Alvarez says his wound is just a graze," Cody told the sheriff, "but have Doc look it over as soon as he's done at headquarters. Don't want it to fester."

"What's the matter, Silver Spurs?" Alvarez asked as

the sheriff ushered him into the jail cell in back. "Are you afraid of losing so famous an outlaw as Diego Alvarez before he even reaches the courtroom?"

Before Cody could answer, Sheriff Burke muttered, "Don't worry, you cow-thievin' bastard. I'll make sure you're good and healthy by the time you reach El Paso. I know how bad they feel when they have to hang a wounded man."

Cody sighed. Burke wasn't a bad lawman, but he wasn't a very pleasant man. The Ranger was leaving the jail when Alvarez called out, "Silver Spurs! I truly hope our paths cross again someday—but under friendlier circumstances."

"For your sake, Alvarez," Cody replied, "I hope they don't." Then he opened the door and stepped back out into the early-afternoon sun. The cool breeze that had swept through the area earlier seemed to be gone now, and he decided he had been wrong about a storm blowing in. He stood on the porch for a moment and looked across the street at the Rio Grande Hotel, where a warm bath and a good meal were waiting for him. And Marie was waiting, too. . . .

He sighed again. Those pleasures would have to wait. He still had the wounded buckboard driver to check on.

Seth Williams was on duty at one of the front desks inside Ranger headquarters. The young, sandy-haired man, who had helped carry the wounded driver in, had been a Ranger for less than three months, telling everyone he was twenty years old—although Cody happened to know he was really two years younger.

Williams was trying to grow a mustache like those most of the other Rangers sported, and when Cody came into the room, the youngster brushed his finger across his upper lip, as if instinctively checking what progress he was making. However, the downy growth proclaimed that it would be a long time before the youth had the maturity or experience to cut the fine figure of a Ranger that Cody did.

"How's that fella you carried in?" Cody asked as he walked over to the desk.

"Don't look too good," Williams told him, straightening in his chair in what Cody knew was an attempt to look a little taller than he actually was. "They're working on him in back, but from the way Doc was talking, it doesn't sound like there's much chance that fella will be driving his wagon home. Likely he'll soon be joining his friend over at the undertaker's." The young Ranger leaned back and rubbed a hand through his long hair, his pale blue eyes narrowing as he tried to adopt a casual tone. "What happened out there, anyway, Cody?"

"Comanche war party. An hour east of here."

"Comanch'? But they don't operate that close to Del Rio."

Cody shrugged and perched on a corner of the desk. "They did this time."

"But why?" Williams persisted.

"Maybe they were after something in particular on that buckboard. Rifles, maybe."

"Naw," Alan Northrup put in, looking up from his papers at a nearby desk. Northrup had helped Williams carry the driver in; then after the body of the other man had been taken to the undertaker's, he had arranged for the care of the wagon and horses. "I got a look at that load of supplies," he went on. "There's nothing much on board—just some bags of grain and crates of vegetables, probably for sale here in town."

At just over five and a half feet tall, Northrup was on the portly side and had to fight a constant battle against the temptations of food and drink. The dark-haired, clean-shaven young man hadn't lied when he gave his age as twenty-one, although he had stretched the truth a little when he listed his weight as one hundred and seventy pounds.

"Well, something got those Comanches stirred up," Cody said. "I just hope that driver lives to tell us what it was."

Abruptly, the two young Rangers sat bolt upright and began shuffling the papers on their desks, clearly trying their best to look as if they were hard at work. Glancing up, Cody saw the reason why: Lieutenant Oliver Whitcomb was striding down the hall from the back of the building, and the young Rangers wanted to look their busiest when the tall, burly, forty-year-old officer passed between their desks, which faced each other on opposite sides of the entrance.

Cody sighed and straightened up from Williams's desk, although he made no effort to stand at attention or salute the captain's assistant. The Rangers were not much on ceremony, but Cody knew the effect a strict disciplinarian like Whitcomb could have on the younger men. While Cody liked to work by himself whenever he could, he realized there were times when the Rangers had to act together in a united front, almost like a military unit. During such times, a man like Whitcomb, despite his shortcomings, was valuable.

Whitcomb came up to Cody, nodded curtly, and stroked his trim black beard as he said, "I heard you ran into some trouble bringing your prisoner in. Nothing a Ranger couldn't handle, I trust."

"I managed," Cody confirmed dryly. Where Whitcomb was concerned, the less said, the better.

"But not without the help of that rustler, Diego Alvarez. Word is you gave him back his gun and let him fight by your side . . . by the side of a Texas Ranger. Wasn't that a little unorthodox?"

"Word travels mighty fast. I don't recollect telling anybody what went on out there."

"But didn't you let that criminal ride right into town without even a rope to bind him?" Whitcomb laced his hands together behind his back. "And anyway, that Mexican half-breed is telling the story right now through the window of his jail cell to some of our men out back. Is it true?"

A muscle twitched in Cody's cheek as he struggled to keep his anger under control. "With ten mad-as-hell Comanches coming at us, giving the man back his gun seemed like the thing to do at the time," he answered. "Alvarez did his share, and he kept his word. He could've escaped, but he didn't. It'll all be in my report."

"See that it is," Whitcomb said testily. "I'm sure Captain Vickery will want to review the incident fully."

"What about that wounded wagoner? Is he alive?"

"He's hanging on, but the doctor isn't hopeful. We'll let you know if his status changes." Whitcomb looked the Ranger up and down, disdainfully eyeing Cody's trail-worn, dirty clothes and three days' growth of beard. "You might want to get cleaned up after the ride. The captain will want to see you as soon as you make yourself . . . a bit more presentable." Nodding, he turned on the heels of his highly polished boots and headed back down the hallway.

Cody watched him go, then looked at the two young Rangers and muttered, "Don't reckon he'll be happy until he's got us all saluting each other and wearing army blue."

"That won't ever happen," Williams said with a grin, but not until he had checked to make sure Whitcomb was out of earshot.

"Seth's right," Alan agreed. "We're Texas Rangers, not some bunch of soldier boys."

"You fellas remember that," Cody told them, then tugged down the brim of his hat and headed for the street.

The three-story Rio Grande Hotel was the biggest and plushest establishment in town, boasting a large saloon and gambling hall and an elegant dining room. Waiting on customers and dealing at the gambling tables were an assortment of women—young and not so young, beautiful and plain, all dressed in the finest and most colorful gowns Texas had to offer.

Upstairs there were thirty rooms for visitors to the city, as well as for permanent residents like Cody. Some of the accommodations had separate dressing rooms with freestanding metal bathtubs, allowing visitors the luxury of bathing in their own rooms—for a nominal fee to cover the cost of lugging dozens of pails of hot water up the stairs, of course. For a few extra dollars, a guest or saloon patron could purchase the services of one of the female employees, if she was so inclined. And most of them were willing, which made the Rio Grande Hotel the most popular stopping place between Brownsville and El Paso. If Cody hadn't been friends with the proprietors and helped keep the peace in the place whenever he was in Del Rio, he could never have afforded to maintain a room there on his salary.

"Cody! Good to have you back!" the thin, gray-haired man behind the desk called out as the Texas Ranger entered the hotel. He was Ernest Palmatier, owner of the establishment. His wife Emily came hurrying out of the back office, her arms opened wide as she rushed around the counter and gave Cody a cheerful hug. Emily was a foot shorter than her husband and rather plump, with black hair worn up in a bun and a matching black dress.

"We were so worried when we heard you had gone after that dangerous Alvarez and his gang," Emily exclaimed as she went back behind the desk. "And now they say you brought him into town with him riding bold as brass alongside you."

"We came to an understanding," Cody explained. "He's over at the jail now, but I'm afraid I wasn't able to corral any of the rest of his gang, and they scattered."

Ernest waved a slender hand. "They're nothing without Alvarez. Just a bunch of drifters with no sense and little to hold them together. You Rangers will round them up soon enough, I daresay."

"Hope it's as easy as that," Cody mused with a slight smile as he accepted the room key Palmatier held out to him.

"Your room is all cleaned and ready for you," Emily

told her guest. "And let me know when you're hungry, and I'll cook you up a little something special."

"You know, ma'am," Cody said, his grin widening, "it was me telling Alvarez about one of your meals that convinced him he ought to come back here to Del Rio with me. You be sure and send some food over to the jail for him, and charge it to me instead of the county." Then he turned and headed for the stairs, leaving Emily nodding and beaming with pride.

As Cody entered his room, he heard the sweet, familiar voice of a woman singing a lilting French lullaby. The song came from behind the door across the room—the door to his private dressing room.

Closing and locking the hallway door behind him, Cody silently went over to the large four-poster bed, where he dropped his hat on the coverlet, unbuckled his gunbelt and hung it on one of the bedposts, and pulled off his boots. He then walked to the dressing-room door and slowly pulled it open.

The tall, statuesque woman had her back to the door and didn't hear his approach, and for a moment Cody just stood there looking at her. A pink silk dressing gown was folded neatly over the clothes rack, and the woman was wearing nothing but a white towel wrapped around her body that hinted at her small waist and barely covered her firm, curvaceous thighs. Her long red hair was draped over her right shoulder, and she was brushing it as she sang.

As she put the brush down on a dressing table beside her, Cody whispered, "Marie," and stepped into the room.

Marie Jermaine let out a small sound of surprise, then turned quickly and came into the Ranger's arms. Cody pushed the door shut behind him with one hand while the other reached up and stroked her luxuriant red hair. Without a word, their lips met in a kiss that began tenderly, then became more urgent and passionate as her hands caressed his shoulders and back. She slipped her right hand around to his chest and began to undo the buttons of his shirt.

"They said you were back," she whispered with a delightfully delicate French accent. "I thought you would like a bath."

Out of the corner of his eye, Cody saw that the large tub was already filled with hot water and piled high with suds. Marie pulled him closer to the tub, and as her fingers undid the last button of his shirt, she slipped it and his vest over his shoulders and let them fall to the floor. Then she took the end of the towel that was tucked between her breasts and pulled it open, tossing it aside.

As Marie stepped back into the bath, Cody stared in wonder at her dazzling beauty—her languorous sea-green eyes, her high, well-rounded breasts, the curve of her thighs tapering to long, sculptured legs. She started to kneel into the piles of suds, but Cody reached out and stopped her, sliding his arms around her waist and then cupping the firm globes of her bottom. He felt the eager prod of her nipples against his chest as he kissed her again.

When he finally broke the kiss, she sighed and rested her face against his shoulder. "I missed you, Samuel," she said, so softly that he almost didn't hear her.

Cody let her slip from his embrace and lower herself into the tub. Her eyes narrowed seductively and a lazy smile played across her full, naturally red lips as she began to rub the suds across her lightly freckled chest. Then she reached out longingly to Cody, her arms urging him to hurry and join her in the bath. Cody didn't need any more encouragement. He reached for his belt buckle.

Somebody rapped loudly on the hallway door.

The sound reached clearly into the dressing room. "Forget them, *mon cher*," Marie begged as he wavered.

But the knocking continued, and Cody shrugged and promised, "I'll just be a minute."

As he walked across the bedroom, Marie began to

sing again—louder this time, and a bawdy French bal-
lad, at that—and he knew it was her signal that the
intruder, whoever it was, was damned well not welcome right now.

Cody paused by the bed on his way to the door and
slipped the Colt out of the holster. Thumbing back the
hammer as he approached the door, he called, "Who is
it?" and moved to one side as he spoke. No point in
taking chances. A greener could blow a good-sized
hole through that door and an even bigger one in him.

"It's me, Seth. Seth Williams."

Cody twisted the key, opened the door, and forced a
smile as he lowered the hammer of the revolver. "Well,
Seth, what do you want?"

"I'm sorry to bother you, Cody, real sorry,"
Williams began, shifting his feet nervously and obviously painfully aware of the sweet singing that drifted
out through the closed dressing-room door. "But you
see, it's about that wounded fella you brought in. He,
uh, he died."

"Damn!" Cody muttered fervently, shaking his
head.

"There's more. Seems he got clearheaded again
there at the last, and he had a heap to say. I don't know
what it's about, but Captain Vickery sent me over to
fetch you right away. The cap'n said it can't wait."
Williams glanced sheepishly toward the dressing-room
door. "Not even for your bath. Those were his exact
words."

Cody had to laugh, although the sound was somewhat bitter. "Just give me a minute to put on my shirt.
Tell the captain I'll be right over."

Williams nodded, backed partway down the hall,
then turned and hurried down the stairs.

Wearily, Cody closed the door and walked over to
the big mahogany chifforobe to get a clean shirt. As he
slipped it on and buttoned it, he stared at the closed
door across the room and sighed. There was something
exciting, electric, between him and Marie Jermaine—
especially at times like this, when he had just returned

from a long assignment—but neither of them called it love. However, that did not diminish the pleasure they took in each other, or the genuine concern they had for each other's welfare. In fact, there were times when they felt more like brother and sister than lovers, joking about the woman who one day would make Cody settle down or the man who would eventually sweep Marie off her feet and offer her a better life.

As Cody returned to the dressing room, Marie looked up from the tub and said, "And now it is our time alone."

"I wish it was, Marie, but the captain's got other ideas."

"But you just got back," she protested. "You aren't leaving town again so soon, are you?"

"Don't know, but it sounds serious. Stay and enjoy the bath. I'll be back as soon as I can."

"I'll be waiting," she replied, forcing a smile. "All day and all night, if necessary." She then added tartly, "Just don't expect the water to be as hot when you return as it is now."

The Ranger could only shake his head and sigh again as he backed out of the doorway, tucked in his shirt, lifted his holster from the bedpost, and walked reluctantly from the room.

As Cody entered the office of Captain Wallace Vickery, the officer stood up and came around his desk to offer the Ranger a firm handshake and a clap on the back. "Good work out there, son," Vickery said heartily. "I knew Alvarez was no match for you—especially with the good Lord on the side of the Rangers."

"Thanks, Captain. Has Lieutenant Whitcomb told you—"

"About that encounter with the Comanches? Yes, indeed. Shame you had to kill some of those savage heathens. Ah, well, what God don't take care of here on the frontier, I reckon ol' Sam Colt does."

A bluff, broad-shouldered, florid-faced man with a

thatch of gray hair and a bristling mustache, Vickery had a keen mind under his rustic appearance. The strain of commanding such a volatile force as the Texas Rangers had worn deep creases across his brow and around his startlingly blue eyes. Dressed in a black broadcloth suit, white shirt, and string tie, he wore a cartridge belt and holster at his waist that held the same massive Texas Paterson Colt he had carried in 1838, during his first term of service with the Rangers. In those days Vickery had ridden with men such as John Coffee Hays and Adam Cody, men who had been responsible for many of the legends that had already sprung up about the Texas Rangers. And now, since the Reconstruction government had been booted out of office and Texas was being run by Texans once more, Vickery was a Ranger again.

During the time when the Rangers were disbanded, he had found another profession—as a hellfire-and-brimstone preacher—and he saw no need later to give up that calling when he rejoined the Rangers. It was an odd combination but strangely appropriate. A fierce foe of savage Indians and lawless desperadoes, Vickery could, in his own words, "shoot 'em, pray over them that's wounded, and bury them that's dead." He was also handy to have around for baptisms and weddings, and he was one of the finest commanders of men Cody had ever known.

Vickery sat down again. Open on the desk in front of him was his thick black Bible, his place marked with a bowie knife in a fringed sheath. He waved Cody to a chair and remarked, "That battle's the talk of the company by now. Sounds to me like you made a wise choice, freeing Alvarez . . . and don't worry, I'll back you up one hundred percent."

Cody nodded his thanks as he sat down.

Picking up the knife, Vickery closed the Bible and then slid the big blade out of its sheath. He tested the sharpness of it with the ball of his thumb, grimacing as it sliced through the top layer of skin. "Hate to do this to you, son," he murmured solemnly.

"Planning on using that knife on me, are you, Cap'n?" Cody asked wryly.

"What? Oh." Vickery put the bowie down and went on, "No, I'm afraid I'm going to have to ask you to go back out into the field, Cody. If you feel up to it, of course. Which I hope you do, 'cause the work of the Lord and the great state of Texas don't ever end."

Cody managed to nod and smile a little, in spite of his tiredness and his disappointment at having to postpone his reunion with Marie. "Reckon I can be ready to go right away if you need me to, Captain," he responded.

"Good. Knew I could count on you, son."

"What is it?" Cody asked, leaning forward in his chair. "Those Comanches?"

Vickery shook his head. "No. I've already given orders to assemble a force of a dozen Rangers that I'll be leadin' myself against those renegades. I've got another assignment for you."

"Concerning that wagon I brought in?" Cody's shrewd mind had been chewing on that problem.

"Exactly. Seth Williams probably told you already that the wagoner came back to his senses just before he crossed the great heavenly divide. The story he had to tell was mighty bothersome, son, mighty bothersome." Vickery stood up and began to pace back and forth, the same way he stalked around behind the pulpits in the various churches where he delivered his sermons. But agitation was driving him now, not religious fervor. "That poor soul's name was Jeremiah Burgess. Said his friend was Rick Forman. They come from a small town called Twin Creeks."

"I've heard of it," Cody said, nodding. "It's one of those new towns north of here—a day and a half, maybe two days' ride. Ranching community, mostly."

"Burgess told us that wagon load of supplies was just a ruse—somethin' to keep from raisin' suspicions when they set out for Del Rio. Seems the real reason they was comin' here was to find the Rangers and get our help."

"What for?"

"Accordin' to Burgess, there's a heap of trouble in Twin Creeks. A gang bein' run by an owlhoot name of Reb Turner has taken over the town and put themselves in as sheriff and deputies. They're makin' life pretty miserable for the townspeople."

"Reb Turner . . ." Cody mused. "Isn't he the fella who caused all that ruckus over in Laredo last year?"

"That's the one, and there's every reason to believe this is the same scoundrel. But he's usually a hired gun, sellin' his gang's services to the highest bidder. It's hard to pin his type down to any crime, and they're always ready to drift when the wind starts blowin' the wrong way."

"Did Burgess say who this Turner is working for in Twin Creeks?"

"No, only that most of the ranchers suspect some wealthy landowner who's been tryin' to buy up some of the neighborin' spreads," Vickery replied. "Burgess ran out of time before he could give us a name. That's where you come in."

Cody drew the obvious conclusion. "You want me to go to Twin Creeks and find out who's behind Reb Turner and his men—without letting on I'm a Ranger."

Vickery slapped a big, callused palm down on the closed Bible. "That's it, Cody. We could send a troop of Rangers in and put the fear o' God into that gang, run 'em out of this part of the country—but we're lookin' to get the man behind all the trouble." The captain straightened and looked intently at Cody. "Seems to me that's a one-man job—your kind of job."

Cody's forehead creased in thought. This would not be the first time he had worked undercover. Such a chore was plenty dangerous but at the same time exhilarating. A man never felt so alive, Cody sometimes thought, as when he was riding with death close by his side.

"Did Burgess give you any contacts I can use in Twin Creeks?" he finally asked.

"Afraid not, son. But he did say that he was sent by

some sort of citizens' committee that's been secretly put together to fight this problem. You shouldn't have too much trouble connectin' with some of the members. You might start by tryin' to find out if Burgess or Forman had a family. Reckon they'd be on the side of law an' order—especially after they find out what happened to their menfolk."

Cody nodded in agreement. "I'll still have to be careful. If Turner or his boss knew the real reason Burgess and Forman were coming here, any link between them and me could give me away."

"Yep. It might be worth your life if the wrong person found out you're a Ranger. But so far there's no reason to believe somethin' like that has happened. There's nothin' unusual about two men drivin' a wagon full of goods to Del Rio. It's just the devil's own luck that the Comanches had to get into the act. Thank God you came along when you did, Cody. Leastways, now their mission hasn't been a complete failure."

Cody stood up slowly, a grim cast to his lean face. "I'd like to make sure those two men didn't die for nothing."

"That's what I thought. And seein' as how you already started this assignment, I figgered you'd want to see it through to the end." Vickery stopped his pacing and came out from behind the desk. "I've given orders for the men to be ready to ride in an hour. There's plenty of daylight left to at least pick up the Comanches' trail before dark. And since that valley where you ran into them is on the wagon road to Twin Creeks, I'd like for you to come with us that far and point out the direction those heathens headed in. I know that don't give you much time to rest, but you ought to have time for a quick bath and a bite to eat. I'll have Seth get your horse ready and pack your supplies."

"Thanks, Captain." Cody took the hand that Vickery extended to him and returned the firm grip. "I'll be ready in an hour."

As the Texas Ranger headed for the Rio Grande Hotel, he thought how nice a good meal would be right now. But if Marie Jermaine was still waiting in his room—as he was certain she would be—he had a far better idea how to spend his last hour in Del Rio.

She was still there, all right—still in the bathtub, in fact. Her lips were set in a pretty pout as she brushed her hand across the few remaining suds, and as Cody stepped into the room, she murmured, "I warned you, Samuel. The water is cool now."

"Well," Cody responded, reaching for the buttons of his shirt, "we'll just have to warm it up again."

CHAPTER

‖‖‖‖‖‖‖‖‖‖‖‖‖‖‖‖‖ 3 ‖‖‖‖‖‖‖‖‖‖‖‖‖‖‖‖‖

A dozen Texas Rangers rode in double file behind Captain Vickery, while Cody rode beside his commander as they headed briskly to the east through a land of gently sloping, treeless hills dotted with mesquite and lined with arroyos. It was May, and the short-cropped grass was a pale greenish-brown; in another month it would be burnished bronze.

As the riders came up over a rise, Vickery raised his arm, and the Rangers pulled to a halt behind him. Cody looked down into the narrow valley below and pointed toward the rutted wagon trace. "There's where the fight was," he stated. "The Comanches must have come back and gotten the bodies of the ones we killed, but you can see they left the dead horse. Just below us is where I finally got the wagon stopped."

Vickery nodded. "Which direction did the renegades head in when they left here?"

"They peeled off and went over that rise to the northeast. It doesn't mean that's the way they went after they retrieved the bodies, but it seems pretty likely."

"Whitcomb!" the captain shouted, turning in his saddle as the lieutenant rode over. "Send a couple of men up over the hill across the way so's they can see if they can pick up the tracks of that war party." He glanced to the west, then added, "I'd gauge we've got a few hours till sunset. We'll head down to the wagon trail and rest the horses for fifteen minutes, then put in a couple more hours before makin' camp."

"Yes, sir!" Oliver Whitcomb briskly replied, then turned his horse and carried out the orders.

As two of the Rangers galloped down into the valley toward the northeast, Vickery kneed his horse forward and waved for the rest of his men to follow.

When the group had reached the wagon road and dismounted, Vickery motioned Cody and Whitcomb over to him. He said to Cody, "I know you were a mite busy at the time, son, but did you notice any markin's in particular on those Comanches?"

Cody had already been thinking about that, casting his memory back over the short but violent battle. His finger traced a jagged pattern across his right shoulder. "They had a red lightning bolt, right here."

"Sounds like Red Thunder's unholy band," Vickery grunted.

"But they've been carrying out their raids north of the Nueces River, in the San Antonio district," Whitcomb protested.

"Apparently they're on the move," Cody rejoined. "Maybe our boys over there have been making things too hot for Red Thunder."

Vickery frowned in thought. "But why would they come all the way over here? You reckon they're on their way to Mexico?"

"Could be," Cody replied. It was hard to tell what a band of renegades like this would do. Since the Battle of Palo Duro Canyon the year before, when Mackenzie's Fourth Cavalry had captured or killed most of the horses being used by Chief Quanah Parker's loose confederation of Comanches, Kiowas, and Cheyenne, many of the warriors had returned to the reservations in Indian Territory. Some of them were still putting up a fight, though, and had pulled back even farther into the wild reaches of what was called Comancheria in the Panhandle and High Plains of Texas. Other bands of renegades, such as the one led by the war chief known as Red Thunder, roamed from place to place, raiding ranches, stealing horses, and killing settlers.

"Well, if they *have* crossed the border," Vickery said, "I'll be more than happy to let them fight it out with the Mexicanos. Texas has had its share of Red Thunder and his pards this past year."

A few minutes later, one of the scouts rode up to announce that they had found a clear trail heading northeast through the hills. Whitcomb took the directions, then sent the man back to join the other scout. Turning to Vickery, the lieutenant asked, "Shall I have the men get ready to ride?"

"That's why we came out here, to track down those Comanches," Vickery snapped.

"Right, sir," Whitcomb replied. He swung up into his saddle and trotted toward the other Rangers, calling, "Mount up!"

As Cody and the captain neared where the rest of the force was forming in double ranks again, Vickery said, "This wagon road heads due north to Twin Creeks, so you'd best continue on alone from here, son."

Cody nodded. "I ought to make it there by tomorrow night."

"Fine. Just see that you get some kind of word back to us by the end of the week. If I don't hear from you by then, we'll be comin' in after you."

"I'll get the job done, Captain."

"I know that. That's why I chose you." Vickery smiled and clasped Cody's arm. "*Vaya con Dios, Cody.*" He tipped his broad-brimmed black hat in an informal salute, turned his horse, and rode out at the head of the other Rangers.

Cody watched with mixed emotions as the force fell in behind the captain and headed off over the hill on the trail of the Comanche war party. There were some things about this life as a Ranger that reminded him uncomfortably of the military. He was a loner at heart, he supposed, and he sought out those assignments that allowed him to operate on his own, shying away from

the organized missions that threatened to turn the
Rangers into the cavalry of Texas.

It was this attitude that annoyed the hell out of Oliver
Whitcomb, who functioned best when he felt the
Ranger command was in total control of its men at all
times, like so many wooden soldiers on a make-believe
battlefield. Captain Vickery, on the other hand, understood and appreciated Cody's considerable talents,
and he gave the Ranger as much of a free hand as possible.

When the other Rangers had disappeared into the
hills, Cody reached into the watch pocket of his denim
pants and pulled out a large gold timepiece, the kind
known as a turnip. Heavy and slightly bigger than
usual, the watch had been bought by Cody a few
months earlier in Corpus Christi, when a job for the
Rangers had taken him over to that Gulf Coast settlement. At the time he had been struck by a possible
second use for the timepiece and had done some modi-
fying on it. This mission was the first chance he would
have to see if it was going to work.

Flipping open the turnip, he paused for a moment
and studied the photograph in the side opposite the
watch face. It was a sepia-toned study of a young girl,
probably eighteen or nineteen, with long, curly blond
hair and undeniably lovely features. The picture had
been in the watch when Cody bought it, and he had no
idea who the girl was.

He twisted the circular gold frame around the picture and lifted it out, photograph and all, revealing a
shallow, hollow space in that half of the watch. Unpin-
ning the Ranger badge from his vest, Cody dropped it
into the hidey-hole, then replaced the photograph over
it. He slipped the watch back into his pocket, confident that no one would find the badge unless he
wanted them to. He took one more precaution. His
vest was made of two layers of leather so that he could
reverse it, and the holes where his Ranger badge had
been pinned would not be visible.

Turning his horse, he headed up the wagon road to-

ward Twin Creeks. He would be riding into the place
like some sort of lone wolf, with enemies on all sides
who would kill him in the blink of an eye if they discovered he was a Ranger—and yet he couldn't help but
grin in anticipation.

The sun was setting when Three Eyes came riding
into the Comanche encampment. His Appaloosa was
winded and lathered, and one of the young braves
came hurrying over to see that the animal was walked
and watered.

As Three Eyes headed silently toward the circle of
warriors where Red Thunder sat, his fingers caressed
the brass telescope that was slung by a leather thong
around his neck. It was this possession—lifted from
the mutilated body of a U.S. Cavalry officer—that had
given him his name and now made him so valuable to
the Comanches as a scout.

Three Eyes was thinner and even shorter than most
of his fellow Comanches, who were generally short
and stocky. And his skin was far darker, for he was one
of the remaining few whose blood had not in some way
mingled with that of Mexicans or Americans. Perhaps
for this reason he was more objective and compassion-
ate than many of the mixed-blood Comanches, who
often turned their anger and frustration into a deep and
brutal hatred of all foreigners, as if trying to wash away
the shame of their mixed blood with the spilled blood
of their enemies.

As Three Eyes reached the circle of warriors, Red
Thunder patted the ground beside him, and the scout
sat down. All the braves assembled here were painted
with a red thunderbolt that ran across the right shoulder and down to the chest—everyone, that is, except
Red Thunder. His bolt of lightning took a different form
and had provided him with his name. It was a zigzagging, flame-red scar that started above his right eyebrow, narrowly skirted his eye, and ended near the tip
of his chin. The scar was a gift of manhood he had

earned at the hands of a Mexican swordsman during Red Thunder's first horse-stealing raid at the age of fifteen, forty years earlier.

Red Thunder looked around the circle from one man to the next, until he had taken in each of the dozen or so who had gathered around him. Then he turned to the scout and asked, "Three Eyes, what has your third eye seen for us?"

"I waited in the west, hidden among the boulders and brush, until the Rangers arrived three hours ago. There were fourteen. Two left at once on the northeast trail, as you said they would. After resting their horses, the others followed—all but one."

"And what of that one?" Red Thunder demanded, leaning forward and scraping at the earth with a short, pointed stick.

"He rode alone to the north, following the wagon trail." Three Eyes paused a moment, then leaned over and gripped Red Thunder's forearm. "There is more," he continued. "This last man was not unknown to me. He was one of the men whose guns kept us from taking the wagon—the one with the rifle. The half-breed was not with him this time."

Red Thunder's eyes narrowed and his expression grew dark. He had lost three good braves to this Ranger, and a fourth was close to death. Equally disturbing was the knowledge that he had failed in his mission to waylay the wagon. He had sent ten of his thirty braves against two white men, and now four were dead—all because that Ranger and his half-breed Mexican friend had interfered.

"What of the captain and his men?" Red Thunder asked his scout.

"I followed them until they made camp. They are still on the trail you laid out for them, and they missed our cutoff to the east."

"Good," Red Thunder grunted, coming suddenly to his feet. He was taller than most of his braves, almost six feet, and his eyes were more hazel than brown. "Tomorrow we will be gone into the wilderness before these Rangers realize the trail we have left them goes nowhere. But tonight we have other business to attend to."

Stepping forward into the circle, Red Thunder addressed the entire gathering. "I will give three of you a chance to avenge our dead brothers. This Ranger spoken of by Three Eyes has taken the wagon road to the north. It should be a simple matter to track him in the full moon and find his campsite before dawn. That camping ground must be the end of his trail."

There was a chorus of approval, and several of the braves stood and came forward to be chosen for the honor. Red Thunder picked three who had been driven off by the Ranger during the attack on the wagon, exhorting each to recover his good name with the blood of this white man.

"Let me ride with them," Three Eyes requested as the chosen warriors headed off to prepare their horses. "I, too, was driven from the battle in dishonor."

Red Thunder smiled and laid his hand on the scout's shoulder. "You have already recovered your honor this night. It is your eyes that I value, not your skill with knife or gun. And I have need of your third eye as we seek to elude our pursuers and return safely to our people."

Though Three Eyes could not agree that his honor had been restored, he knew there was wisdom in his leader's words, so he forced a smile and nodded his acceptance of Red Thunder's decision.

"Good," the war chief declared, clapping Three Eyes on the back. "Then let us get something to eat. Though we can make no fire tonight, cold food warms the soul as readily as hot."

Cody pulled up in a small arroyo and looked at the night sky. A full moon was rising—the stalking moon as the settlers had come to call it, because the Comanches loved to raid by its light. Better to make camp now, the Ranger decided, than to push his luck by continuing on the trail to Twin Creeks. That was why he had left the wagon road and found this gully, about a quarter of a mile west of the rutted trail.

At a small stream that trickled along the bottom of the arroyo, he watered his horse but didn't unsaddle it. The animal would have been more comfortable without the heavy saddle on its back, but with Comanche renegades in the area, Cody didn't want to have to waste any time if he had to light out of here. He hobbled the horse's front legs with a short length of rope that could be cut with one quick slash of a knife, then turned the animal loose to graze on the sparse grass beside the stream.

Even though it was May and summer wasn't far off, the air was cool, almost chilly, this evening. A fire would have felt good, not to mention some warm food, but that was out of the question. Cody unfolded his bedroll and spread it out, then tugged off his boots, unbuckled his cartridge belt, and climbed into the bedroll, where he made a quick, cold meal of some jerky and cornbread from his saddlebags. That done, he settled down and closed his eyes, drifting off to sleep rapidly.

Usually he slept lightly, waking up a couple of times an hour at the slightest sound. But he hadn't gotten much rest while he was bringing Diego Alvarez to Del Rio, and tonight, exhaustion getting the better of him, he slept deeply—far more deeply than he would have liked.

It was shortly before dawn when the three braves sent by Red Thunder approached Cody's camp. In the bright moonlight, they had had little trouble tracking the Texas Ranger's movements and finding the spot where he had turned off the trail.

Leaving their horses well beyond the arroyo, the three Comanches approached the campsite on foot. One carried a pistol, but the others preferred the silence of tomahawk and knife. As they slipped down the

bank of the wash, one of the braves pointed to the
sleeping man lying on his side and motioned to the
other two braves to approach the Ranger from behind.
Meanwhile, he would skirt around to the other side,
cutting off any chance of escape.

As the three Comanches crept ever closer to him,
Cody was dreaming of Marie Jermaine, once again
with her in his room at the Rio Grande Hotel, taking
that long-awaited bath together. He was cupping her
breasts in his hands, spreading suds over her large pink
nipples with his thumbs as she wrapped her legs
around him and lifted herself onto his thighs, ready to
join with him . . . but even in his dream, that damned
knocking started on the door again.

Reluctantly, he climbed up out of the tub and, drip-
ping wet, stalked over to the door and flung it open—
and was shocked to see his horse standing in the hall,
nickering and whinnying and prancing around in nervous excitement.

"Dammit, not now, boy!" Cody groaned, trying to
hang on to the image of Marie waiting for him in the
bathtub. But as the horse continued to stomp and
neigh, he knew it was too late. The delightful image of
Marie was slipping from his mind, and there was no
way he could summon it back.

As Cody stepped out of the room, he felt the cold air
of the hallway wash over his naked skin—then suddenly felt an equally cold sensation of dread shudder
up his spine. The dream vanished abruptly, and he
found himself lying in a bedroll in the middle of nowhere.

Cody slowly opened his eyes. Careful not to move a
muscle as he listened intently to the faint night sounds,
he knew right away that what had awakened him was
the noise of his horse stirring skittishly and whinnying
in fright.

Ever so slowly, he slid his left hand out of the bedroll
and drew his Colt from the holster beside his head.
Shifting the revolver to his right hand, he then slipped
the bowie knife out of its sheath with his left, pulling it

down inside the bedroll. He managed to keep his breathing calm and under control as he tried to figure out a way to turn around and see if there was anything behind him.

Cody let a few seconds pass, and for a moment he wondered if it might have been just another animal that had frightened his horse. But then he clearly heard the soft scraping sound of something approaching from behind. And whatever it might be, it was dangerously close to his back.

Holding his breath, Cody forced himself to count to three. Then he hurled himself sideways in a roll, raising his gun in the same motion.

He never saw the Indian who was poised above him with a tomahawk raised and ready to strike, for the warrior was standing so close and was taken so completely by surprise when the Ranger came barreling into him that he was thrown forward off his feet. What Cody *did* see was another brave standing behind the first, holding a pistol in his hand.

Cody and the Indian fired together, but the brave had been aiming at the place Cody had been lying, and his frantic effort to alter his shot threw it wide, almost hitting the warrior who had been knocked over. Cody's first shot caught the man in the shoulder, gouging flesh and smashing bone. The second bullet was to the heart, and the brave was thrown back off his feet, dead before he hit the ground.

The first brave was back up again. Cody was still trapped in the bedroll, and as he struggled to tear free of it and bring his gun around, the Comanche kicked his enemy's arm and sent the Colt spinning into the night. Flinging himself on top of Cody, the Indian slashed down with his tomahawk to finish off the Ranger, but Cody twisted his head and threw up his arm barely in time to ward off the blow, then managed to grab hold of the man's wrist as the brave tried to raise the tomahawk for a second strike.

Cody's left hand, holding the bowie, was caught inside the bedroll, held in place by the weight of the body

on top of him. As the Indian reached with his free hand
for the knife on his own belt, Cody gave a fierce heave
and threw the brave to the side, freeing his left hand to
thrust from inside the bedroll. He felt the covers tear,
followed an instant later by the dull pressure of the
blade sliding into the man's belly.

In the moonlight, Cody saw the look of surprise and
pain on the brave's face. The Indian still grabbed at his
own knife, but as it came out of the sheath, it slipped
from nerveless fingers and clattered to the ground.

As Cody heaved the dead man off him, ripping free
the bowie, he heard another Indian shouting somewhere close by. This third warrior was the one who had
begun to skirt around the campsite, but he had circled
back to try to calm the Ranger's horse when it started
whinnying.

Cody gave a swift uppercut through the bedroll, slicing it in half and freeing himself from the covers. Just
then the third Comanche came hurtling through the
predawn darkness, tomahawk raised in one hand and
knife ready at his side in the other. With time to do
little more than scramble to his knees, Cody threw his
bowie knife with a practiced flip of the wrist at the
onrushing form.

The blade whipped through the air and caught the
warrior squarely in the chest, only ten feet from where
Cody was kneeling. The man stumbled, weaved the
final few yards, twisted around, and fell on his back in
front of the bedroll, his hands still clutching his weapons as he thrashed at the air a few times and then
slowly became still.

Grabbing the hilt of the bowie, Cody ripped the
blade free as he scrambled toward his Colt, which he
had spotted lying on the ground a few feet away. He
scooped up the revolver and put his back against the
rocky bank of the arroyo. His pulse was hammering in
his head, but he listened intently over that roar for any
more threatening sounds in the night.

For a good five minutes he crouched there, the barrel of the Colt trained on the sprawled forms of the
three Comanches, just in case there was a spark of life

left in any of them. Finally, he figured that they were undoubtedly dead and that there hadn't been any other warriors with them.

Approaching the bodies, Cody cautiously checked all three of them. Dead, sure enough, he saw. He reached for his boots and slipped them on, then gathered up the weapons the Indians had intended to use on him. The sky was gray now, with sunrise not far off, and there was enough light for Cody to see the jagged bolts of lightning painted in red on the right shoulders of the dead braves. That was no surprise, and Cody was also fairly certain he had seen these particular Comanches during the attack on the wagon.

He wondered whether Red Thunder had sent them after him, or if they had acted on their own, trying to redeem what they might see as their lost honor. Didn't matter either way, Cody supposed. He was still alive, and they were dead.

He picked up his holster, thrust the knife into its sheath, and buckled it on. His horse was still kicking up a fuss, so he went over to it and patted its flank, talking quietly to the animal until it calmed down. He checked the mount quickly to make sure the Indians hadn't done anything to hurt it. As he expected, the horse was fine. The Comanches sometimes called themselves the Horse People, and they weren't likely to harm any animal they could steal.

As Cody walked back toward his campsite, he looked to the east and saw that the sky was turning red with the approach of the sun. It was going to be a bloody sunrise this morning, he thought, glancing at the sprawled bodies.

No point in trying to go back to sleep, he decided. He could be on his way before much longer, as soon as he had gathered his gear and eaten. It might not be very pleasant, having his meager breakfast next to a trio of dead Comanches, but he'd taken meals in worse spots.

And then he still had a long day's ride to Twin Creeks in front of him . . . where his real work was waiting for him.

CHAPTER
||||||||||||||||||||||| 4 |||||||||||||||||||||||

Evening was coming on again when Cody walked his horse down the main street of Twin Creeks, Texas. The settlement was a typical cow town—a single main street fronted by business establishments, with the townspeople's houses on lanes intersecting that broad, dusty avenue. Many of the commercial buildings were adobe, but there was a smattering of frame structures, among them the Ace High Saloon, Margulies's General Mercantile, Cole's Apothecary, the Bon Ton Milliners, and Gomez's Feed and Hardware.

Scanning the signs, Cody noted that the sheriff's office was a squatty adobe next to the hardware store. At the north end of town were a couple of cantinas, and even though night had not fallen, the sounds of singing and guitar music were already drifting from them. The houses on the cross streets were a fairly even mixture of frame, stone, and adobe structures, although a few tents were mixed in. Twin Creeks was beginning to acquire a look of permanence, but there were still such reminders of its relatively recent beginnings.

Since leaving the arroyo early that morning, Cody hadn't seen any more Indians or even any tracks of unshod ponies, and the rest of the ride to Twin Creeks had been peaceful, if a little boring. When the Ranger pulled his horse to a stop in front of the Ace High, he wanted a drink, something to eat, and information—not necessarily in that order.

The saloon was a large building, maybe the biggest in town, occupying half a city block. Two entrances led into it, one fronting the main street, the other around the corner on a side street. Swinging down from the saddle, Cody flipped the reins around the hitchrack in front of the main door. He stepped onto the boardwalk, glancing at the set of antelope antlers fastened to the wall above the batwings and several large drawings of the ace of spades that decorated the glass in the big windows.

Somebody was playing a piano inside, and as Cody headed for the entrance, he judged that the professor of the keyboard, whoever he was, didn't have a whole heap of talent, but it sounded as if he was enjoying his work. The tune was rowdy, raucous, and very enthusiastic.

Shoving open the batwings, Cody paused with a hand on each door and looked around the big room. A large chandelier hung from a chain in the center of the ceiling, and there were smaller lamps suspended here and there around the room; all of them were lit, even though shadows were just now starting to creep through the street outside. A polished hardwood bar ran almost the entire length of the wall to Cody's right, while to his left, the piano sat on a small platform in the angle formed by the front and side walls of the building. The cloth-covered tables for the drinkers in the front half of the room were separated from the gambling tables to the rear by a small open space that could serve as a dance floor. The hour was early, but there were already quite a few customers in the place.

Cody glanced at the piano. The man pounding the keys had his back to the room and appeared to be absorbed in the music, for his head with its thinning sandy hair bobbed to the rhythm. He wore dark trousers, a white shirt, and a fancy vest with gilt brocade on the front that was just visible from where the Ranger stood. Cody could only see the side of his face, but he seemed to be in his late thirties.

The Ranger's survey of the room took only an instant before he stepped inside, letting the batwings slap closed behind him, and headed for the bar, where a dozen men were drinking. Two bartenders in red aprons were behind the bar, and five saloon girls in short-skirted, low-necked, spangled outfits circulated among the tables, some of them delivering drinks, others flirting with the customers and leaning over to give the men a good luck at the treasures contained in the bodices of their gowns. At the tables in the back of the room, several games of chance were going on, including poker, faro, and black-jack.

All in all, Cody thought as he sauntered over to the bar and found a vacant spot at the brass foot rail, the Ace High looked like dozens of other saloons he had been in. A little cleaner and newer, maybe, but that was the only difference.

One of the red-aproned bartenders ambled up in front of him and asked, "What can I do for you, cow-boy?"

"Beer," Cody grunted, pleased that the man had taken him for a simple range rider.

The bartender filled a mug from a keg under the bar and slid it across to Cody, some of the thick foam that topped the amber brew sloshing out as he did so. "Four bits," the man stated.

Cody frowned. "Bit steep on the price, isn't it?" he asked.

"I don't set the prices, mister," the bartender re-plied with a shrug. "Fella who owns the place figures he's got to make a living. Ain't that a bizarre notion?"

"Reckon not." Cody dug some coins out of his pants pocket and pushed them across the gleaming surface. "Since you brought it up, just who does own this place?"

"Turn around and you'll be lookin' at him. He's over there in the corner, at the piano."

Cody glanced over his shoulder. The piano player had finished his previous number and launched into an-other one, but this tune was much slower, more melan-choly. It fit the twilight that was settling over the town.

"The piano player owns the saloon?" Cody asked, surprised by that revelation.

"Yeah. Name's Andre Duval," the bartender told him. The man's voice hardened slightly as he went on, "This any of your business, mister, or are you just curious?"

Cody took a sip of the beer—cool instead of cold, but not bad—and then placed the mug on the bar and held his hands up slightly, palms out. "Just curious," he said, his tone as placating as his gesture.

"I wouldn't make a habit of it, was I you."

"Thanks for the advice, friend. I'll remember it."

The bartender nodded and moved on to serve one of the other customers.

A voice to Cody's left said, "He was right, you know."

Casually, the Ranger sipped the beer again and turned to look at the man who had spoken. Somewhere in his late twenties, Cody gauged, he was hunched over the bar, intently regarding a shot glass of whiskey, and even in that position, he was obviously a good-sized, brawny individual. A cream-colored Stetson was tilted back on his head, revealing thick dark hair. His clothes were of good quality, but they were also rumpled and slightly dirty, as if he had been sleeping in them for several nights. He wasn't wearing a gun.

"You talking to me, mister?" Cody asked the man.

"That's right. You're the only stranger here. Ever'body else knows it's not smart to start askin' too many questions in Twin Creeks these days."

The man's voice was thick and somewhat slurred, and Cody would have been willing to bet the drink in front of him was not his first of the day—not by a long shot. The Ranger said mildly, "Didn't mean to rile anybody. I just stopped for a drink and a bite to eat." He grinned. "Got the drink. Now, you know where a man can get a good meal?"

The big man ignored the question. He tossed back the rest of the whiskey and thumped the empty glass down on the bar. "'Nother one, Harley," he said to the bartender. "And leave the goddamned bottle this time."

The bartender took a bottle from under the bar, but he frowned and hesitated before pouring another drink. "You got enough money to pay for a bottle, Tom?" he asked.

"'Course I do." The big customer awkwardly thrust a hand into his pants pocket and came up with a double eagle. He tossed the coin on the bar and said, "Take it outta that." He grinned bleakly. "That's all that's left of my last month's pay as sheriff of this here town. Sad, ain't it?"

Cody kept his face impassive, trying not to show the sudden interest he felt. If this man had been the sheriff of Twin Creeks before Reb Turner showed up and took over, he might be an excellent source of information—provided he was sober enough to answer a few questions, that is.

The bartender put down the bottle and picked up the coin, the double eagle disappearing deftly in his fingers. "Ain't none of my business, but you better take it easy, Tom," he muttered.

"You're right, Harley. It isn't any of your goddamned business."

The bartender grunted and walked off again, leaving his customer to splash more whiskey into the empty glass. The ex-sheriff did so, then glanced over at Cody and lifted the bottle. "Have a drink on me?" he invited.

"Thanks. Maybe when I finish this beer," the Ranger replied.

"Suit yourself." The big man polished off the fresh whiskey in two swallows.

"Heard you say you were a lawman," Cody said slowly.

"Not anymore. So if you're on the dodge, you don't have anything to worry about in Twin Creeks. The man who's wearing the badge now ain't interested in catching owlhoots."

"Never said I was an owlhoot," Cody remarked.

"You never said you wasn't." He looked pointedly at the well-worn walnut butt of Cody's .45. "You appear to be a man who's good with a gun. Reckon I just jumped to a conclusion. Sorry if I offended you."

Cody shook his head. "No offense, Mister . . . ?"

For a long moment, the other man didn't answer. Then, finally, he said in a low voice, "O'Rourke. Tom O'Rourke."

"Glad to meet you." Cody extended his hand. "I'm Sam Cotton."

O'Rourke hesitated, then took Cody's hand. The big man's grip was slack, but Cody sensed that at one time—before he had dived headfirst into a bottle of booze—there might have been a great deal of power in it.

"You passing through, Cotton?" O'Rourke asked as he released Cody's hand.

"As a matter of fact, I was looking for someplace to settle down. Maybe you could tell me a little about the town, seeing as you used to hold office here."

"Sure," O'Rourke said, shrugging. "Why don't we go sit down?"

"Sounds good to me."

Cody picked up his beer, noting as he followed O'Rourke to an empty table that the big man was weaving slightly as he walked, but he didn't seem too unsteady on his feet. Cody figured O'Rourke had already put away a lot of whiskey, but he was big enough and his constitution strong enough that the liquor hadn't made him falling-down drunk—not yet, anyway.

O'Rourke was a good three inches taller than Cody and probably outweighed him by fifty pounds. The man certainly *looked* capable, but Cody suddenly wondered how much of a fight O'Rourke had put up when Reb Turner and his cronies came to Twin Creeks and took over.

They sat on opposite sides of the small table, and O'Rourke poured himself another drink. He swallowed a healthy slug, then asked, "What is it you want to know, Cotton?"

"Well . . . what kind of place is this to live?"

"Used to be a good place." A grim expression settled over O'Rourke's face. His features might have been handsome once, but now they were muddied and swollen by alcohol. "A damn fine place—until Turner came along."

"Turner?" Cody echoed.

"Reb Turner. Ever hear of the son of a bitch?"

A man at a nearby table stood up suddenly and hurried out of the saloon, and Cody glanced at him, noticing that he was roughly dressed and had a fringe of beard stubble on his lean jaw. Thinking that the man's departure was more than coincidental, Cody told himself to keep an eye on the door, then turned his attention back to O'Rourke's question. Turner was a fairly well-known gunman; it might look suspicious if Cody denied ever hearing the name. He said, "Sounds kinda familiar, but I can't really place him. The way you're talking, he must be a regular badman."

"Bad enough," O'Rourke grated. "Him and his gang showed up a while back and paid visits to me and the mayor and the other important folks in town. Turner had himself a plan—I was going to resign as sheriff, and then the mayor was going to appoint the owlhoot acting sheriff." The big man finished his drink, poured another one, but left the glass on the table. "Hell, I wasn't just about to turn over my badge to some outlaw. I was duly elected, and I'd been a good sheriff. A damn good sheriff, if I do say so myself—not that it did a bit of good."

He fell silent, glowering down at the tabletop. Cody sat in silence for a few moments, waiting for O'Rourke to resume his story, but the former lawman stayed quiet. He was solemn and seemed a bit more sober now, as if the bad memories had burned away some of the liquor in his body.

"What happened?" Cody finally asked.

"You're a curious sort, aren't you?" O'Rourke muttered. "Harley and I both told you it's not a good idea to ask too many questions around here."

Cody's wide mouth quirked in a grin. "If I'm going to settle down in a place, I like to know something about it."

"You don't want to settle down in Twin Creeks. I can promise you that. But, since you asked . . . I tried to stand up to Turner. Told him to get out of town. He just laughed at me and went for his gun, right in the middle of Main Street. I always thought I could handle a shooting iron pretty good, but Turner's fast, mighty fast. He put a slug into the ground between my boots before I had my Colt halfway out of the holster. He laughed again and waited to see if I was going to finish my draw before he killed me." O'Rourke swallowed, pain etched on his face now as the memories obviously played themselves out in his head.

"I looked around to see if anybody was going to help me," he went on. "Hell, all the townspeople had scurried off the street like a bunch of scared rabbits. Bastards turned their backs on me, left me out there to face Turner and his men. There was nothing I could do. I . . . I let my gun back down in the holster, took it off, and left it there—along with my badge. Came straight here to the Ace High and started drinking. Haven't stopped for very long since."

Cody took a deep breath. "Doesn't sound to me like there was anything else you could do," he said.

O'Rourke shook his head. "You don't understand. Sure, I was outgunned and nobody would back me up. But I was still the sheriff. Folks trusted me. I should've done something to get rid of Turner—and if I couldn't do that, I should've died out there on the street."

A footfall scraped on the floor to Cody's right, and he was suddenly aware that the piano had fallen silent while O'Rourke was talking. A man's voice said softly, "That would not have done anyone any good, *mon ami.*"

Cody looked up to see Andre Duval, the piano player who owned the Ace High, according to the bartender. The slender, sandy-haired man stepped up to the table and put a long-fingered hand on O'Rourke's shoulder.

O'Rourke shrugged off the hand. "Leave me alone, Duval," he growled. "I didn't see you out there, siding me against those owlhoots."

The saloonkeeper shook his head and rejoined, "I am a musician, not a pistol artist." He turned to Cody. "You are new in Twin Creeks, eh?"

"Yeah, but I don't know if I'm going to stay around or not," the Ranger said. "Don't sound like much of a town."

"Do not judge us too quickly, sir. Things could always change. . . .For now, though, I must return to my piano." Duval gave a little half bow and turned around to walk away.

"Things could change," O'Rourke repeated dismally. "Sure." He didn't sound convinced.

"I reckon Turner and his men are sort of running roughshod over everybody now," Cody remarked after a few seconds.

"You reckon right. Turner's collecting protection money from most of the businesses in town, throwing folks in jail on trumped-up charges and making them pay big fines to get out—hell, just generally making things rough for everybody but him and his pards. Deputies, they are now." The big man laughed humorlessly. "This's probably the first time any of those galoots have been on that side of a badge, but I'll bet they've seen plenty in their time."

Cody nodded, deep in thought although he was still trying to appear just idly curious. The whole situation was shaping up just as Captain Vickery had relayed it. So far there had been no real surprises in Tom O'Rourke's story, and all Cody had accomplished was to confirm the tale that Jeremiah Burgess had told with his dying breaths. He was no closer to the identity of the man behind Reb Turner's guns.

And it looked like he wasn't going to get any closer right now, either, because O'Rourke straightened abruptly, got a stony look on his face, and picked up his glass. Downing the whiskey, he turned his head away from the door.

Cody glanced in that direction, movement and a flash of color catching his eye, and saw a young woman pushing aside the batwings and entering the saloon. She was lovely, but that was the only resemblance between her and the saloon girls who were moving around the floor of the Ace High. Her beauty had an innocence about it that had long since departed from the other women in the room. She had long, softly curled chestnut hair and wore a gingham dress with a red sash around her trim waist. As she came toward the table where Cody and O'Rourke sat, the Ranger couldn't help but admire the flash of spirit in her eyes—and the thrust of her breasts against the fabric of her dress. She looked like the kind of girl a man might have to marry to get into bed, but once he got her there, he'd have his hands full.

The Ranger stood politely as she reached the table, and she nodded at him, then looked down at O'Rourke, who had remained seated. "I thought I'd find you here, Tom," she said. "We were supposed to have supper together, remember?"

"That was your idea, Sally, not mine," O'Rourke replied. Setting down the empty glass, he reached for the bottle. "This is all the food and drink I need now."

The girl grasped the neck of the bottle and moved it out of O'Rourke's reach. "Why don't you come back to the house with me?" Sally asked. "I can heat up the food—"

"Dammit, just forget it, Sally!" O'Rourke said hotly. "Now, give me that whiskey."

"No." Her voice was cool, but it trembled slightly from the emotions that she had to be feeling.

"Blast it, girl! You want everything to be nice and proper—even when the whole world's gone to hell around us. . . ."

Sally sighed. "Tom, I'm sorry. I just want to help you—"

O'Rourke interrupted, demanding, "By spying on

me? Hell, there was no need to do that. Anybody in town could've told you where to find me, Sally. Where else would a stinking coward ex-lawman be except in a saloon?"

"You're not—"

O'Rourke's palm came down sharply on the table. "The hell I'm not," he said grimly. Pushing his chair back, he stood up and added, "Just leave me alone, Sally. I'm not worth it, and I'm sure as blazes getting tired of you trying to . . . to . . . whatever the hell it is you're trying to do!"

With that, he pushed roughly past her, stalking to the door and slapping the batwings aside to disappear into the darkness.

Cody was left standing beside the table with the young woman. He shook his head and said, "I'm sorry, ma'am. I reckon I got him stirred up. He was telling me about what happened with this fella Turner—"

"There's no need to apologize, Mister . . ."

"Cotton. Sam Cotton."

"I'm Sally Edwards."

"Pleased to meet you, ma'am."

Sally's face was pale and drawn, pain showing clearly in her eyes. "I'm afraid Tom doesn't need an excuse to behave like that these days." She summoned up a weak smile. "Well, I'd better be getting home. It's obvious I won't be having a guest for dinner tonight."

Cody tugged his hat off and regarded her solemnly. "I'd be glad to walk you, Miss Edwards."

"Thank you, but—"

"From what your friend was saying, Twin Creeks has gotten a mite rough lately," Cody pointed out. "I don't mean to be forward. I just thought you might like to have a gentleman see you home safely."

"And are you a gentleman, Mr. Cotton?" she asked.

Cody smiled. "I can approach the general vicinity of it, ma'am, when I try real hard."

She laughed softly, and Cody thought he heard some genuine amusement in the sound. "All right. Thank you."

Cody settled his hat back on his head and fell in step beside her. But they hadn't gotten halfway to the door when three men shoved abruptly through the entrance.

The one in the lead would have been handsome except for a nose that had been broken sometime in the past. He had blue eyes, curly blond hair, and wide shoulders. A two-gun rig was strapped around his hips, and he hooked his thumbs behind the belt as he came to a stop just inside the door. He wore a faded red shirt, tan pants, and a brown Stetson. His companions, who came to a halt just behind and to either side of him, were similarly dressed, although they both wore vests and carried only one gun apiece. One of them, Cody realized, was the man who had hurried out of the Ace High earlier when O'Rourke had started talking about Reb Turner.

All three men wore badges, but Cody didn't need that to tell him who they were. He had already guessed that he was facing Reb Turner and two of the gunman's cronies.

Turner had looked angry when he first came in, and Cody suspected he had been told that Tom O'Rourke was here in the saloon, talking about him. But the outlaw's attitude changed completely when he glanced around, saw that O'Rourke was gone, and then let his gaze fall on Sally Edwards. A smile broke out on his face.

"Howdy, Sally," he said, touching a finger to the brim of his hat. "What are you doin' in here?"

She swallowed and said, "I was . . . looking for someone, if that's any of your business, Sheriff."

One of the other men said harshly, "Ever'thing's the sheriff's business."

Turner waved him to silence. "Hush now, Jack. No need to get upset. Why, if anybody in Twin Creeks knows about the importance of respectin' law and order, it's Miss Edwards here. Ain't that right, Sally?"

The man's mocking tone sent anger surging through Cody. He kept a tight rein on himself, though, and stood as casually as Turner. He was well aware that all three of the outlaws-turned-lawmen were looking him over, trying to figure out who he was and if he represented any danger to them.

Sally flushed and didn't answer Turner's question. She started to go around him, saying, "I was just on my way home."

Turner shifted subtly, keeping himself between her and the doorway. "You don't want to be walkin' the streets by yourself," he said. "Somebody might take you for a whore. Better let me walk you."

Flushing even more at the sheriff's bold language, Sally opened her mouth to protest, but Cody beat her to it. He said coolly, "No need to worry, mister. I'll be walking the young lady home."

Turner looked at him directly for the first time. His lips twisting into a sneer, he demanded, "Just who the hell are you?"

"Name's Sam Cotton—" Cody began.

"He's my cousin," Sally suddenly interjected. "He's just come to Twin Creeks for a visit, that's all."

A faint crease marked Cody's forehead at her words. Unsure why she had spoken up and lied to Turner, he decided to play along for the moment. He nodded when Turner looked at him again and asked, "Is that so?"

"That's right, Sheriff," Cody answered. "And I'm not looking for trouble."

The stubbly-faced deputy called Jack stepped forward, and after glancing at Turner and evidently getting some sort of signal, he planted a hand on Cody's shoulder and gave the Ranger a hard shove. "Well, that's just what you're goin' to get, if you give the law a hard time."

"Watch it!" Cody snapped angrily, reacting as any man would under the circumstances.

Jack crowded closer, thrusting out his jaw and demanding, "Are you resistin' an officer of the law?"

"No, I just don't want you pushing me around," Cody replied, then added in a whisper that only Jack could hear, "you chickenshit son of a bitch!"

Jack reacted just as Cody knew he would. His eyes widening in surprise, the deputy mouthed a curse, and then he jerked his Colt from its holster and swung it viciously at Cody's head.

Cody's left hand clamped around Jack's wrist, stopping the blow short in midair. An instant later the Ranger's right fist crashed into the man's jaw, and Jack flew backward, stumbling into Reb Turner. Beyond the sheriff, Cody saw the other deputy snatching out his pistol.

In the wink of an eye, the Ranger's Colt was drawn and pointed, hammer pulled back under his thumb. Cody heard rapid footfalls behind him as the saloon's customers scurried to get out of the line of fire. He ignored that, concentrating on the three men in front of him. "Hold it!" he barked. "I said I wasn't looking for trouble."

"Well, then, you've got a damned unusual way of goin' about it, mister," Turner said, shoving aside the deputy Cody had punched.

"I didn't start this fight," Cody pointed out, "but I don't aim to be pushed around, either. Your man was out of line, Sheriff. I reckon you can see that. All Cousin Sally and I wanted to do was leave peacefully."

"That's right," Sally agreed. "This . . . this isn't my cousin's fault, Sheriff."

Turner glanced once around the room, and then his gaze returned to the rock-steady revolver in Cody's fist. He took a deep breath and muttered, "Reckon it wasn't." Turning to the deputy, he went on, "What the hell did you think you were doin', Jack? Just 'cause you're wearin' a badge don't mean you can go around assaultin' innocent citizens!"

Jack was clutching his jaw, and he held on to it as he tried to speak. When his words came out as gibberish, Cody felt some grim satisfaction as he realized his punch had broken the man's jaw. Jack wouldn't be repeating what Cody had said to provoke him anytime soon.

"Never mind," Turner snapped disgustedly. "Asa,

put your gun up and get Jack out of here. Take him over to the doc's."

The second deputy followed the sheriff's orders, leading his cohort out of the saloon. Before he was fully out the door, Jack cast a venomous glance back over his shoulder at Cody, and the Ranger knew he had made an enemy. More than one, in fact, for he could see the hatred shining in Turner's eyes, too, though the sheriff was not going to push the matter at this point. Cody would have to watch his back, but that was nothing new.

Glowering at Cody, Turner warned, "You can have your visit, Cotton, but you'd better make it a short one. I want you out of Twin Creeks in a week's time. And don't get into any more trouble while you're here."

"Sounds fair enough," Cody stated. He hammered down and lowered the Colt into its holster, but he kept his hand on the butt just in case.

"Remember what I said." Turner's eyes flicked back to Sally. "The Edwards family has already had enough trouble lately. You don't want to add to their problems. Sally, if he doesn't know already, you'd better tell your cousin what happened to your father."

With that, Turner wheeled around and walked out of the saloon. Silence hung over the large room for several long seconds. Then Andre Duval started playing the piano again, and the crash of chords made several people in the room jump nervously.

Quietly, Cody said to Sally, "I'm not sure what's going on here, ma'am, but I reckon we can talk about it while we're walking back to your house."

"Yes, I think we should," the girl agreed. "But there's one thing that should be clear already, Sam: You're not going to like being a member of my family."

CHAPTER
||||||||||||||||||||||||||| **5** |||||||||||||||||||||||||||

Full darkness had fallen by the time Cody and Sally Edwards left the Ace High Saloon, and there was less traffic on the main street of the town now, since quite a few of the businesses had already closed for the day. The saloons were open, however, and bright light and music spilled from all of them.

Cody wondered if he should take Sally's arm as they strolled down the boardwalk, but he decided against it. She seemed like a rather independent-minded young woman and probably wouldn't appreciate the gesture. As he walked along beside her, he asked, "What was it that Turner said about your father?"

Sally sighed deeply, and Cody could hear the pain in the sound. "You have to understand, Mr. Cotton—"

"Better make it Cousin Sam," Cody reminded her. "And by the way, you haven't explained why you told Turner I was a relative."

"It just occurred to me that he might not try to push you into a fight if he thought you were related to me. If he had known you were a stranger in town, there's no telling what he might have done. I'm sure he and his men have robbed and killed people who were simply passing through Twin Creeks."

Cody frowned. "That's a pretty strong accusation."

"Turner is nothing but an outlaw—a cruel, vicious outlaw. There's nothing I could accuse him of that would be beneath him," Sally responded vehemently.

"Could be you're right. Which brings us back to your father . . . ?"

"Yes." They were passing one of the lanterns hanging at intervals on the posts supporting the awnings over the boardwalk, and in its flickering glow, Cody could see the grimace on Sally's face as she spoke the word. "Like everyone else in town, Dad didn't . . . didn't stand behind Tom O'Rourke when Tom faced up to Turner. But that doesn't mean the citizens aren't opposed to Turner. They are. Practically everyone in town would like to see that criminal gone, except for the other hardcases who've drifted in lately, so the townspeople started getting together quietly, trying to figure out what to do about the problem. I guess you could say they formed a sort of citizens' committee."

Cody nodded. "Not the first time that kind of thing has happened. Lots of times folks have had to take the law into their own hands, especially when the law they've got to start with turns bad."

They had reached another corner. Sally motioned to the cross street and said, "We turn here. The house is just about a block down." After a moment, she continued, "My father was one of the leaders of the movement to do something about Turner. That alone would have been enough to make Turner hate him, once the *sheriff*"—her voice was filled with scorn—"got wind of what was going on, but . . . well, there was me, too."

"You," Cody stated, not making it a question.

"That's right. Turner likes me. He . . . I suppose you could say he wants me, to be blunt about it."

Cody couldn't really tell in the darkness, but he was sure from her voice that she was blushing again. She pushed on, saying, "My father made it perfectly clear to Turner that he was to have nothing to do with me. I agreed, of course. I was repulsed by the man, and I still am—now more than ever, since I've seen the kind of awful things he's capable of doing."

Sally Edwards's personal life wasn't really any of his business, Cody thought, but at the same time, if he was going to get to the bottom of the mess in Twin Creeks, it would help to know where everyone stood. He said, "Looked to me like there might be a little something between you and that O'Rourke fella."

The young woman didn't answer right away. When she finally did, her voice was stiff. "Once, maybe, you would have been right, Mr.—Cousin Sam. But after everything that's happened . . ."

"O'Rourke backing down when Turner drew on him, you mean."

Sally stopped short and turned to face him, anger making her movements abrupt. "That's not what I mean at all." Her tone was equally brusque. "It wouldn't have helped anyone for Tom to get himself killed. I certainly didn't want that. But once it happened, once it was all over, there was no reason for Tom to start trying to drink himself to death, now, was there?"

The Ranger regarded her solemnly in the moonlight and slowly lifted a hand to stroke his mustache. "O'Rourke struck me as a proud man," he said after a few seconds. "It's hard for a man like that to back down. When he has to, it sticks in his craw."

Sally just looked at him, then shrugged and turned to walk on. Obviously, his argument just didn't reach her. "Getting back to my father," she said, "after he'd told Turner to leave me alone, I was afraid that Turner would do something to try to get even with him. I was right. A week ago, when Dad was on his way home from work one evening, someone grabbed him and pulled him into an alley. Several men were waiting there, and they beat him—beat him dreadfully. When they dumped him on our front porch afterward, I . . . I thought he was already dead. He had blood all over his face—"

The trembling words came to a sudden halt, and Cody could tell that recounting this story was taking a toll on Sally. But he had to know what had happened.

"Your father?" he gently prodded. "Did he . . . ?"

"Did he die?" Sally shook her head. "No, thank

God. My brother, Patrick, ran for the doctor and brought him quickly. Dad had some broken ribs, and he was bruised and cut pretty badly, but Doc says he'll be all right with plenty of rest. That's what he's been doing for the last week, recuperating in bed."

"The men who did that to him—did they say anything while they were working him over?"

"They said . . . they said this would teach him to stick his nose into things that didn't concern him. You could take that to mean his involvement with the citizens' committee—or him standing up to Turner and ordering him to leave me alone."

"Or both," Cody muttered.

"Or both." Sally indicated a small, neat frame house behind a recently planted lawn. Some narrow, white-washed boards lay scattered haphazardly along the boundary between the street and the yard. "This is our house. And that was our fence. The men who hurt Dad kicked it down and trampled it when they brought him home. I haven't felt like trying to clean it up."

"You mentioned a brother. Tell him to do it."

Cody saw her smiling broadly for the first time. "Patrick is twelve years old, Cousin Sam," she told him. "He has better things to do, and besides, twelve-year-old boys never do what their big sisters tell them to do."

"Reckon I've heard that," Cody agreed, chuckling with remembrance.

"Well, I appreciate you walking me home. . . ."

Cody knew that she was on the verge of saying good night, but he didn't want this conversation to end just yet. Quickly he asked, "This citizens' committee your father's a part of—has it come up with anything to get rid of Turner?"

She hesitated for a long moment, then said, "I'm not sure. There's a Ranger post at Del Rio, south of here, and it was decided that a couple of men would go down there to try to get some help. They left a few days ago and haven't gotten back yet, so it's too soon to tell if that's going to do any good or not." She took a step toward the house. "I have to be going in now."

"Wait," Cody said, stepping after her and moving into the shadow cast by one of the trees in the front yard. She was starting to get a bit skittish, and he knew she had to be wondering if she had talked too much to him. After all, despite the "Cousin Sam" lie, he was a complete stranger to her. He went on, "Don't worry, Sally. I just want to ask you one more question."

"You ask a lot of questions, Mr. Cotton."

He noticed the change in how she referred to him and knew she was more nervous. "This one's the most important of all," he said. "Why'd you tell me all of this? For all you know, I'll go back to Turner and repeat it. That'd be a way of getting on his good side after that run-in at the Ace High."

She gave a brittle laugh. "That did occur to me. But . . . I don't know, for some reason I just trusted you. You seem like an honest man, and that's something we don't see that often in Twin Creeks these days. I . . . I hope you're not going to disappoint me."

"I do, too," Cody replied dryly. His fingers slipped into his pocket and came out with the big turnip watch. As he flipped it open, he added, "There's something I want to show you."

Just as Sally had when she told him what was going on in Twin Creeks, he was acting on instinct, for as a Ranger, he had to be a shrewd judge of character—and he was sure he was doing the right thing. Deftly, he plucked the picture from the watch and removed the badge behind it, pressing it into her hand. Even in the darkness, she could recognize by touch the five-pointed star in the silver circle.

Her breath caught in her throat. "A Ranger!" she whispered. "Then the men got through—"

"Not without trouble," Cody said, his hand closing over Sally's. "I'm afraid I've got bad news. Both the men who were sent to Del Rio are dead. Comanches jumped them on the way. They killed one of the men in the fight and wounded the other one, but he got to Del Rio, and before he died he told us something about what was going on up here. I've been sent to find out the whole story and put a stop to it."

Her voice was shaky as she said, "You mean Mr. Burgess and poor Rick Forman . . ."

"Afraid so, ma'am. By the way, my name's Cody, but I reckon I'd better stay Cousin Sam for the time being, just to keep things simple."

"You mean you don't want me to tell my father or Tom or—"

Cody cut in, "You can tell your father who I am, I reckon, but not anybody else. For certain, not Tom O'Rourke—though we'll have to come up with some story as to why we didn't immediately know each other as kinfolk." His face was grim in the darkness as he went on, "O'Rourke may have been a good man once, but he drinks too much to trust him now."

He sensed more than saw Sally nodding her head. "I suppose you're right, although I hate to admit it. I won't tell anyone else but Dad, not even Patrick."

"Good idea. Youngsters like to gab and try to impress their friends."

"Yes, they do." Sally managed to laugh softly. "And Patrick would certainly think it was impressive if he could boast to his friends that a Ranger was staying with us."

Cody frowned in surprise. "What was that, ma'am?"

"Well, you're my cousin, aren't you? So you'd better get used to calling me Sally, instead of ma'am, and where else would you stay while you're in Twin Creeks but with your relatives?"

"Reckon there's a hotel—"

"But your story will be a lot more convincing if you stay with us. Dad will play along, I know he will. He'll do anything to help, once he finds out you're a Ranger. And as for Patrick, well, he can't know all of our relatives. I'll make up some story to explain the visit of a cousin he's never heard of. And speaking of stories, I suppose we can tell Tom that we've only known of each other by name and have never met before, which is why we didn't recognize each other in the saloon. We can tell him that it was only after he left and we introduced ourselves that we realized we were cousins, and that you had recently written to say that you'd be coming to Twin Creeks to look for work."

Cody considered the suggestion for a moment, then told her, "I reckon that's a reasonable explanation, and staying with you is a good idea, all right—but things might wind up with you and your family being in danger."

"We're already in danger, as long as Reb Turner is in charge. Every decent citizen in Twin Creeks is in danger."

She had a point there, Cody thought. He took a deep breath and said, "All right. You've got a deal."

Sally reached out and briefly took his arm. With a forced note of brightness in her voice, she declared, "Then come along inside, Cousin. I'll introduce you to the rest of the family."

She handed the Ranger badge back to him, and he slipped it into its hiding place in the watch, returning the timepiece to his pocket as they walked up to the house. A small front porch had what looked like the beginnings of a flower garden around it—though Cody had a hard time being sure of that in the darkness—and a lamp burned behind lace curtains in the front window. The place looked homey, even at night.

Opening the front door, Sally called, "It's just me, Dad! Patrick, where are you?"

Cody removed his hat as he stepped into the foyer behind Sally. He heard a door open and shut somewhere in the house, and then rapid footfalls sounded in the hallway that faced the front door. A boy about twelve years old appeared around a corner, coming toward them fairly rapidly, but he stopped in his tracks when he saw the tall, lean, gun-wearing man with his sister. A look of fear and anger flashed through his brown eyes, and he started to lift the carbine he held in his hands.

"Wait a minute, Patrick," Sally said quickly, putting herself between Cody and the boy. "This man is a friend. In fact, he's even a relative. Now, put that gun down."

"Don't pay to take chances," the youngster countered truculently. "What do you mean he's a relative? I've never seen him before!"

"Have you seen every single one of our relatives?" Sally asked tartly.

Patrick hadn't lowered the carbine, but he hadn't brought the barrel up any higher, either. Frowning, he finally answered, "No, I reckon I haven't."

"Well, then, I'd like for you to meet our cousin, Sam Cotton, from—"

"From over San Antone way," Cody finished for her, wanting the story they told to be not only one he wouldn't have any trouble remembering but one it would be hard to prove was a lie. Not many people were going to trip him up if they started asking questions about San Antonio. He'd spent several years there, right after the end of the Civil War. He went on, "Glad to meet you, son. You must be Patrick. I've heard a heap about you."

Patrick frowned suspiciously. "From who?"

Cody gestured toward Sally and said, "Why, from your sister here, for one. She's told me quite a bit about you." That was a lie. Cody knew only Patrick's name and the fact that he was twelve years old. But he supposed twelve-year-old boys were alike the world over, at least to a certain extent.

Patrick Edwards was sturdily built, which was evident despite his loose bib overalls and muslin shirt, and he had a shock of brown hair, a smattering of freckles across his face, and bright, intelligent brown eyes. The casual way he handled the carbine showed that he was familiar with the weapon and had used it before, and Cody imagined he was pretty good at potting squirrels and rabbits. Shooting at a man was a different story.

His eyes still narrowed in suspicion, Patrick asked,

"If you're my cousin, how come you've never come to visit us before?"

Cody chuckled. "Well, I've been a mite busy, Patrick. Man's got to make a living, you know. I've been running cattle on a spread over close to San Antone, and that takes most of my time."

"You're a rancher? Have you been on a cattle drive?"

"Sure. I've taken a few herds up the trail to Kansas."

"To Abilene and Dodge?" Patrick was showing more interest now. "Did you ever see Wild Bill Hickok?"

"Have I seen Hickok? Why, I was in a saloon in Abilene one night when he came in, looking for some desperadoes that were wanted for murder. They were there, all right, but they weren't partial to the idea of being arrested. They threw down on Wild Bill, four men against one, but I never saw a man draw as fast as Hickok did that night."

Cody's voice became more animated as he got caught up in the flow of the story he was making up as he went along. "His arms were a blur as he reached for those Navy Colts he kept in a sash around his waist. He uses a cross-draw, you know, but he can get his guns out quicker than most men can blink. Well, Patrick, most of the folks in that saloon hit the floor when the shooting started, but I stayed where I was so I could watch Wild Bill trade lead with those outlaws. He's fast, but he's good, too, and nearly every shot he got off hit something. Those bandits started going down—"

"I think that's about enough of that tale, Cousin Sam," Sally interjected. "I don't want Patrick having nightmares about gunfights."

"Aw, Sally!" the youngster exclaimed. "I wasn't gonna have nightmares! Let Cousin Sam finish his story!"

Cody grinned. As he had hoped, Patrick had also gotten caught up in the yarn, and the barrel of the carbine was pointing toward the floor again. The boy wasn't going to argue about whether or not the stranger was related to him, not if he had such exciting stories to tell.

"Your sister's right," the Ranger told Patrick. "I'll finish telling you what happened some other time."

"But—"

Cody shook his head. "Don't argue about it, son. There'll be time for storytelling later."

"All right, dammit," Patrick muttered.

"Patrick!" Sally burst out. "What did you say?"

"Nothing, sis," Patrick answered quickly. "You need me for anything else?"

"No, you can run along and get ready for bed. And don't complain about it being too early."

Patrick was muttering again as he disappeared down the hall. Cody smiled and said to Sally, "He's a good-looking youngster. Seems smart as a whip."

"He is. Too smart for his own good, I sometimes think. It hasn't been easy, raising him since my mother died six years ago. But Dad and I do the best we can."

"It appears you're doing a fine job," Cody assured her. "Now, I want to meet your father."

"Come on. I'll take you to his room."

She led Cody down the hallway to a bedroom in the rear of the house. After knocking softly, she opened the door slightly and asked quietly, "Dad? Are you awake?"

"Come in, Sally," a tired voice answered. Cody could hear the weariness and pain in it.

Sally opened the door wider and ushered Cody in. Martin Edwards was lying in a big bed, and he turned his face toward his daughter. The flame in the room's single lamp was turned down low, making the bruises on the man's face somewhat less conspicuous, but Cody thought that in the light of day, the signs of the beating Edwards had endured a week earlier would still be painfully obvious. Bandages were wrapped tightly around his torso, and Cody recalled Sally saying that some of her father's ribs had been broken in the attack.

Edwards had crisp gray hair that was somewhat disheveled at the moment and a lean, weathered face. His cheeks were hollow, giving him a gaunt look, but his eyes were alert as he studied Cody and asked, "Who's this, Sally?"

Just in case Patrick was somewhere close by, Cody said, "Reckon you don't remember me. I'm your cousin, Sam Cotton, from San Antonio."

Edwards frowned and began, "But I don't have—"

Sally stopped him by stepping forward, shaking her head, and pressing a finger to her lips. Cody was already reaching for his watch. In a matter of seconds, he had the Ranger badge out, the silver emblem glinting in the light from the lamp on the bedside table. Edwards's eyes widened in surprise when he saw it.

"Cousin Sam has come to pay us a visit, Dad," Sally said. "Isn't that nice?"

"It . . . it certainly is," Edwards answered hesitantly. Cody's revealing himself as a Ranger had apparently cleared up some of the older man's confusion, but not all of it by a long shot.

Sally stuck her head out the door again and looked up and down the hallway. She turned back to the two men and said in a low voice, "It's safe enough, I think. Patrick doesn't seem to be anywhere around. I told him to get ready for bed, so he's probably in his room."

"What in blazes is going on?" Edwards demanded, keeping his own voice soft. "Are you really a Ranger, mister?"

"That's right," Cody assured him. Quickly, he filled the older man in on what had happened to Jeremiah Burgess and Rick Forman, and Edwards's eyes filled momentarily with grief when he learned about the tragic end of his friends' lives. Cody finished with an abbreviated version of the encounter in the Ace High with Turner and his "deputies." The Ranger concluded, "We've not been formally introduced. My name's really Cody, not Cotton."

Edwards took the hand that Cody extended to him.

"I'm Martin Edwards," he said. "And I'm mighty pleased to meet you, Mr. Cody. I just hope you haven't bitten off more than you can chew. Turner's got quite a few men on his side, and there's only one of you."

Cody shrugged. "One Ranger's usually enough. And another dozen men from Company C aren't that far away. I'd like to clean up this mess and get to the man responsible for it before Captain Vickery gets here, though."

"The man responsible . . ." Edwards grunted and gave a grimace as if he'd just bitten into a rotten apple. "That'd be Ben Bigelow."

"Don't reckon I know the name," Cody mused with a shake of his head. "Who is this Bigelow?"

"He owns a spread west of here. His ranch is big enough that I guess you'd call him a land baron. He showed up in the area about the same time the rest of us did, a couple of years ago when Twin Creeks was founded. He bought up a lot of land, and I guess he figured his wealth ought to buy him power and influence, too. Had it in his head that he was going to be in charge of things around here. He ran for mayor and was convinced he'd win without any trouble. But he lost." Edwards shook his head. "That was the start of all the trouble. Maybe Bigelow had never lost anything before, never had anybody stand up to him and say, 'No, you can't have that just because you want it,' because he swore the town would regret not electing him."

"Fella sounds a mite greedy, all right," Cody agreed. "But that doesn't mean he brought Turner in here."

Edwards leaned his head back against the pillows that were propped up behind him. It was obvious that talking tired him out, but he forced himself to go on. "I don't suppose we can prove anything against Bigelow. But he's been expanding his holdings all along, buying up some of the smaller spreads around his at ridiculously low prices."

"No crime in making a good deal," Cody pointed out.

"But Bigelow always made his offers right after a Comanche raid. Folks are scared, especially the smaller ranchers. Bigelow has a big crew, and they're tough. The renegades seem to leave him alone and go after the other settlers." Edwards shrugged. "Maybe Bigelow *doesn't* have anything to do with it, but he's certainly profited by the situation. The townspeople and the smaller ranchers are convinced he's behind all the trouble that's been plaguing us."

Cody frowned, turning his hat over in his hands. "You're saying folks believe he's working with the Indians?"

"It's a possibility. . . ."

Cody had to admit that it was. From the sound of things, Ben Bigelow was indeed the most logical candidate to have brought in Reb Turner and the other gunmen. The Ranger asked, "Has anybody ever seen Bigelow and Turner together?"

Sally answered that question by shaking her head and saying, "If they're working together, they're keeping it quiet. But Turner could ride out to Bigelow's ranch and report to him without any of us in town ever knowing about it."

"May have to keep an eye on Mr. Bigelow and Mr. Turner," Cody murmured, as much to himself as to the other two. "And Bigelow sounds like his background could do with some looking into." He smiled down at Martin Edwards. "Thanks. You've given me a good starting place."

"I suppose you want me to keep my mouth shut about you being a Ranger."

"For the time being," Cody confirmed with a nod. "I'll be more likely to get to the bottom of this if folks don't know who I really am."

Sally asked, "Will it be all right for Mr. Cody to stay here with us, Dad, while he's in Twin Creeks?"

"Of course. In fact, it's a fine idea. I—"

The sound of a footfall in the hall made Edwards stop abruptly. A knock sounded on the door, and Sally opened it to reveal Patrick standing there. The boy looked up at Cody, then said to Sally, "I know you told me to go to bed, but I got to thinking. . . . Cousin Sam, how about I show you around town tomorrow?"

"That'd be just fine, Patrick," Cody replied. "I can finish that story about Wild Bill then."

A grin broke out on Patrick's face. "That's what I was hoping you'd say. I'll see you in the morning."

"Good night, Patrick."

"Yes, good night, son," Edwards added. Sally went with Patrick to the boy's room to see that he was tucked in, a procedure that Patrick protested all the way down the hall.

Martin Edwards closed his eyes and sighed. "I thank God you came to help us, Mr. Cody," he said. "I hate to think what might have happened to Twin Creeks if you hadn't been there to help poor Jeremiah and Rick."

"Just because I'm here doesn't mean the trouble's all over," Cody warned. "Turner won't back down, and from the sound of it, Bigelow's not likely to, either. It'll be a fight all the way to put things right again."

"I have confidence in you, though. After all . . . you're a Ranger."

A moment later, Sally returned and told Cody, "I'll show you the spare bedroom. It'll be yours while you're here."

"Thanks. Is there a place around here where I can stable my cayuse?"

"There's a livery stable on Main Street, but we have a small barn out back. That might be better," she suggested.

Cody nodded. "I'll amble back down to the Ace High and fetch him, once I've seen that room." He turned back to Sally's father and went on, "Good night, Mr. Edwards. We'll talk some more tomorrow."

"Good night, son." Edwards's soft voice was hard to distinguish. He seemed almost asleep already, and Cody assumed the man had probably been dozing off a lot the last week, trying to regain the strength he had lost in the attack.

Still carrying his hat, the Ranger followed Sally into the hall, and she led him to a room several doors away. "It's a bit small," she apologized before opening the door.

"Room for a bunk's all that matters to me," Cody told her. "However small it is, it'll beat hard ground."

As she showed him the narrow little room, she said, "There's one more thing I'm curious about. That watch where you keep your . . . well, you know . . ."

Cody nodded. "What about it?"

"There's a picture of a girl in it. Who is she?"

He hesitated a moment, then said, "My sister. She's back home in Bandera."

"Oh. She's certainly lovely. I thought . . . maybe she was your sweetheart—or your wife."

Cody grinned. "Never had one of those."

"A wife, you mean? Or a sweetheart?"

"A wife. I reckon I've had a few sweethearts in my time."

"Yes," she said, nodding in thought. "I imagine you have." Pausing in the doorway, she pointed to another room across the hall. "My bedroom is right over there . . . in case you need anything during the night."

Cody hesitated. "I'll remember that."

CHAPTER
6

Despite Sally Edwards's thinly veiled invitation for him to pay her a visit during the night, Cody stayed in his own room. Sally was plenty attractive, but he had a feeling the main reason she had said what she had was that she was still mad at Tom O'Rourke. Cody had never bedded a woman just to spite another, and he didn't want anybody using him that way, either. Besides, he was sure that if he *had* accepted the offer, her upbringing would have prevented anything from happening and she would have been horribly embarrassed.

Between thinking about Sally and mulling over everything he had discovered about the situation in Twin Creeks, it took Cody quite a while to doze off. But he felt fresh and rested when he got up the next morning, and he had a rough idea how he was going to proceed.

Sally was quiet during breakfast, but Patrick made up for it. Excited and talkative, the youngster was anxious to get started on the tour of the town that he had promised Cody.

"How long are you going to be staying with us, Cousin Sam?" he wanted to know.

"Well, that all depends," Cody replied. "I reckon I'll be here for a few days, anyway. There'll be plenty of time for us to get to know each other, Patrick."

"I hope you don't wait so long before visiting us again."

"I do, too, son," Cody said with a smile. "I do, too."

When they were through with the meal—hotcakes and ham and eggs, all fresh and a whole heap better than the chuck Cody ate on the trail—Sally stood and said, "I'll take a tray in to Dad."

Cody scraped his chair back, and he stood as well. "And Patrick and I will take a look at the town."

Sally hesitated in the doorway to the kitchen. "Be careful," she said.

"Aw, sis, don't worry," Patrick told her. "Turner and his men won't bother us, and even if they do, Cousin Sam's tough enough to handle them. Aren't you, Cousin Sam?"

"A smart man doesn't go looking for trouble, Patrick," Cody told the youngster, adding silently, *unless he's a Ranger and it's his job.* To Sally, he went on, "We'll watch ourselves."

Patrick was dressed as he had been the night before, with the addition of a broad-brimmed hat. He reached for the carbine that was leaning in a corner of the front hall as he and Cody started to leave the house, but the Ranger shook his head and told him, "We won't need that."

"Yeah," Patrick agreed with a meaningful glance at the Colt on Cody's hip. "I reckon we won't."

Cody hadn't meant it quite that way, but he didn't see any point in arguing with the boy. They set out from the house, heading toward Main Street.

The morning was fairly warm, with lots of fluffy white clouds in the sky. As Cody and Patrick reached Main Street, the Ranger saw that there was some horse and wagon traffic on the thoroughfare, but overall the place wasn't as busy as a growing cow town should have been. That had to be because of the way Reb Turner had taken over. The townspeople would be lying low, to a certain extent, and the ranchers from the surrounding area probably didn't come into town as often as they had in the past.

As they walked along the boardwalk, Patrick pointed out all the businesses to Cody, filling the Ranger in on who owned what. Patrick knew quite a bit of gossip, too, and he wasn't shy about repeating it. Cody filed away all the information in his mind, well aware that a man could never know for sure what might turn out to be valuable later on. And Patrick, like many children, knew a lot more about what was going on around him than most adults—including his sister—probably realized.

As they neared the Ace High Cody saw that the saloon was already open, for its doors were thrown back, leaving just the batwings across the entrances, and he could hear piano music drifting from inside the building. Andre Duval was at it again, playing a soft, simple melody. Anybody who was drinking at this hour of the morning was probably trying to cure a hangover with a little hair of the dog, and they wouldn't want any music that was too loud.

As they passed the entrance that fronted on Main Street, Cody heard a sudden scraping of chairs and a crash as a table was overturned. "Watch it, you bastard!" somebody shouted, and the piano music fell abruptly silent. There was a rush of footfalls, a thud, then a groan.

His face suddenly grim, Cody said to the boy, "You wait here, Patrick. I'm going to have a look inside."

Patrick looked dubious. "Sally said to be careful. And you said a smart man doesn't go looking for trouble."

"Never claimed I was smart," Cody replied with a slight smile. He pushed the batwings aside and stepped inside.

His gaze flicked rapidly around the room, taking in everything. Only one bartender was behind the bar now, a different man from either of the bardogs who had been on duty the night before. Three customers were standing at the bar, but all of them had turned around to put their backs to the hardwood. None of the tables in the front half of the room were occupied, but men were clustered around one of the gambling tables in the back. The table was overturned, with playing cards, coins, and bills scattered around it.

Andre Duval was standing beside his piano, and as Cody entered the room, the saloonkeeper called out to the men in the back of the big room, "Stop it! Stop it, please!"

"Stay out of this, Frenchy," Reb Turner growled. He stood on one side of the overturned poker table with two other men. They were not the same ones who had been with him the night before, but they were cut from the same cloth: unshaven, roughly dressed, and with an air of brutality about them. More so-called deputies, Cody figured.

On the other side of the table were four men, ranchers from the look of their clothes. One of them was holding his head while two of his companions gripped his arms and kept him from falling. Blood from a long gash oozed between the fingers of the wounded man.

The fourth man stood a little in front of the others, glaring at Turner, and this man exclaimed, "You didn't have to pistol-whip him, you scoundrel! He wasn't going to—"

"He came at me," Turner interrupted. "That's resistin' an officer of the law." The sheriff's lips curled in a mocking smile as he drawled, "I'd've been within my rights to shoot him down, and you know it."

"I don't know anything of the sort," the other man responded hotly. "We were just playing a friendly game of poker—"

Again Turner didn't let him finish his statement. "I heard the four of you arguin'. I call that disturbin' the peace. That's why we came in here to break it up."

Duval took a few steps away from his piano. "They were not fighting, Sheriff. I know these men; they are old friends. They might insult one another, but it is all in fun—"

"I told you to stay out of it, Duval," Turner rasped. He looked past the saloonkeeper, his blue eyes gazing at Cody. "What the hell do *you* want?"

The Ranger shrugged. "I heard something going on in here and thought I'd step in to see what it was."

"None of your damned business, that's what it is. Now haul your ass out of here, mister."

Slowly, Cody shook his head. "I don't think so. You don't have any right to arrest these men. They claim they weren't fighting, and Duval backs them up. Maybe you'd better just let it go, Turner."

"Why, you son of a bitch," Turner breathed. "No right? I'm the sheriff of this town, ain't I? That's all the right I need!"

Cody said quietly, "Maybe somebody ought to do something about that."

Turner's face flushed with rage. He had forgotten about the four cardplayers; all of his anger was now directed at Cody. He leveled a finger at the Ranger and ordered, "Arrest that rabble-rousing bastard!"

The two deputies started toward Cody, grins of anticipation on their faces. The Ranger waited for them, standing easily just inside the door of the saloon, his thumbs hooked casually behind his belt. When the deputies got close to him, one of them held out his hand and growled, "Hand over that gun, mister."

"Take it," Cody challenged.

The deputy's hand balled into a fist and shot toward Cody's head. Cody moved smoothly to his left, letting the punch go harmlessly past him. While the deputy was off balance, Cody stepped forward and drove a fist into the man's belly, then followed it with a sharp left cross to the jaw. The deputy's head jerked around from the impact of the blow.

The other deputy let out a curse and reached for his gun, but Cody grabbed the lapels of the first man's coat and swung him around, giving him a hard shove that sent him staggering into his companion, delaying the draw. Cody pulled his own Colt, but not to fire the gun. He stepped forward, lashing out and down with the revolver, and its barrel cracked across the wrist of the second deputy. The man howled in pain and dropped his gun.

Instinct warned Cody and he swiveled slightly, pushing the two deputies aside. Turner's gun was out, and it was coming up fast.

For a split second, Cody thought about firing. But he didn't have any proof yet that Ben Bigelow was the force behind Turner, and until that was settled, he wanted the sheriff alive. So he lined his sights on Turner's breast pocket and shouted, "Hold it, Sheriff!"

Turner hesitated. He could probably get a shot off, but even if he did, Cody would down him, sure as hell. His voice shaking with fury, Turner railed, "Drawin' on an officer of the law puts you in big trouble, mister! You'd better just drop that gun now, and maybe it won't go so hard on you!"

"I don't think I'll do that," Cody responded, aware that everyone else in the room had ducked for cover. They were all still listening intently, however, to see how this confrontation was going to end. He wished he knew for sure that Patrick Edwards had obeyed him and stayed outside the saloon. Even though he hadn't known Patrick for long, Cody figured the boy might have ignored him and slipped through the batwings to watch—but he couldn't take his eyes off Turner to check. Taking a deep breath, Cody went on, "I've told you a couple of times now that I don't want trouble, Sheriff, and I meant it. But I'm not used to being shoved around, even by the law. Maybe I butted in on something that wasn't my business, like you said. Seemed to me those fellas weren't doing anything but playing cards and enjoying themselves, but maybe I was wrong. Why don't we all just put up our guns so people can go about their business, and let it go at that?"

"You're crazy," Turner snarled. "You attacked my deputies, resisted arrest—"

"And I'm mighty sorry," Cody cut in with a smile. "That satisfy you? Or do we have to start shooting and maybe all die?"

Turner licked dry lips. It was apparent to Cody that the sheriff knew somebody would die if any gunfire broke out, all right—him. Cody could see the man weighing the odds in his mind, deciding whether or not his pride was worth his life.

Suddenly, Turner lowered his gun and jammed it back in its holster. "You've got more goddamn gall than anybody I've ever seen, mister," he snapped. "Someday it's going to catch up to you."

"But not today."

"Not today," Turner agreed reluctantly. He turned to his deputies, who were standing to one side of Cody, nursing their bruises. "Get on back to the office, dammit!"

"What about the card game?" Cody asked, knowing that he was pushing.

"I still say these men were disturbing the peace," Turner insisted. "But I'll let them off with a warning this time, if they'll get out of town."

Cody nodded, willing to let Turner save some pride for the moment. "Sounds fair enough to me."

A couple of the stockmen began to grumble, but a hard look from Cody silenced them. If not for his intervention, they would be in jail now if not worse, and they knew it. Silently, they filed out of the saloon after the crestfallen deputies, turning toward the doctor's office to get some medical attention for the head wound Turner had inflicted with his pistol's gunsight.

The sheriff gestured toward Cody's Colt. "You going to put that up?" he asked.

"Might as well," Cody replied, slowly lowering the gun. "The trouble's over, isn't it?"

"Yeah," Turner grunted. "All over."

But it was clear from the look in the sheriff's eyes that it wasn't over. Turner had disliked him before; now, after this humbling encounter, he would regard the Ranger as a bitter—and permanent—enemy.

Turner stalked to the side entrance and slapped the batwings out of his way. He left the saloon without a backward glance, his spine stiff and the back of his neck brick red with anger.

Andre Duval heaved a long sigh as he looked at

Cody. "You have done an unwise thing, *mon ami*," he stated. "That one will never forget that you forced him to back down."

"Good," Cody responded. "I don't want him to forget it."

A whistle of admiration came from behind him, and he looked around to see Patrick standing just inside the front entrance. "Hot damn!" the youngster exclaimed. "I never saw anybody draw like that before!"

"Well, you'd better not let your sister hear you talking like that," Cody warned him, "or you won't ever see much of anything again. And you'd better learn to do what grown-ups tell you to do, too."

"Aw, I just wanted to see what was going on. I never figured you'd turn out to be a gunslinger, Cousin Sam!"

Cody shook his head. "I'm no gunslinger. Now you run along outside and wait for me. We'll get back to that tour in a few minutes."

"Can't I wait for you in here?" Patrick asked.

"Nope. Now, do like you're told."

The boy trudged reluctantly out of the saloon, and Cody turned back to Andre Duval. "Who were those men Turner was trying to put the run on?" he asked.

"Cattlemen from ranches north of here," the saloonkeeper replied. "Chadwick was the one who was standing up to Turner; Searles had the cut on his head from Turner's gun, and their friends Owen and Gardner were holding him up. Good men, all of them."

"They've managed to hold out and keep from selling to Ben Bigelow, then?" Cody queried.

Duval shot him a sharp glance. "Who told you about Ben Bigelow?"

"I'm staying with my relative, Martin Edwards," Cody said quietly. "He told me a little about what's been going on."

"If you came for a visit, you picked a bad time. Things in this part of the country, they are bad right now. It would be better, perhaps, if you rode on."

Cody smiled. "Don't reckon I can do that. I've dealt

myself in; I've got to play out the hand." He paused for a second, then asked, "Does Turner usually give the honest ranchers as much trouble as he did today?"

Duval shrugged expressively and said, "It has become harder and harder for men such as Chadwick and the others to carry out their business. They are harassed when they come to town, which is why they all came in together today to buy supplies. While their wagons were being loaded, they came over here for a friendly game of cards. You saw how that turned out."

"Yeah," Cody grunted. "I sure did." The Ranger rubbed his chin in thought. "If folks can't buy supplies without trouble, they're going to have a hard time keeping their ranches going. Might have to sell out to a bigger spread like Bigelow's."

"You said that, not I, *mon ami.*"

"Sounds like this fella Bigelow is the man to see if you want to get along around here."

The saloonkeeper's face stiffened, and his voice was cool as he said, "If a man had no qualms about who he associates with, that might indeed be true."

"Sometimes a man can't afford to be too picky," Cody countered. He waved a hand as he started toward the doorway. "I'll see you around."

"Yes. I am sure you will."

So far, so good, the Ranger thought as he shouldered out past the batwings. He had established himself as a touchy hombre who was tough enough not to let himself be pushed around. Of course, in the process he had made an enemy out of Reb Turner, but that might not be a bad thing. The next step was to find out more about Ben Bigelow. . . .

Patrick was waiting for him on the boardwalk. Cody grinned, slapped the boy on the shoulder, and suggested, "Well, let's get on with it, why don't we?"

Across the street and half a block away, Reb Turner stood in the shadowy doorway of the sheriff's office and jail, watching as the tall gunslinger walked away with Patrick Edwards. Hatred smoldered in Turner's eyes, and it took an effort of self-control not to yank out his pistol and put a bullet in the man's back. There would be time enough for that later, once he found out what Sam Cotton was really doing in Twin Creeks.

"C'mere, Hayes," Turner said over his shoulder, summoning one of the deputies in the office. When the man appeared at Turner's side, the sheriff went on, "I want you to keep an eye on that bastard while I go talk to Bigelow."

"Why don't I just get a Winchester and put a slug in the son of a bitch's back?" Hayes asked harshly, rubbing his sore wrist where the stranger had hit it with his six-gun.

Turner shook his head. "No, I don't want him dead . . . yet. I want to find out what he's up to first."

"You reckon he's got somethin' to do with Bigelow?"

"No reason to think that," Turner replied. "But Bigelow don't tell me everything he's doing." A wry smile plucked at the phony lawman's lips. "Of course, we don't tell him everything either, now, do we?"

Hayes chuckled. "He's gonna be mighty surprised when we clean out the town bank and then leave him holdin' the bag."

"Won't he, though," Turner agreed, nodding. "It'll be a good payoff for us—as soon as the time is right. But first I want to milk this for all it's worth. In fact, I think it's time for Bigelow to up the ante a bit more." He stepped onto the boardwalk and added over his shoulder, "Watch Cotton, like I told you. I'll be back after a while."

Turner's horse was tied at the hitching post in front of the jail. Jerking the reins free, he swung up into the saddle, then turned the animal and galloped north along Main Street, heading out of Twin Creeks.

He would be glad when he could put this place behind him for the last time. Working for Bigelow paid well, and double-crossing the rancher was going to pay even better, but Turner still had a funny feeling about this job. It was like cold fingers up and down his spine, and the sensation had gotten more intense since Sam Cotton had ridden into town.

Yeah, Reb Turner thought, he would be very glad to leave Twin Creeks for good.

"How's our visitor this morning?" Martin Edwards asked his daughter, when Sally brought him a tray with his breakfast.

"Just fine, I suppose," Sally replied. "He and Patrick are out taking a look at the town. Patrick is certainly excited to have him here."

Edwards smiled tiredly. He had slept late and had not been awake long, but already the day was taking a toll on him, Sally thought. "He'd be even more excited if he knew Mr. Cody was a Ranger," Edwards said.

"Let's hope he doesn't find out," Sally rejoined, laughing softly. "If he does, the whole town will know about it." She became more serious. "I hope they don't run into any trouble."

"Cody struck me as the sort who can handle just about any kind of trouble. They'll be all right, Sally."

"I suppose so."

While her father ate, she went back to the kitchen and started cleaning up the breakfast dishes. As she worked, her mind kept coming back to Cody.

She felt herself flushing as she recalled the blatant invitation she had issued to him the night before. At least it had seemed blatant to her. She had still been full of anger at Tom O'Rourke, and it wasn't just because he had forgotten about dinner. She was mad because of the way he was letting himself sink deeper into self-pity.

Still, she was glad Cody hadn't come to her room after all. Instead of the shameless hussy she had pretended to be, he would have found a scared, inexperienced girl.

Well, maybe it was time she stopped being so fright-

ened, she told herself. Maybe it was past time she
stopped being a girl and started being a woman—

The knock at the back door made her head jerk
around sharply. She swallowed, deciding the visitor
probably wasn't Turner or one of his men. They would
have just barged in without knocking. "Who is it?" she
called.

"Tom . . . Tom O'Rourke."

Sally took a deep breath as she stepped over to the
door. What would she see when she opened it? He
hadn't sounded drunk, but it was hard to tell with Tom.

Opening the door, she found O'Rourke holding his
hat in his hands and looking contrite. He turned the
Stetson over nervously and nodded to her. "Morning,
Sally. Can I talk to you for a few minutes?"

He seemed sober. She hesitated, then stepped back.
"All right. But only for a few minutes. I have a lot of
work to do today."

O'Rourke nodded again and came into the kitchen,
leaving the door open behind him. "I just wanted to
say I'm sorry about last night," he began. "I remember now that we were supposed to have dinner together. I reckon it just, uh, slipped my mind."

"You mean you forgot because you were drunk."
The words came out sharper—meaner—than she had
intended, and she saw pain flare in his eyes.

But then his jaw tightened and he admitted, "Yeah,
that's right. I was drunk."

"That seems to be a common occurrence with you
these days."

"I didn't come over here for a sermon, Sally,"
O'Rourke snapped. "I just came to apologize. You can
accept it or not, that's up to you."

She looked down at the floor. "All right. I accept
your apology. But it would mean more if you'd quit
trying to drown all your problems in whiskey."

Coming a step closer, O'Rourke reached out and
grasped her arm. "Who are you to judge me?" he demanded as she gasped in surprise. "You don't know

what it's like to have everybody turn on you! Nobody
had the guts to back me up when the showdown came
with Turner, but afterward, I heard all the comments.
People thought I was a coward, just because I didn't let
myself be gunned down like some sort of sacrificial
lamb!"

Sally shook her head. "No one thought that, Tom,"
she told him. "No one but you. We didn't want you to
get killed—"

"That's what would've happened if I'd gone up
against Turner and all his men."

"I know." For a moment, she felt a surge of pity for
him, but she forced it back. That wasn't going to do
him any good. What he needed now was strength.
"There are other things you can do now. You could
support the citizens' committee. They're trying to get
rid of Turner."

O'Rourke laughed. "How? By sneaking around and
patting themselves on the back while they stay out of
the line of fire?"

Sally bit her lip. She could tell him that the committee had sent for help and that even now a Texas Ranger
was in Twin Creeks, working to free the town from
Turner's tyranny. But Cody had made a point of asking
her not to tell O'Rourke who he really was, and she
had to honor that request. "I'm sure someone will
think of something," she murmured.

"Yeah, and it'll just get somebody else hurt, like
what happened to your father. That's how anybody
who opposes Turner will end up."

"My father is a brave man," Sally insisted. "He
stood up for what he thought was right. You could use
some of his courage, Tom." He flinched at her blunt
words, but she pressed on, "Even a stranger in town
has shown more courage than you have lately."

"You're talking about Cotton?"

"He's my cousin from San Antonio."

O'Rourke frowned in surprise. "Cousin? I didn't
know that. I heard he had a run-in with Turner last

night after I left the Ace High, but nobody said anything about him being related to you."

"Well, he is, and he's staying with us awhile."

O'Rourke's frown became a glare. "Staying with you? Are you out of your mind? If he's put himself on the opposite side from Turner, that's just going to cause trouble for you and your family. Isn't what happened to your father enough?"

"You sound like Turner now."

O'Rourke's words seemed to catch in his throat at the comparison to the hated sheriff. His hand tightened on Sally's arm, and he finally warned, "I'm not going to argue with you, girl. You can't let Cotton stay here. Sooner or later, Turner will come gunning for him."

"If—*if*—that happens, then we'll face up to it," Sally insisted. "Nobody can run scared their whole life, Tom . . . except maybe—"

He let go of her arm and stepped back abruptly. "Shut up!" he hissed. "You're just like the others. You think I'm a coward, too. One of these days I'll show you—show the whole bunch of you!"

With that he turned and stalked out through the open kitchen door, not looking back as he left. Sally watched him go, her insides knotting up in confusion. There had been a time when she was convinced that she loved Tom O'Rourke, but now she felt mostly anger and pity, and that was a horrible mixture. Somewhere under his own chaotic emotions she sensed that there was still a good man. But whether or not that good man would ever show himself again, Sally couldn't say.

The only thing she was sure of at the moment was that she hated Reb Turner—for what he had done to Tom O'Rourke, to her father . . . to all of them.

CHAPTER 7

Not surprisingly, Cody's instincts warned him that somebody was following him. He paused on the boardwalk and put a hand on Patrick's shoulder. "Wait a minute, son," he said as he glanced back.

Cody caught sight of a bulky shape darting off the boardwalk into the doorway of a store, and a slight smile tugged at the Ranger's mouth. Although he had only caught a glimpse of the follower, he had recognized one of Turner's deputies, the man he had disarmed with a blow from his Colt. Turner had probably ordered the deputy to keep an eye on him.

Looking up the street, Cody spotted the sheriff himself, riding quickly out of town. That was interesting, he thought, and wondered where Turner was going. To report to the man who had hired him, maybe?

The Ranger's horse was in the barn behind the Edwards house, several blocks away. "Come on," Cody told Patrick, increasing his pace. "Sorry, but we've got to cut this short."

"But you didn't finish telling me about Wild Bill Hickok," the youngster reminded him.

"Later," Cody promised as they walked quickly toward Patrick's house, his hand still on the boy's shoulder to hurry him along. Patrick complained a bit, but he obviously sensed that Cody had something else on his mind now and kept quiet for the most part.

Throwing an occasional glance over his shoulder, Cody saw that the deputy was staying about half a block behind them. That was a problem that would have to be dealt with, and pretty damn quickly at that. Turner would already have a good lead on him, although Cody was fairly confident he could easily close the gap enough to trail the sheriff.

Cody and Patrick turned into the cross street where the Edwards house was located. On the corner of the intersection was a feed store, and several heavy sacks of grain were stacked up along the side wall of the building. An idea came to Cody when he saw them, and he said to Patrick, "Keep going toward your house. And don't look back."

"But—"

"I need your help, Patrick. Do as I say."

The boy nodded abruptly, cast one more puzzled glance at Cody, then started on down the boardwalk, which played out at the end of this building. Cody flattened himself against the wall, just beyond the sacks of grain. He heard approaching footfalls and knew the deputy was hurrying to bring his quarry into sight again. Twisting around, Cody put his shoulder against the sacks, which were piled up taller than his head.

The deputy turned the corner just as Cody shoved with all his strength, and the Ranger couldn't tell if the man even saw him before the sacks began to topple. The deputy had time to let out a yell, but then the top sack—which had to weigh at least eighty pounds— slammed into him, followed closely by several more. One of the sacks split, sending a shower of grain down on the man as he was knocked to the boardwalk by the miniature avalanche.

The man's face was covered with grain, and he was coughing and pawing at the stuff as Cody pulled his Colt and stepped up to him, then rapped the butt on the deputy's head. That would hold him for a while, Cody thought as the man went limp.

Holstering his gun, the Ranger turned and ran toward the Edwards house, finding that Patrick had stopped not far up the street and was watching wide-eyed. As Cody came up, the boy exclaimed, "That deputy's going to hate you, Cousin Sam! That's twice this morning you got the best of him."

"I'll worry about that later, Patrick. Right now I need my horse. Why don't you lead him out of the barn while I get my saddle?"

"Sure!"

With Patrick's help, it took Cody only a couple of minutes to get the horse saddled and ready to ride. As he mounted up, Sally appeared in the back doorway of the house and called out, "Cousin Sam! Where are you going?"

"Got an errand to run," Cody replied. "I'll be back later." He heeled the horse into a trot, guiding it around the house.

By the time he reached the northern end of Main Street, Turner was out of sight. The road turned into a trail that curved to the left, and Cody decided to follow it. Turner could have veered off at any time, but the Ranger remembered Martin Edwards saying that Bigelow's ranch was west of town. The trail headed in the right general direction, anyway. Putting his horse into a gallop, Cody urged top speed from the big dun, which responded eagerly, glad for a chance to stretch its legs.

Half an hour after leaving Twin Creeks, Cody topped a rise that commanded a good view of the rolling hills to the west. He squinted in the morning sunlight and spotted a rider about half a mile ahead of him. That would be Reb Turner, Cody decided, recognizing the sheriff's shirt from the flash of color. With a grim smile on his face, the Ranger slowed his own mount. It wouldn't do to get too close to Turner and risk being noticed, so Cody was willing to hang back and follow at a distance.

In another fifteen minutes, the terrain leveled out slightly into a broad valley, and Cody judged that the line of green on the horizon marked the course of the Rio Grande. Well to this side of the border river, a magnificent house surrounded by cottonwoods reared into view. Built of whitewashed timbers freighted in from either east Texas or New Mexico Territory, the house rose three stories, and in a land of squatty adobe structures, it was quite a sight. Cody didn't doubt for a second that he was looking at the home of Ben Bigelow.

And at the moment, Reb Turner was riding into the clearing in front of the ranch house.

Cody reined in, hooked a leg around the saddle horn, and studied the lay of the land. The rolling hills of Bigelow's range were covered with grass that was still thick. The heat of summer would start to dry it out in a few weeks, but right now it was prime grazing land, and accordingly, the hills were dotted with longhorns. Cody could see probably a couple of thousand head just from where he was sitting. North of the ranch house was an area of mesquite and thick chaparral, and there would be even more of the half-wild cattle lying up in there, he supposed. A man could approach the place unobserved from that direction, if he didn't mind doing a little brush popping.

Overall, Bigelow had a fine-looking spread, and most men would have been more than satisfied with it. But from what Martin Edwards had said, Ben Bigelow wasn't the type to ever be satisfied with anything he had. He would always want more and more, his greed driving him on. Some men with that force eating away their insides became outlaws, Cody thought; others became land barons. Sometimes there wasn't much difference between the two.

He might be judging Bigelow too quickly, he reminded himself. The fact that Turner had ridden out here to see him didn't look good for the rancher, but it wasn't really proof of anything.

Cody stayed where he was, watching patiently as Turner dismounted, handed his horse over to a man who emerged from a bunkhouse near the big frame building, and went to the front door of the house. Someone answered his knock and let him in.

Close to an hour passed before Turner reappeared. He came out onto the porch of the house accompanied by a smaller man in a suit. At this distance, it was hard for Cody to be sure what was going on, but Turner and the other man were talking animatedly. Finally, Turner nodded, got on his horse, which had been tied to a small hitchrack in front of the house, and rode away without looking back.

Cody looked around for some cover. The large area of chaparral north of the house extended in several fingers away from the main growth. Cody rode toward one of them, easing his horse into the thick, scrubby growth. He stopped and turned his horse around when he was far enough in so that he couldn't be easily seen from the trail. Penetrating much farther into the thorny stuff would have been hard on both him and his mount.

A flurry of hoofbeats reached his ears as Turner rode past. When the noise had faded completely away, Cody eased his horse out of the chaparral and turned it toward the ranch house. It was time to pay a visit to Mr. Bigelow.

As the Ranger drew closer to the ranch headquarters, he could see that there were quite a few outbuildings—a bunkhouse for the hands, a cookshack, a blacksmith shop, and several sheds that were probably used for storage. More signs of Bigelow's wealth, Cody mused, and he wondered what made a man who already had so much want even more.

But that wasn't the important question. The only thing that mattered at the moment was how he was going to stop Bigelow, assuming the rancher was the man behind the trouble in and around Twin Creeks.

Three men emerged from the bunkhouse, and when they saw the stranger riding in, their slouching, casual attitudes disappeared. Straightening, they strode quickly toward Cody, and he noticed that all three men kept their hands close to their guns.

"Howdy, mister," one of the men called as Cody reined in about halfway between the bunkhouse and the main house. "Somethin' I can do for you?"

Cody studied the man briefly. He was middle-aged, with plenty of gray in his dark hair and mustache. His face had the seamed, leathery look of a man who had spent practically all of his life outdoors. A Remington revolver hung on his hip, and he looked as though he knew how to use it.

"Maybe you can help me," Cody said. "You the range boss around here?"

"That's right. Name's Garrison. But if you're lookin' for a ridin' job, we ain't hirin' right now. Sorry."

Cody rested his hands on the saddle horn and leaned forward slightly. "Well," he said with a grin, "I might be looking for work, but I've never been much of a one for punching cows. I want to see the owner of this place."

His eyes narrowing, the foreman said, "Just what sort of work was you lookin' for, then?"

"Reckon I'd best take that up with the head man."

Garrison exchanged a glance with his two companions. All three of the hands appeared to be tough and capable, bad men to cross, but they didn't strike Cody as hired guns. Garrison spat in the dirt of the ranch yard and said, "Ain't just anybody who can waltz in here and see the boss. You got a name, mister?"

"Cotton. Sam Cotton." Cody paused for a second, then went on, "Your boss may have heard of me, real recent-like."

Another glance passed between Garrison and the other two. They were probably aware that Reb Turner had been in the main house just a few minutes earlier, and now this stranger was hinting that he might have been the subject of the sheriff's conversation with Bigelow. Garrison nodded thoughtfully and said, "Maybe you ought to get down off that horse for a while, Mr. Cotton. I'll see if anybody inside wants to talk to you."

"'Preciate it," Cody murmured as he swung down from the saddle and then led his horse over to the hitchrack. He looped the reins over the rail while Garrison went up onto the veranda of the house and knocked on the door.

Cody caught a glimpse of a man in a suit when the door opened and Garrison went inside, but it wasn't the same man who had been talking to Turner on the porch earlier. While the Ranger waited, the two cowboys stood silently nearby, obviously intending to watch him while Garrison was gone.

After a few minutes, the front door opened again. The foreman didn't appear, but the man in the suit did, and he said stiffly and formally, "Please come in, Mr. Cotton."

Cody went up the steps and through the door, taking off his hat as he did so. The man in the suit was tall and balding and carefully expressionless, and Cody realized he was some sort of servant. Butlers, the Ranger thought—that was what they called such fellas back east, wasn't it?

"Follow me, sir."

Trailing along a hallway behind the man, Cody was struck by how cushiony the rug was underneath his feet. He felt as if he were walking on thick grass. The walls of the corridor had some sort of gilt-embossed paper on them, on which paintings were hung at intervals, and a couple of delicate and highly polished tables held vases of fresh-cut flowers. Cody saw a stairway at the end of the hall, but the butler stopped before he got that far. The man opened a door and stepped aside so that Cody could enter the room.

"Someone will be with you shortly," he told the Ranger.

Cody frowned and nodded. Something was wrong with this setup, but he couldn't quite figure out what. The butler closed the door behind him as he stepped into the room, and the thought flashed through the Ranger's mind that this might be some sort of trap.

However, no one was inside the room, which was a good-sized chamber papered in pale blue with a large bay window that overlooked a flower garden. Carefully arranged about the room were several brocade-covered armchairs, a love seat upholstered with the same fabric, and more of the small, intricately carved tables, these covered with fancy lace doilies. A large credenza placed against one wall displayed a selection of fragile ceramic figurines.

Cody turned back toward the door, thinking that a mistake must have been made. No rancher would greet a visitor in such a place. This was a woman's room. However, before he could reach the door to the hall, a smaller door on the far side of the room opened, and a female voice asked, "Mr. Cotton?"

Cody stopped in his tracks and looked over his shoulder. He had been right. He knew instinctively that the woman who had just come into the room had been responsible for its furnishings.

She was tall and stately and just about the most beautiful woman he had seen in a long time. Honey-blond hair fell in soft curls to her shoulders and then tumbled halfway down her back, and her lips were full and red, while her eyes were a smoldering blue. She wore a burgundy gown that was cut daringly low, revealing the tantalizing beginning of the valley between her breasts. Cody put her age somewhere around twenty-five, and he felt the impact of her beauty all the way to the pit of his stomach. Some men would die for a woman like this. And some would kill. . . .

"I'm Gloria Bigelow," she said as she came across the room, extending her slender hand to him. "I understand you want to talk to my husband."

"That's right, ma'am." Cody found his tongue after a second's hesitation. He took her hand for a moment, and her fingers were as cool and smooth as he would have expected.

"I hope you'll forgive me for telling Phillips to show you in here first." Her voice was soft and slightly husky, and it packed almost as much punch as her looks, Cody thought. "I've heard of you, and I wanted to speak to you for a moment before my husband does."

"Heard of me? I'm not sure how, ma'am. I'm not what you'd call famous."

She smiled. "Oh, no? The man who has faced down

Reb Turner not once but twice? I'd say you're becoming famous in this part of the country, Mr. Cotton."

Obviously, she had either been part of the meeting between her husband and Turner, or she had eavesdropped on their conversation. Cody had no idea which, and it didn't really matter. As beautiful as Gloria Bigelow was, he had come here to see her husband.

"Well, fame's not something I ever set out after, ma'am," he began.

"Call me Gloria. And you're . . . Sam?"

Her voice became even more throaty as she spoke his name, and he realized she was putting on her seductive air deliberately. He frowned. What the hell was going on here?

Heavy footsteps sounded outside the hallway door and saved Cody from having to come up with an answer for her. The door opened and a man whom Cody recognized as the one who had talked with Turner stepped inside. His dark gray suit and vest were obviously of the finest cut, and light from the big window struck the diamond in the stickpin on his cravat and reflected brilliantly. His graying hair was slicked down, and his face had something of a houndlike appearance. His gaze went from Cody to Gloria and back again.

"Mr. Cotton?" he said. "I'm Ben Bigelow. Glad to meet you."

Cody took the hand that Bigelow thrust at him. "Sam Cotton," he replied. "I appreciate your seeing me, Mr. Bigelow."

The rancher waved off the thanks. "It's my pleasure, sir. I'm just sorry you got sidetracked in here." Looking at his wife, he told her, "Gloria, you can run along now. Thank you for entertaining Mr. Cotton."

"I don't mind staying, Ben—"

"That won't be necessary," Bigelow said coldly. "If I need you for anything, I'll send Phillips for you."

Gloria caught her lower lip between even white teeth for a moment, then nodded and went to the smaller doorway. "Good-bye, Mr. Cotton. I hope you come again soon," she said, looking at Cody with a different kind of invitation all too evident in her eyes.

He nodded and said politely, "Ma'am," then turned his attention back to Bigelow. If the rancher had noticed how his wife was playing up to the visitor—and Cody didn't see how Bigelow could have helped but notice—he wasn't showing any signs of being bothered by it.

Cody suddenly wondered how Mrs. Bigelow and Reb Turner got along.

As the door into the adjoining room closed behind Gloria, Bigelow hooked a thumb in his vest pocket and gestured at the furnishings with his other hand. "If you don't mind talking business in such highfalutin' surroundings, Mr. Cotton, perhaps you could tell me what brings you to the Box B."

"The Box B . . . that's your brand?"

"That's right."

"Nice-looking spread you've got here, Mr. Bigelow. Reckon you'd hate to see anything happen to it."

Bigelow frowned. "And what does that mean? I have to tell you, Mr. Cotton, some people might construe your comment as a threat."

Cody wondered idly if Bigelow was packing a gun under his coat. It was possible that the rancher had a small-caliber pistol in a shoulder rig—but Cody didn't intend to find out just yet. He said, "No threats. I just meant that you're risking quite a bit by working with a man like Reb Turner."

The rancher's frown deepened. "What do you know about Reb Turner?"

"I know he's an overrated blowhard," Cody said bluntly. "He thinks he and his gang are the toughest bastards this side of the Rio Grande, but he's wrong."

"Oh?" Bigelow smiled slightly now. "And how is he wrong?"

"*I'm* the toughest bastard on this side of the river—and on the other side, too."

Bigelow chuckled and said, "You're certainly one of

the most audacious, Mr. Cotton. Tell me what brings you to Twin Creeks."

"I've got relatives there," Cody replied with a shrug. "But I wouldn't have wasted my time visiting them if I hadn't heard there was a chance a man like me might find work around here."

"A man like you . . ." Bigelow repeated. "To be honest, you look like a cowboy to me, Mr. Cotton, and I have plenty of cowboys working for me."

Cody shook his head. "I told your foreman I don't punch cows." He put his hand on the butt of his Colt.

Bigelow took a cigar from his shirt pocket and stuck it in his mouth without lighting it or offering one to Cody. "This is ridiculous," he grated around the stogie. "Are you offering me your services as a hired gun?"

Cody shrugged again. "Figured you were in the market. You took Turner on."

"I don't know how you found out about that, but it's true," Bigelow admitted. "Turner is working for me. And I'm quite pleased with his results so far. Why should I hire you?"

Cody looked around the room with its feminine furnishings. "Can't very well show you in here."

"Well, let's go outside, then. I must admit, you've got me curious, Mr. Cotton."

Bigelow ushered the Ranger out of the room and down the hall to a rear door. They stepped out onto a large patio paved with stones. On the other side of the patio, about thirty feet away, was a circular fountain similar to some of the ones Cody had seen in missions back in San Antonio. Unlike those fountains, though, this one had a statue of a naked youth in the center of it. The hands of the statue held a pitcher, and water poured from it to splash into the pool at the base of the sculpture.

Cody turned to face Bigelow as the rancher said, "I assume you wanted to come outside to demonstrate your skill with a gun." He pointed past Cody with the cigar and continued, "My wife insisted I buy that statue, and I've always hated it. Use it for target practice, and I'll have a good excuse for getting rid of the thing."

Cody hesitated. "You're sure? I wouldn't want to offend the lady—"

"Don't worry about that," Bigelow snapped. "Show me what you can do, or get on your horse and quit wasting my time."

Cody jerked his head in a terse nod. Abruptly, he spun around, the Colt sliding out of its holster smoothly and rapidly. The Ranger fired three times, the shots so close together they seemed to blend into one long roar. Lowering the gun, a wisp of powder smoke trailing from its muzzle, Cody faced Bigelow again and asked, "How's that?"

The rancher looked past him, raising his eyebrows as he saw the two bullet holes where the statue's eyes had been. The third bullet had gone considerably lower, smashing to powder the sculpture's stone manhood.

A laugh burst out of Bigelow. "Quite effective, Mr. Cotton!" he exclaimed. "My wife may be a bit disappointed, especially in your choice of targets, but you've proved your ability." A serious expression came over the rancher's face. "You've yet to prove your trustworthiness, though."

"Give me a job," Cody suggested. "You'll see quick enough that I ride for the brand."

"I believe I will hire you. But not to take Turner's place. I need someone here on the ranch, someone I can trust just in case Turner gets a little too ambitious. Do you get my drift, Mr. Cotton?"

Cody nodded solemnly. "I sure do. And I can tell you, Mr. Bigelow, if that ever happened, it'd be a pleasure to take care of it for you."

"I imagine it would. I heard about your encounters with Reb. He said you were—let's see, how did he phrase it?—just about the proddiest son of a bitch he'd ever seen."

"Coming from him, I'll take that as a compliment," Cody remarked with a grin.

"All right," Bigelow said, his voice becoming brisk and businesslike. "The pay is a hundred a month, with the possibility of several bonuses if things go the way I want them to. You'll bunk here. Shad Garrison is the foreman, and I'd advise you to get along with him, but your real orders will come from me, understand?"

"Sure. I'll just ride back in to Twin Creeks and pick up my gear. Be back later today."

"What about your relatives? The Edwards family, correct? What will they think of you going to work for me?"

Turner must have given Bigelow a full report, Cody thought, including the identity of his alleged relatives. Martin Edwards and the citizens' committee stood in the way of Bigelow's plans, and Cody didn't want the rancher thinking that he had any sympathy for their cause.

"Who gives a damn what they think?" Cody replied. "I came to this part of the country to work, not to sing hymns and bitch about how the poor folks are being mistreated. You'll see I've got a whole heap more loyalty to the man who pays my wages than to somebody who accidentally happens to be related to me."

"Money means more than kin, eh?" Bigelow asked with a smirk, obviously fairly certain that he had Cody pegged now.

"Reckon you could say that."

"Very good. We'll see you later in the day, then."

Cody nodded. Bigelow led him back through the house and out the front door. The Ranger didn't see Gloria again, and he was glad of that. Until he had a better idea of what was going on here at the Box B, he didn't need the distraction of a beautiful, restless woman.

Swinging up into the saddle, Cody nodded to Bigelow, then turned and rode away from the ranch house. He had taken the next step in his plan, and things were becoming increasingly clearer. Bigelow had already admitted that Turner was working for him, but the Ranger had a hunch there was still more to discover under the surface. Bigelow talked like a man with big plans, and Cody wanted to know what they were before he made a move to stop the rancher.

Sooner or later, though, the showdown would come, with Bigelow and Turner both—and Cody was looking forward to it.

CHAPTER
8

Back in Twin Creeks, several townsmen showed up at the Edwards home at intervals during the day, and Sally Edwards admitted them and took them to her father's room. She knew all of them—Mr. Margulies from the general store; Mr. Cole, the apothecary; Mr. Hendryx, the blacksmith; Mr. Gomez, who ran the feed store; and Reverend Morris Ogden, the pastor of the local church—and Sally knew as well that, along with her father, they were the leaders of the citizens' committee that wanted to rid the town of Reb Turner and his gunmen. Although she didn't sit in on any of the discussions her father had with the men, she had a good idea what they were about.

That afternoon, when the final visitor had left, Sally took some tea to her father's room. He was propped up on his pillows, and his face was even paler than usual, for the parade of visitors had worn him out.

"Maybe you should get some sleep, Dad," Sally suggested. "I can wake you when it's time for supper."

Martin Edwards shook his head. "No, there's no time to sleep now. Just pour me a cup of tea and let me collect my thoughts. We're going to have a meeting tonight."

"But you've been talking to the other members of the committee all day," Sally protested, frowning. "Why do you need to have a meeting?"

"I haven't talked to everyone, only the other leaders . . . if we're even worthy of the name after the way we let Turner come into our town and take it over. The others are spreading the word about the meeting, so there should be a good crowd, maybe even some people who haven't come over to our side yet." Edwards's voice strengthened. "This could be the beginning of something very important, Sally. This could be the beginning of Reb Turner's end."

Quietly, Sally asked, "Are you going to tell them about Mr. Cody?"

Edwards sighed and shook his head. "Not without his permission. And he hasn't come back from wherever he rode off to, has he? I've been listening for him."

"No, I haven't seen him since this morning. He didn't say anything to Patrick about where he was going, just that he had some business to attend to. I'm sure it had something to do with his mission here."

"Well, if he shows up in time, I'll ask him if I can reveal his identity to the other members of the committee. If not, I'll keep silent about it for the time being."

Sally agreed with that plan. Pouring a cup of tea for her father, she left him sipping it and returned to the kitchen. She paused in her work and looked out the window for a moment, wondering where Cody was. The instinctive faith she had felt in him the night before was still there, and she was sure that wherever he was, whatever he was doing, he was trying to help the citizens of Twin Creeks.

The pattering footfalls behind her told her that Patrick had just entered the room. Turning, she smiled at her young brother and said, "I haven't seen much of you today. Where have you been?"

"Down in town, waiting for Cousin Sam to come back," Patrick replied as he sat down at the kitchen table. "He's supposed to tell me the rest of that story about Wild Bill Hickok. But I got tired of waiting, so I came back."

"You really like your cousin, don't you?"

"Shoot, yeah," Patrick answered. "Why wouldn't I?"

"No reason. He seems like a good man."

"You said you don't really know him, right?"

Sally nodded and got some potatoes from the bin, then sat down across from her brother to peel them. "That's right, I don't. As I told you, I'd never met him until last night myself. But I'd like to get to know him better."

Patrick grinned. "Sounds to me like you're gettin' sweet on him."

"I'm doing no such thing!" Sally protested. "Besides, he's our cousin." That was two lies, she told herself.

Patrick suddenly shoved his chair back and stood up. "I hear a horse," he declared. Running to the window, he peered out and exclaimed, "It's Cousin Sam! He's back!"

Sally got to her feet and joined her brother at the window. Cody came riding around the house, but instead of putting his horse in the barn, he reined in at the back door. Sally frowned. Something about the Ranger's actions bothered her.

He came in the door a moment later, grinning at both of them. "Afternoon," he said. "Everything quiet here in town?"

Sally wanted to tell him about the committee meeting that night, but she couldn't with Patrick in the room. The boy knew of the committee's existence, of course, but Sally tried to keep him apart from their activities as much as possible so that he would be safer.

"Everything's fine," she replied. "Patrick, why don't you go see if Dad needs anything else? He's probably through with his tea by now."

"But I want to talk to Cousin Sam—"

"It'll only take you a minute," she said firmly.

Patrick sighed, nodded, and went out. When he was gone, Cody said, "I reckon something's up, or you wouldn't have sent the boy out."

"The citizens' committee is going to have a meeting here tonight," Sally explained quickly. "Can you come? Dad wants to tell them you're a Ranger, but he won't without your permission."

Cody shook his head, a somber look coming over his face. "I won't be here tonight, and I'd rather your father didn't say anything about me to the other folks just yet."

"Won't be here?" Sally repeated. "Where are you going?"

"To work for Ben Bigelow," Cody answered.

She stiffened in shock. "Bigelow?" she managed to say after a moment. "You're working for Bigelow now?"

"Not really," Cody replied with a shake of his head. "But he thinks I am. Your father and the others were right about him; he's the one who brought Turner here. But he's got something else up his sleeve, and I want to find out what it is before I make a move against him."

Sally took a deep breath. "I suppose that makes sense. But won't it be dangerous for you, being right in the middle of all those gunmen?"

"Won't be the first time," Cody told her, smiling. "Don't worry, I'll keep an eye on my back."

Patrick entered the room, carrying his father's cup, in time to catch the last part of Cody's statement. He stopped short and said, "Sounds like you're going somewhere, Cousin Sam."

Cody nodded to the youngster. "I've got to leave for a while, Patrick. I need some money, and I was offered a few days' work at a ranch not far from here. So I'll still be around. I'll see you again 'fore I leave this part of the country."

Patrick looked upset. He asked, "What ranch?"

Cody exchanged a quick glance with Sally, then answered, "Fella named Bigelow owns it."

"I knew it!" Patrick exclaimed. "Don't go out there, Cousin Sam. They'll kill you!"

Cody grimaced, asking wryly, "Now, why in the world would anybody want to do that?"

"Because they'll find out you're a Ranger!"

Sally caught her breath. "Patrick! What . . . what are you talking about? Cousin Sam's not a—"

"Oh, hell, he is, too." Patrick's voice shook with the depth of his emotion. "I'm not deaf and blind, sis, and I know a lot more than you give me credit for. I heard the two of you talking last night before you ever came in the house."

Cody had stiffened at Patrick's initial outburst, but now a grin spread across his face. "You little hellion," he said with a chuckle. "So you knew all along!"

Patrick shrugged. "Sure. But I figured it'd be better if I let all of you think you had me fooled. Besides, it was . . . it was kind of nice to pretend I really did have a Cousin Sam who was a Texas Ranger."

Sally looked at her brother for a long moment, then sighed and shook her head. Turning to Cody, she asked, "What are we going to do now?"

"Nothing much we can do," he replied pragmatically. "We'll have to trust Patrick to keep the secret—"

"I will," the boy promised. "I swear I will. But I still don't want you to go out to Mr. Bigelow's ranch. My dad thinks he's the one behind all the trouble."

Cody pulled out a kitchen chair, reversed it, and straddled it, motioning for Patrick to sit down at the table as well. "Your dad's right," the Ranger said as Patrick took another chair. "But I've still got work to do, and a Ranger doesn't back down just because the trail gets a little rough, son. Your sister and your dad haven't backed down. I can't, either. But I'll be careful, and I'll be all right."

"You promise?" the boy asked solemnly.

"Sure. You got the word of a Texas Ranger on it, Patrick."

The youngster smiled. "I reckon that's good enough for me. But I'll miss you while you're gone."

Cody stood up. "Reckon I'll miss you, too. Now, you've got to promise me that you'll take care of your sister and not do anything foolish."

"You've got my word on it."

Cody clapped the boy on the shoulder. "I reckon that's good enough for *me*." He turned to Sally. "I've got to get my gear together, and then I'll be riding."

She nodded, unable to say anything. Now that she'd had a chance to think about what Cody was doing, she was as frightened for him as Patrick had been. If Bigelow found out that Cody was a Ranger—

That kind of thinking wasn't going to do any of them any good. Forcing lightness into her voice, she told Cody, "I'll fix you a little something to eat on the way back out there."

"Thanks." Cody smiled at both of them and left the room.

"It'll be all right, Sally," Patrick said when Cody was gone. "Cousin Sam can take care of himself." Pausing, he added, "That's the way I'm going to think of him. You reckon he'll mind?"

She smiled and shook her head. "No, I don't think he will."

She got out some bread and ham to make a couple of sandwiches for Cody to take with him. The chore was just something to keep her mind occupied, but that was how she was going to have to proceed until this was all over. She would stay busy, and maybe she wouldn't worry so much.

A soft knock came at the back door. They were certainly getting the visitors today, Sally thought as she wiped her hands and went over to see who was there. The committee members had all come to the front door, she recalled. Tom O'Rourke was the only one who came to the back. . . .

And he was here again, she saw as she opened the door.

"Hello, Sally," O'Rourke said. "May I come in and talk to you for a minute?"

She wasn't sure what he would have to say to her after their conversation that morning, but politeness made her step back to let him in. "Of course," she replied.

O'Rourke came into the room and saw Patrick sitting

at the table. "Hi, Pat," he said in a friendly tone. "How are you?"

"Fine," Patrick replied sullenly, not looking at O'Rourke.

"Haven't seen much of you lately. What have you been up to?"

"Not much." Patrick's voice was still cold. "I don't get into the saloons very often."

O'Rourke's jaw tightened, but other than that he seemed to ignore the boy's gibe. Turning to Sally, he said, "I want to talk to you about that meeting tonight."

"Meeting?" she echoed.

"Don't play dumb with me, Sally," he countered. "People all over town are whispering about the citizens' committee meeting here tonight. If they're trying to keep it a secret, they're not doing a very good job. And you can bet that if I know about the meeting, Turner sure as hell does."

"What's your point?" she asked, trying not to show how disturbed she was at the news he had brought.

"I want you to call it off."

She blinked in surprise, then said, "I . . . I can't do that."

He frowned, took a step toward her, then stopped. "You've got to. You've got to talk to your father and tell him that somebody's going to get hurt—hurt bad— if he and his friends keep stirring up trouble."

Sally started to shake her head, but O'Rourke hurried on, "Don't you see the danger your family is in? It's bad enough that your father is the ringleader of those troublemakers, but then you have to go and take in that gunfighter—"

"He's not a gunfighter," Patrick cut in, and for an instant Sally was afraid he was going to blurt out Cody's real identity. But then the boy looked down at the table again and repeated, "He's not a gunfighter."

"Well, whatever he is, he's trouble," O'Rourke grunted. Turning back to Sally, he continued, "You've got to think about yourself, Sally, and about Patrick. The chances you're taking—"

Again Patrick interrupted. "I'm not afraid," he said sharply, standing up. "I'm not a coward like some people!"

It was obvious whom he was talking about. O'Rourke paled under the lash of the boy's words.

Suddenly, Sally found herself turning to face her brother. Her hand came up, seemingly of its own volition, and slapped Patrick's face. She had no idea why she had done such a thing, why she would defend Tom O'Rourke, and she gasped, every bit as surprised as Patrick.

Tears welled up in the boy's eyes, but they were tears of hurt and anger, not pain. "Fine!" He threw the word at his sister. "Maybe you can't make up your mind about things, but I damn sure can!" He whirled around and ran from the room before she could say a word to him—even if she had known what to say.

"I . . . I'm sorry, Tom," she told O'Rourke after a moment. "I don't know what made Patrick say that. He didn't hear it in this house, I can promise you that."

O'Rourke's face was stony. "It doesn't matter," he muttered. "Maybe the boy's right. But I still want you to get your father to call off the meeting."

"I can't. I just can't."

A new voice said from the doorway, "Sally's right. Things have gone too far. Calling off one meeting's not going to change anything."

O'Rourke spun around as Cody stepped into the room. "You!" the former sheriff exclaimed. "You're the one who's to blame for all this! Why the hell are you goading these people into getting themselves killed?"

Cody shook his head. "I'm not goading anybody into anything. Open your eyes, O'Rourke. When folks start fighting back, it's because they're damn sick and tired of being stepped on."

"No." O'Rourke was breathing heavier now. "You

can spout all the words you want, mister. All I know is that everything got worse when you came to town. I think you ought to leave."

"Can't," Cody said simply. "Not yet."

"Then maybe somebody needs to throw you out!" O'Rourke's eyes narrowed, and he clenched his fists as he took a step toward the Ranger.

"Tom! No!" Sally cried.

She was too late. O'Rourke was already swinging a punch toward Cody's head.

O'Rourke wasn't drunk now, and he still possessed some of the speed and skill he'd had before he started putting away so much whiskey. Cody tried to get out of the way, but O'Rourke's fist grazed the side of his head, and the blow made him take a staggering step before he was able to catch himself.

Sally's heart was pounding in her chest as O'Rourke closed in on his opponent, throwing another punch. She didn't want to see either man hurt, but unless O'Rourke came to his senses—

Cody was able to sidestep O'Rourke's second blow. While the big man was off balance from the miss, Cody stepped in and hammered a fist into his belly. O'Rourke bent forward, grunting in pain, and an instant later his face caught a sharp jab from Cody's left that straightened him again. The Ranger then brought his right around in a looping blow that slammed into O'Rourke's jaw. Eyes glazing over, O'Rourke stumbled back a couple of steps and then fell to one knee.

With his fists clenched, Cody waited to see if O'Rourke was going to get up and come back for more. Seizing the chance, Sally darted between the two men and rested a hand on Cody's chest, begging, "Please! Please don't—"

O'Rourke got to his feet. "Get out of the way, dammit!" he growled, shaking his head. "You don't have to protect me, Sally. I'm not scared of him."

Sally turned quickly to face him. "Did you ever stop to think that I don't want my kitchen torn up by a couple of fools acting like a pair of old bulls?" she demanded hotly. "I won't have any fighting in my house!"

"Sorry, Sally," Cody said. "I don't want trouble, either, but I won't back down from it."

O'Rourke's hat had been knocked off in the scuffle. He bent over, picked it up, and jammed it on his head. "You people are all crazy," he muttered. "It's not worth fighting over." He looked at Sally. "Remember what I said about calling off that meeting. You're risking all of your lives." With that, he turned and stalked out of the house.

Sally sighed, then realized she still had her hand on Cody's chest. Taking a quick step backward, she said, "I'm sorry. I don't know what got into Tom. . . ."

"Pride," Cody said. "Like we talked about before, this whole situation is eating at him. He's striking back at whatever target happens to be convenient—like me."

"Are you . . . ready to go?"

He nodded. "I've got everything together."

"I don't suppose you know how long you'll be out at Bigelow's ranch?"

"No telling," Cody responded, shrugging. "Depends on how the job goes."

"You promised Patrick you'd be all right. I want you to promise me, too."

A smile tugged at the Ranger's lips. "Sure. But you know a man in my line of work can't really promise anything of the sort."

"I know," Sally said softly. "I just want to hear it."

Cody put a hand on her shoulder and squeezed gently. "I promise."

Word had gotten around town about the trouble in the Ace High that morning, and business in the saloon was unusually slow this evening. Not many people wanted to risk being harassed by Turner and his deputies. When Tom O'Rourke pushed through the batwings, there were only half a dozen customers in the place—and two of them were Turner's deputies.

The deputies gave O'Rourke an idle glance as he walked in and slumped into a chair at one of the tables. At one time, they might have taken more notice of him, but none of Turner's men regarded him as much of a threat now. The deputies turned their attention back to their drinks.

Andre Duval was behind the bar tonight, leaving the piano silent. That silence contributed to the gloomy atmosphere in the place. As O'Rourke caught Duval's eye and signaled for a drink, the other men who had been at the bar left, casting contemptuous looks at the former sheriff as they filed out. At least, that was the way O'Rourke saw the glances. Maybe they were just pitying him, he thought, but that was just as bad.

The two deputies were left alone at the bar, and one of them said in a loud voice, "Looks like folks around here think they're too good to drink with us, Harvey."

"I'd say you're right, Nate," the other man replied. "'Cept for ol' Tom back there. He ain't too good for anybody."

"I'd say he's no good at all," the one called Nate quipped, laughing.

O'Rourke heard the words clearly, and deep inside, a flame of anger sprang into life. But Duval was bringing over a bottle and a glass, and O'Rourke knew from experience that the whiskey would soon put out that fire.

It was funny, he thought. Throw whiskey on a regular flame and it would burn that much brighter. It didn't affect *him* that way.

As Duval set the bottle and glass on the table, he remarked quietly, "It is not good you are here tonight, *mon ami*. Perhaps for once—"

"I should forget about drinking?" O'Rourke grasped the neck of the bottle and jerked the cork from it with his other hand. "I don't think so, Duval. I tried sobering up and talking sense to people, but it didn't do anybody a damn bit of good, least of all me. Just got me in trouble. From now on, other people's problems are their own lookout."

Duval regarded him for a long moment, then went back to the bar. As O'Rourke tipped the bottle and splashed liquor into the glass, he glowered at the saloonkeeper. Duval was just a slimy little French piano player, O'Rourke thought as he tossed back the drink. The man didn't have any right to look down on him.

Might as well, though. Everybody else did. Sally hated him, and that fella Cotton figured him for a worthless coward, just like the rest of the town. The way Sally felt was what hurt the worst, O'Rourke mused. There had been a time when the two of them—

No point in thinking about that. Those days were long gone. He had seen the way she looked at Cotton. He could tell how she felt about the gunslinging stranger.

And yet, she had defended him when her brother called him a coward. Why would she do that, unless she still had some feelings . . . ?

Sure, she had feelings for him, O'Rourke told himself bitterly. Pity, mostly.

As he poured a second drink, the voices of the deputies penetrated again, and he caught the end of a question from the one called Harvey. "—think Reb'll do to those stupid townies?"

"I ain't sure what he's got planned, but I reckon it'll be fun," Nate replied. "And when we're through, they'll think twice about havin' any more of those damned committee meetin's."

O'Rourke's fingers tightened on the glass. So, Turner *had* found out about the meeting at the Edwards house tonight, just as O'Rourke had feared. And obviously, from the way the deputies were talking, Turner planned to do something about it.

Knowing the so-called sheriff as he did, O'Rourke was sure that that something would be violent. Turner would break up the meeting and try to throw such a scare into the townspeople that they wouldn't even attempt to organize against him again.

O'Rourke drained the whiskey glass, feeling the
warm shock as the fiery stuff went down his throat. He
had tried to warn Sally that this was coming. If there
was trouble, it would be on her head.

He waited for the pleasant haze that usually accompanied his drinking to steal over his brain, but tonight,
for some reason, it didn't come. Despite a third slug of
whiskey and then a fourth, his thoughts remained crys-
tal clear—and they were thoughts of what might happen to Sally when Turner made his move against the
committee.

O'Rourke glanced at the deputies again. They still
weren't paying any attention to him. Taking a deep
breath, he stood up clumsily, then headed toward the
door, swaying slightly as he walked so that anyone
looking at him would think he was drunk. He didn't
even glance at Harvey and Nate, but instead kept his
head down, his eyes deliberately unfocused.

When he reached the boardwalk, he kept up the act
until he was a good block away from the Ace High, just
in case anybody was watching. Then he straightened
and began walking faster.

Within half a minute, Tom O'Rourke was running.

Several hours had passed since the ugly incident
with Tom O'Rourke, and Sally Edwards was completely calm now. At least she tried to tell herself she
was. She had fed Patrick an early supper and sent him
to his room, then helped her father get dressed and
walk from his room to the parlor. No sooner had she
gotten him settled in a comfortable armchair than the
first soft knock had come on the door.

Now the room was full, with townsmen filling all the
chairs and the rest of them standing. Sally counted
nearly thirty men in the parlor, and not all of them were
businessmen from Twin Creeks. Quite a few of the
smaller ranchers from the surrounding area were also
there. It was a good group, quite representative of the
honest citizens in this part of the country.

She was the only female in the room, and for a moment she was afraid that her father would try to chase her out, but instead he said, "Sally, why don't you tell everyone what's going on?"

"All right, Dad." She moved to the center of the room, feeling somewhat embarrassed and nervous because of all the eyes on her. Before Cody had left for the Box B again, they had worked out the details of what the committee would be told, and now Sally began, "As you know, several days ago two men were sent to Del Rio to try to get help from the Rangers there. We've found out that they got through, or at least Jeremiah Burgess did. Rick Forman was killed along the way in an attack by Comanche renegades."

A murmur of shock and regret went through the room. Most of the men here had known and liked Forman.

"Mr. Burgess was mortally wounded, too," Sally went on, "but before he died, he reached the Ranger post and told them about our problem. There are . . . indications that the Rangers are already in this area, working to restore law and order."

"Indications?" one of the men echoed from the back of the room. "What sort of indications?"

"I really can't say right now," she replied. Cody had agreed that she could tell them that much, but that she should not mention him by name or reveal his pose as her cousin. "I can assure you, though, that things are starting to turn our way."

It was clear from the grumbling that went on in the next few minutes that most of the committee members were not satisfied with her vague statements. Sally wished she could tell them more, but she had to abide by her promise to Cody.

The front door of the house opened suddenly. Sally looked toward the foyer, expecting that the new arrival was a latecomer to the meeting, but it was Tom O'Rourke's big figure that loomed in the doorway to the parlor, a grim expression on his face.

"You've all got to get out of here," he announced.

"Turner and his men plan to break up this meeting. There could be violence."

Sally looked for some sign that O'Rourke was drunk, but he seemed sober enough. His normally slack-looking face was stiff with anxiety.

"How do you know this, Tom?" Martin Edwards demanded. "Everyone here was sworn to secrecy—"

O'Rourke snorted in disgust. "Most of these busybodies couldn't keep a secret if they were the last person on earth." He scowled at the group. "You all get together to twitter about how sorry things are, but don't do a damn thing to change them."

Edwards straightened in his chair. "See here!" he snapped, with some of his old fire. "You've got no call to talk to us that way, Tom. We *are* trying to change things. That's why we sent for the Rangers—"

The front door was suddenly forcefully opened, crashing back against the wall. Sally let out a cry of surprise as Reb Turner strode into the room, followed by half a dozen of his deputies.

Everyone tensed, but for the moment all Turner did was hook his thumbs in his belt and regard the gathering with a mocking smile on his face. "You folks get together for a little prayer meetin'?" he asked snidely.

Edwards swallowed, then said, "You've got no right to come busting in here like this, Sheriff. This is a private home—"

"I've got a right to come in anywhere I think there's criminal activity going on, Edwards," Turner cut in.

"But we're not doing anything illegal!" Edwards protested. "This is just a gathering of friends!"

"Got a permit for it?" Turner demanded.

"This is my home! I don't need a permit to have a few friends come over!"

Sally moved closer to her father and put a hand on his shoulder. In his condition, he couldn't afford to get too angry or excited. He was still too weak for that. Weak from the beating Turner's men had given him, she thought, staring coldly at the outlaw.

Turner came a few steps farther into the parlor, his

men close behind him, and the committee members drew back to give them room. Planting his feet in front of Edwards's armchair, Turner growled, "You need a permit now, mister. New rule, just established by the sheriff's office. So if you don't have one, you're all breaking the law, and I'd be within my rights to haul you all into jail."

Sally saw the fury and hatred in her father's eyes, and her hand tightened on his shoulder. But he ignored her and grated, "Get out of my house, you bastard!"

"Resisting an officer of the law, eh?" Turner retorted, grinning. He reached out and grabbed Edwards's collar, declaring, "Well, you can be the first one tossed behind bars, you old buzzard!"

"No!" Sally cried, leaping forward. She caught at Turner's arm and tried to wrench his grip loose. "Let him go!"

Scowling, Turner put his other hand on her face and shoved.

As she staggered back, she heard a roar of anger; then someone crashed into Turner, knocking him loose from her father. Sally caught her balance against the wall and saw Tom O'Rourke swinging a malletlike fist at Turner's head.

The blow never landed. One of Turner's deputies drew his gun, stepped up quickly behind the former sheriff, and slammed the weapon against the back of O'Rourke's neck. He let out a groan and slumped forward into the arms of more of Turner's men, waiting to catch him. They held him upright while Turner threw a couple of savage punches into his belly.

Other fights were breaking out around the room as a few members of the committee tried to stand up to the deputies, but they were no match for the hardcases.

Martin Edwards had slumped back into his chair, and Sally knelt beside him, an arm around his shoulders. Tears rolled down her cheeks as she watched Turner pummeling the helpless O'Rourke, who seemed to be barely conscious now, his head hanging limply on his shoulders and his face streaked with blood. The other men who had fought back were faring equally badly.

After what seemed like an eternity but must have been only a couple of minutes, Turner stepped back from O'Rourke and barked, "Take him to jail! Take all these other bastards, too! Maybe a night behind bars'll teach 'em a lesson!"

One of the deputies gestured toward Sally and her father. "What about the old man?"

Shaking his head, Turner replied, "Leave him be. I'll handle him." The sheriff strode over to the armchair and glowered down at Edwards. "I know you're the ringleader of this bunch, but I've decided I'm not going to throw you in jail. You just think about all your friends behind bars, though. You never know what might happen to them while they're there."

"You . . . you inhuman . . ."

"Better watch that mouth of yours," Turner warned with a tight grin. "It's already caused a heap of trouble." He turned to Sally. "As for you . . ."

His hands—stained with Tom O'Rourke's blood— caught her arms and pulled her against him. His mouth came down hard on hers, his tongue insistent against her lips. She writhed and tried to pull out of his grip, but he was too strong. Finally, she tore her mouth away from his, and he laughed.

"You'll give me what I want, girl," he told her in a low, harsh voice. "You'll give it to me—or I'll take it. You've got one more day to make up your mind."

Numb, almost overcome by revulsion, Sally looked past Turner and saw O'Rourke being dragged out of the room by the outlaw deputies. The members of the committee were being herded out at gunpoint, except for a couple of men who had been knocked out cold during the fighting and were also being dragged.

O'Rourke's eyes met Sally's for an instant, and she saw the pain in them—not only pain from the beating, she realized, but also from what he had just witnessed. And then he was gone.

"Remember," Turner's voice prodded her. "One more day."

Releasing her arms, he turned to stride out of the parlor, his walk jaunty with self-satisfaction.

For the first time in her life, Sally Edwards wanted to kill somebody. If she'd had a gun in her hand at that instant, she would have emptied it into the bastard's back without hesitation.

Her head slumped. She didn't have a gun. And she and her father and their friends had done everything they could to fight back against Turner's reign of terror, without success.

It was all up to Cody now.

CHAPTER

9

Cody arrived back at the Box B earlier that afternoon, and as he rode up, Shad Garrison, the foreman, and several other hands were standing beside the corral. Neither Ben Bigelow nor his wife, Gloria, were anywhere in sight. Reining in and swinging down from the saddle, the Ranger smiled at Garrison and remarked, "Looks like I'm working here now. Reckon I can turn my horse into this corral?"

"Sure," Garrison grunted. "Mr. Bigelow told me you'd signed on, Cotton. I just got one thing to say to you."

"Let's hear it." Cody waited.

"Do what you're told and keep your nose clean, and you won't have no trouble with me. But you best remember—I've seen gunslicks come and I've seen 'em go, usually in a pine box. So I ain't scared of you."

"No need to be," Cody replied with a grin. "I'm a peaceable man, Shad."

The foreman grunted again and walked off as Cody began unsaddling his horse.

All his gear was in his saddlebags. When he had placed the saddle itself on a sawhorse in the barn, he slung the *bags* over his shoulder and picked up his sheathed Winchester. Coming outside again, he spotted one of the Box B punchers and walked over to the man, asking, "Where's a fella supposed to sleep around here?"

The man didn't answer for a moment, his expression

hard and unfriendly in the gathering twilight. "Bunkhouse is full," he finally replied curtly. "Reckon you can use one of those cabins." He inclined his head toward the small buildings Cody had previously assumed were used for storage.

Shrugging, the Ranger walked toward the nearest cabin. The chilly reception he got from Garrison and the cowboys wasn't unusual. He was an outsider, and he would be one until he had proved himself. That was typical among hardened crews like the one Bigelow had put together.

The door of the small building had no lock. Unlatching it and stepping back, letting what was left of the daylight into the cabin, Cody saw that his assumption had been partially correct: A bunch of crates was stacked inside the room, taking up most of the floor space. But there was a narrow aisle between the piles of boxes, and in the back of the room, under the building's single window, was a bunk. These storage cabins apparently served double duty as living quarters whenever the bunkhouse was full.

Cody wondered briefly if the bunkhouse was really that crowded, or if the hands just didn't want him bunking in with them. Not that it mattered, he thought as he stepped into the cabin and dropped his saddlebags on the thin blanket covering the bunk. He'd slept in a lot worse places.

Still, looking around at the narrow confines of the shed, he felt a little shiver go down his spine. He'd never liked being closed in too much, ever since he had gotten stuck in a cave he was exploring on his parents' ranch as a boy. The torch he'd taken with him had burned out, and he'd been left there with rock pressing in around him on all sides. Finally, he had managed to slither through the tight space—with the sweat of fear coating his body—and found his way back to sunlight and the world. But the terrifying memory of the experience had stayed with him for a long time, and it still cropped up every now and then. That was why he liked riding the open range, he supposed.

Forcing his mind away from those childhood memories, Cody hoped he could get closer to a few of the cowboys. If they let their guard down, they might be able to tell him more about what was going on here at the Box B.

The growling in his stomach reminded him that it had been many hours since breakfast. He had missed lunch while he was riding back and forth from Twin Creeks to the ranch, and Tom O'Rourke's visit had interrupted Sally's sandwich making. Cody went in search of something to eat, and as luck would have it, the cook stepped out of the main house at that moment and rang a bell on the back porch. Cowboys emerged from the bunkhouse, ready for supper.

The hands ate in a big dining room next to the kitchen, and while the long table was crowded, the men managed to leave an empty chair on each side of Cody. He frowned. This was carrying unfriendliness a mite too far, he thought. No one spoke more than two words to him during the meal.

After supper, the cowboys ambled back outside. Some of them sat on the back steps and rolled quirlies for an after-dinner smoke, enjoying the warm evening air, while others returned to the bunkhouse to repair their tack or play cards or turn in early.

Cody spotted Shad Garrison over by the corral and strode toward the foreman. "Evening, Shad," the Ranger said as he came up to him.

"Don't recall us bein' on a first-name basis, Cotton," Garrison snapped. He turned away from Cody and leaned on the pole fence, watching the horses inside the corral.

Cody put a hand on his arm, and Garrison stiffened. "Look, I didn't come here to cause trouble for anybody," Cody said. "Now, how about telling me why everybody's got their back up. I've seen Comanche war parties that were friendlier."

The foreman jerked his arm free and turned to glare at Cody. "You want to know why we ain't welcomin' you with open arms, is that it?" he asked sarcastically.

"Hell, a man in your line of work oughtn't to be surprised when folks ain't overly friendly."

Cody did not dispute the man's assumption that he
was a gunslinger; however, he countered, "I've looked
over the rest of this crew, and there's not a man among
you that don't still have the bark on him."

"Maybe so, but we been with the boss a long time. It
was bad enough when he brought in that fella Turner
and those other men, but hell, at least they stay in
town. What're you doin' here on the ranch, Cotton?"

Cody drew a deep breath. So that was it. The Box B
hands didn't like Turner, and they saw him as more of
the same, only intruding even farther into their territory. Maybe he could turn those feelings to his advantage.

"If you're worried about Turner and me being
friends, you don't have to," Cody said. "Him and me
have already had a couple of run-ins." He considered
carefully what he was about to say next, then went on,
"If you ask me, the boss doesn't trust Turner too much
himself. He wanted me on hand just in case there was
trouble."

Garrison's eyes narrowed as he studied the tall
Ranger. "Is that a fact?" the foreman finally said. "I
ain't overly fond of Turner. He ain't nothin' but an
owlhoot."

"That's the way I size him up, too." Cody could
sense that Garrison's hostility was receding somewhat.
"And another thing, Shad—I'm not here to take anybody's place on the ranch. I've never been much for
punching cows, like I told you this morning. When my
job's done, I'll be riding on."

Garrison nodded. "Fair enough. What'd you say
your first handle was?"

"Sam," Cody answered, grinning. "Sam Cotton."

"All right, Sam. I'll spread the word 'mongst the
boys that you ain't aimin' to take over. Hope for your
sake that you're tellin' the truth."

Garrison walked away without saying anything else,
but at least his back wasn't as stiff as it had been ear-

lier. Cody wondered for a second if the foreman was just trying to fool him, wondered if Garrison was really as hostile toward him as ever. He didn't really think so; Shad Garrison struck him as a blunt, straightforward man, not the type for a lot of deception and double-dealing.

Cody strolled around the ranch headquarters, looking up at the stars and letting the warm breeze wash over him. Once again he thought that this was mighty pretty country, and the way the sky spread out above his head, it seemed as though there ought to be plenty of room for everybody. A man like Bigelow, who wanted it all and was willing to go to any lengths to get it, had to be stopped. That was one reason he had become a Ranger. That was also why his father had joined up with Jack Hays and Bigfoot Wallace and the original Rangers.

Cody knew he had some big shoes to fill. Even though Adam Cody had died before he had a chance to see the kind of man his son would become, the Ranger liked to think that, somehow, his father knew. Cody could have been back on the ranch near Bandera, content to tend to his own little corner of the world and let other folks deal with their own problems. But there was something inside him that would never be satisfied with that, and he had always known it.

Still, he didn't put any fancy words on it. He was no knight in shining armor, like those English guys in that fella Walter Scott's stories. He was just a Ranger, a man with a job he was good at and that he wanted to do for as long as he was able. That was all there was to it.

Cody walked back to his cabin and sat on his bunk. A candle sat on one of the boxes, but he didn't light it. He'd put in quite a few miles today, and even though it was early, he decided to get some sleep. He had hoped that Bigelow might want to see him again, maybe tell him what he had in mind for Cody to do to earn his pay, but that didn't seem to be forthcoming.

Shucking his hat, boots, and gun belt, the Ranger took the .45 from the holster and slipped it under the thin pillow. It might make for a hard place to rest his head, but he wanted the Colt close. Enough moonlight came in through the window to let him see the stacks of crates, and he wondered briefly what was in them, then dozed off.

Campaigns against the Indians had taught him how to sleep. Except on rare occasions like the other day, when he had been exhausted enough to fall into a deep sleep, he slumbered lightly, and a part of his brain remained alert. He judged that two or maybe three hours had passed when he suddenly came fully awake.

Cody's ears strained, listening for any telltale signs of whatever had awakened him. He knew it had to have been a noise of some sort, and something out of the ordinary, at that. The normal sounds of a ranch at night wouldn't have disturbed him.

A tiny scrape of a foot on the ground came from just outside the door of the cabin. That was what he had heard, Cody decided as he slipped his hand under the pillow and closed his fingers around the revolver's butt. Somebody had approached the cabin, and now he was standing out there. Was he trying to decide whether or not to come in? Maybe making sure Cody was good and asleep before busting in and ambushing him?

The latch on the door clicked. Whoever the visitor was, he no longer hesitated.

The cabin was no more than eight feet long. In a flash, Cody had rolled off the bed, come up lightly on his feet, and lunged down the aisle between the supplies. As the door swung open, revealing a figure silhouetted against the moonlit night, Cody reacted automatically. Reaching out with his free hand, he grabbed a strange-feeling fabric and jerked the intruder inside. He thrust his foot between the person's ankles, and whoever it was went down. Leaning over his captive, the Ranger thumbed back the hammer of his gun, the click loudly ominous in the darkness.

"My goodness!" a throaty voice exclaimed.

Cody realized that the material in his hand was not the rough fabric of a cowboy's shirt—it was too soft, too silky. And the intruder didn't smell like a cowboy, either. A light, delicate scent like fresh flowers drifted to his nose. The startled exclamation confirmed the visitor's identity.

"What the hell are you doing here, Mrs. Bigelow?" he demanded. "Dammit, I could've shot you!"

"Yes, but you didn't, Mr. Cotton," she replied, sounding a bit more calm now. "And if you'll let me up, I'll be glad to explain."

Cody let go of her silk robe—that was what the garment had to be, he decided—and stepped back, easing the hammer down on the Colt. "Sorry," he muttered. "Reckon I shouldn't've jumped you. But it's not very smart, coming up quiet-like where a fella's sleeping."

"I know that. I'm the one who should apologize." Gloria Bigelow got to her feet and brushed herself off. Now that she was standing, he could see that she was indeed wearing a dressing gown, which was belted tightly around the waist and clinging to her slender figure. Cody was relieved that the light in the cabin was dim and he couldn't see any more than that.

"Please, Mr. Cotton, sit down," she requested. "I hated to disturb you, but it's very important that I talk to you."

Cody had to brush past her to sit down on the bunk, and when he did so, he felt the warmth of her body through the robe. As he had also guessed, there didn't seem to be much—if anything—under it except the lady.

He sat down, slipping the pistol back under the pillow, and then she sat close beside him, which didn't come as a surprise, either. Turning slightly, she reached up and opened the buttons of his shirt, then spread it back, baring his chest, and began to massage him. Her strong, slender fingers playing through the mat of dark brown hair worked a special sort of magic, and he felt himself responding to her touch.

After a few moments, Cody reached up and caught her wrists. She flattened her palms against his chest and pressed hard with them as she leaned forward. Her lips found his in the darkness. They were hot and sweet and wet, and she tasted damned good.

He was going to hate to put a stop to this.

Taking his mouth away from hers, he said, "I thought you said you came here to talk to me."

"This is much more enjoyable, isn't it?" she whispered.

"Damn right it is—but your husband just hired me. I don't figure to get in trouble with him this soon."

"How do you know he didn't hire you to do . . . this?" She leaned against him again, lowering her head so that her tongue could flick out and tease the skin of his throat.

Cody chuckled, despite the effect Gloria was having on him. "I'd say Ben Bigelow likes to handle such chores for himself. Now, tell me what's going on."

"Later," she breathed, pressing herself against him again. She slid her wrists out of his grasp, then took his hands and held them to her breasts. He felt her nipples prodding against his palms through the flimsy fabric of her robe, and she let out a low moan when his fingers cupped and squeezed the sensitive mounds of flesh.

He could feel her heartbeat. It was slugging as hard as his own. If he didn't put a stop to this soon—

Letting go of her, he stood up, and Gloria let out a soft cry of disappointment. Cody turned to face her, and his voice was angry as he said, "Dammit, I know you didn't come out here because you found me irresistible. I'm not *that* fond of myself. So, boss's wife or not, you can tell me the truth, lady, or you can get the hell out!"

His harsh words had the effect he had been hoping for. She stared up at him for a few seconds, and then her face suddenly crumpled, and she began to sob, lifting her hands to her face as tears rolled down her cheeks. He had sensed that she was holding herself on a tight rein, and now that her control had broken, near hysteria washed over her.

Cody stepped to the bunk and sat down beside her, putting his arms around her. But there was nothing sensuous about this embrace; he was just one human being comforting another. For long minutes, Gloria cried softly in his arms.

Finally, she hiccuped a couple of times and managed to say, "I . . . I was so scared. I wanted you to help me, and . . . and this was the only way I knew. . . ."

"Sssh," Cody whispered, stroking her hair. "If you need help, ma'am, I'll be glad to do what I can. But what's wrong? Your husband's a rich man, and it looks to me like you've got a mighty fine life here."

"He's a monster!" she burst out. "You don't know him—you can't know how he is, what he does to me!"

Cody felt a cold wave of anger go through him. It didn't surprise him to hear that Bigelow mistreated his wife, but it still made him mad.

Gloria drew in several deep, ragged breaths, and some of her composure returned as she explained, "I was very young when I married my husband, Mr. Cotton."

"Sam."

"Thank you. Sam. As I was saying, I wasn't much more than a girl. I was . . . very innocent, too. And Ben was a successful rancher."

"Was this before he started the Box B?" Cody asked.

"Yes. He had a spread up near Waco. We'd been married about six months when we had to leave suddenly. There was some trouble about a deed and a man who had been killed in some sort of accident. . . .But Ben had plenty of money, and he said we wouldn't have any trouble starting over. He started this ranch, and it's been very successful, I have to admit that." She turned her tearstained face toward the Ranger, and even in the dim light, he could see the fear in her eyes. "But I found out later he'd killed that man in Waco and stolen his land. Ben even *bragged* about it!"

Cody nodded. If he got out of this job alive, he'd have to check on Bigelow's background in central Texas and maybe help clear up a few criminal cases there.

"I found out that Ben's the kind of man who just takes what he wants," Gloria was saying. "He was . . . nice to me at first, but then— Oh, God, the things he makes me do! And it's like I'm a slave, not allowed to go out of the house or have any friends. . . ."

What she described sounded like a miserable existence, all right, but it fit the picture Cody was getting of Ben Bigelow. He asked, "Why'd you come to me?"

"I heard the sheriff talking to my husband earlier today. Turner was upset about some stranger who had come into town and made him look bad. The man sounded like he was absolutely fearless." A weak smile tugged at the corners of her mouth. "And then, just a few minutes after the sheriff left, you came riding in. It was like . . . like some sort of omen. I knew then that you were the man to take me out of this hell. And no price would be too great to pay for that, Sam. No price at all."

"Including your body," he grunted.

She solemnly admitted, "Including my body. But— for what it's worth—I really do like you."

Releasing her, he stood up abruptly, his mind whirling. He turned back to face her, then queried, "You know what your husband has been doing around here, don't you? You know that he hired Turner to take over the town and terrorize it?"

Gloria nodded. "I think he's trying to punish Twin Creeks for not electing him mayor. That really hurt him."

"What about the Comanches?" Cody asked, playing a hunch. "Does he have anything to do with the raids those renegades have been carrying out around here?"

"I . . . I'm not sure. One night I heard some strange noises, and I looked out to see several Indians on horseback. They had ridden right up to the house, and Ben was on the front porch talking to one of them."

"Could you tell anything about him? The Indian, I mean?"

Gloria shook her head. "It was too dark. But I heard

Ben call him by name. It was . . . Thunder . . . something."

"Red Thunder," Cody stated.

She nodded. "I think that might have been it." Frowning, she went on, "Why are you asking me all these questions?"

Cody took a deep breath. He didn't want to tell her that he was a Ranger just yet. "Let me ask you one more," he said after a moment. "If I take you away from here, is Bigelow the kind of man who'd come after you?"

"Oh, Lord, yes. I don't think he really loves me, but if you took me away, he'd hunt us down and try to kill us."

"Then we've got to make sure he can't do that," Cody said. "And the only way to be sure is to put him in jail. If you got the chance, would you testify against him?"

Gloria licked her lips anxiously, hesitating. Finally she said, "I would. You're right. That's the only way."

"Good. But we have to bide our time. We can't do anything to make him suspicious just yet." He had seen the eagerness spring up in her face, and he wanted to make sure she understood they would not be leaving the Box B tonight. "You said you're not supposed to leave the house. I reckon you slipped out tonight without anybody seeing you?"

"Yes. I've gotten pretty good at sneaking out, if I do say so myself. Sometimes I've just got to get away from Ben and get some fresh air." She sighed. "If you're wondering why I've never stolen a horse and tried to escape, well, I'm afraid I don't have that kind of courage, Sam."

"Seems to me you've got plenty of courage," he remarked, stepping closer to her and running a fingertip over her soft cheek. She looked up, moonlight coming through the window and shining on her blond hair. She was a beautiful woman, there was no doubt about that, and sitting there on his bunk with her robe half-open like that— Well, she made the prettiest picture he'd seen in a long time.

"I meant what I said," she whispered.

"And so did I. You don't have to buy my help, Gloria. Not that way." He took her hands and lifted her to her feet. Bending over, he kissed her softly on the lips and then on the forehead. "You go on back inside. Hold on to your nerves, and wait until I let you know when the time's right to make our move. It'll be soon, I promise you."

"I hope so." Her fingers slid lingeringly out of his. "Good night, Sam. And . . . thank you."

"Good night," he said, making his voice gruff so she wouldn't be able to tell how much he wanted her.

She made it to the door and then stopped. "Sam . . ." she said softly, turning back to him.

Cody heard a whispery sound and knew she had untied the robe and let it fall around her feet. She walked into the rectangle of illumination again, and he could see the lovely interplay of light and shadow on her bare skin. In a tight voice, he said, "I thought we agreed—"

"You agreed," she cut in, stepping up to him and resting a finger on his lips. "Not me."

"But there's no need—"

"There's the biggest need in the world," she told him, moving into his arms and molding her body to his.

"When everything is cleared up here, I'll have to be riding on," he said. "There's no future for us."

"Tonight is all the future I'm interested in," she murmured. Her arms went around his waist and tightened. "But—"

"Dammit, hush up and make love to me!"

Well, Cody thought with a wry grin, just before he kissed Gloria Bigelow, he'd never been one to argue with a lady.

CHAPTER
10

Dawn was just breaking. Out in the Texas wilderness some ten miles east of Twin Creeks, Captain Wallace Vickery was saying grace over a cold breakfast of jerky and biscuits—as difficult as it was to offer thanks to the Lord for such unappetizing fare—when the scouts he had sent out the night before came galloping into the Ranger camp. Vickery broke off his prayer in midsentence and hurried over to meet the two tired riders.

"What'd you find, boys?" the captain asked as the men slid down from their mounts.

"You were right, Cap'n," one of the scouts said. "Those red devils've been leadin' us on a false trail. The main bunch is a half-day's ride northwest of here. Looked to be at least twenty braves."

The other man added, "And they didn't appear to be in any hurry to break camp and move out, neither."

"Praise the Lord!" Vickery exclaimed, clenching one hand into a fist. Mustache bristling, he turned to Lieutenant Oliver Whitcomb, who had followed him to hear the scouts' report, and instructed, "Have the men get ready to ride. We'll have our breakfast in the saddle today!"

"Yes, sir," Whitcomb replied crisply, then turned to carry out the captain's orders.

Seth Williams and Alan Northrup were among the band of Rangers, and they exchanged glances as they lifted blankets and saddles onto the backs of their

horses. Neither of the young men was a stranger to
violence, having grown up on the frontier, but neither
had they ever gone into battle against a superior force
of Comanches. Everybody knew the Comanches were
about the fiercest warriors of all the tribes, and nobody
was their equal when it came to fighting on horseback.
The Rangers would likely have more firepower, since
they were all armed with Colts and Winchesters and
some of the Indians would probably have only bows
and arrows, but that might not be enough to make a
difference.

Still, there was nothing Williams and Northrup
could do but follow orders and try to keep up their
courage. They *were* Rangers, albeit not seasoned ones
yet.

Captain Vickery stepped between the young men,
putting his right hand on Northrup's shoulder and his
left on Williams's. "No need to be worried, lads," he
told them in a quiet voice. "The Psalms say, 'Yea,
though I walk through the valley of the shadow of
death, I will fear no evil, for the Lord is with me.'"

Northrup swallowed and responded, "Yes, sir, I recollect hearing that passage before. But do you think
there were any Comanch' in that valley the fella was
writing about?"

"Could've been, son," Vickery declared, squeezing
the stocky young Ranger's shoulder. "There sure
could've been. Just be as brave as you can, and let the
Lord do the rest."

"Yessir," Northrup said, and his comrade nodded in
agreement.

Within ten minutes, the troop of Rangers had their
gear packed and their horses saddled, and they were
ready to mount up. Vickery swung into his saddle,
waved for the other men to do the same, and then led
the way out of the camp, following the directions given
to him by the scouts. The sun was barely over the horizon.

Before it set again, Vickery knew, some of these
brave men—maybe all of them—would likely be dead.

* * *

After breakfast in the main house that morning—just hours after Gloria Bigelow had paid her visit to his cabin—Cody wandered out to the corral, where Shad Garrison caught up to him and said, "Boss wants to see you."

"Thanks," Cody responded. He turned and walked back toward the house.

Phillips, the butler, was waiting for him just inside the rear door. Cody hadn't seen the distinguished-looking, sobersided Phillips the night before; evidently the servant didn't associate with the Box B cowhands. Greeting the Ranger with a nod, the butler said, "Mr. Bigelow will see you in his study, sir. If you'll follow me, please."

"Sure," Cody said as he took off his hat.

Phillips led the Ranger down the central hallway to a different room from the one he'd been in last time. This one was dominated by a large hardwood desk in the center of the room and had dark wooden walls, although the wall behind the desk had large windows overlooking the sweep of valley down to the Rio Grande. To Cody's left was a massive gun cabinet displaying rifles and pistols of all kinds, from an ancient Kentucky flintlock to the most modern Winchester. The Ranger glanced the other way and saw a tall bookcase.

Phillips backed out the door behind him and closed it; there was no sign of Ben Bigelow. Cody got to look at guns all the time, but books were more of a rarity, so he ambled over to the bookcase to scan the volumes in Bigelow's collection.

Cody's mother had seen to it that he attended school until he was fourteen, so he could read better than a lot of men on the frontier. His sisters had been well educated, too, and with their help he had learned even more. Ever since he could remember, he had loved to read; it didn't matter what sort of book his hands fell on, he would read it avidly.

He saw now that the books in Bigelow's collection were a mixed lot—histories, novels, treatises on the sciences—and all in fine bindings. Cody took down one of the volumes and frowned when he saw the dust on it. Obviously, the book hadn't been disturbed in a long time. Opening it, he flipped through the pages, only to discover that many of them had never been slit apart.

Cody replaced the book and checked several others. All of them were in the same condition: unread. The Ranger snorted. Bigelow must have bought the books for show, never intending to read them. Seemed like a damned waste to Cody.

The study door opened, and Bigelow stepped in. He frowned in surprise when he saw Cody standing there with a thick book in his hands. "Looking for something to read?" he asked sarcastically.

Cody suddenly realized that Bigelow might think he was searching for something worth stealing. Slapping the book shut, he answered, "As a matter of fact, I do like to read. Wouldn't mind going through your collection while I'm here—if there's time and you don't object, that is."

Bigelow grunted and went behind the desk. "I think you're going to be too busy for that, Mr. Cotton."

Before the rancher could continue, Phillips appeared in the open doorway and announced, "Here is the other gentleman you sent for, sir."

One of the cowboys came into the study as Phillips stepped back. Cody had seen the man at supper the night before and breakfast this morning, but they hadn't exchanged a single word so far. The newcomer was lean-faced, with a dark stubble of beard on his gaunt cheeks. His clothes were the usual range outfit, maybe slightly more worn and mended than most, and like all the Box B hands, he had a pistol belted around his hips.

"Do you two know each other?" Bigelow asked.

"We haven't been introduced," Cody replied, glancing at the other man, who shook his head.

"Cotton, this is Bart Seeley. Sam Cotton, Seeley."

The two men nodded to each other. Seeley's eyes weren't friendly, Cody noted, but they weren't particularly hostile, either. Neither man offered to shake hands.

"You're going to be working together this morning," Bigelow went on. "I have some business for you to tend to on a couple of neighboring ranches. Seeley, you know where Hazlett's and Morton's spreads are, don't you?"

"Sure, boss," the cowhand replied.

"You and Cotton are going to pay a visit to both of them. I heard that Hazlett and Morton got hit by Comanches last night and lost some horses. I offered to buy them out a while back, and they turned me down. Maybe this bad luck will convince them to change their minds."

Cody kept his face carefully impassive. Bigelow had all but acknowledged that he was working with the Comanches and was responsible for their raids. There hadn't been any visitors to the ranch this morning, so the only way the rancher could have known about the attacks on the nearby spreads was if he'd had advance knowledge of them. Cody glanced at Seeley. If the puncher had come to the same conclusion, you couldn't tell it from his face, which was just as mask-like as Cody's.

"Of course," Bigelow added, "some time has passed since I made my original offer. I want you to tell Hazlett and Morton that I won't pay a thousand dollars anymore. The offer is now eight hundred."

"Eight hundred for a whole spread?" Cody asked, unable to keep the question in.

"I think the offer is reasonable, under the circumstances," Bigelow said smugly. He looked intently at both men. "I'm counting on you men to convince Morton and Hazlett of the same thing. Use whatever methods of persuasion you have to."

In other words, terrorize and browbeat them into accepting Bigelow's ridiculously low offer, Cody thought.

Anger at the man's arrogance burned fiercely inside him, but he kept it hidden as he nodded in understanding of Bigelow's orders.

Seeley was nodding, too, but then he asked, "What if they won't go along with it right away, boss?"

I'm willing to give them a couple of days to come to their senses, but no more," Bigelow snapped. "Before you leave either place, make sure the bastards know how unwise it would be not to cooperate."

"Sure," Seeley said shortly. He glanced over at Cody. "You ready, Cotton?"

"Soon as I saddle my horse," the Ranger answered. "Is that all, Mr. Bigelow?"

The rancher nodded and waved a hand in dismissal. He pulled some papers from a stack on the desk and began to study them as Cody and Seeley left the room.

This was a test, Cody thought as he saddled up and got ready to ride. Bigelow had hired him primarily as an insurance policy against Reb Turner, but the rancher had to find out just how loyal Cody was. He would prove himself by helping Seeley drive off a pair of small ranchers. It was going to be a tricky proposition, and he had to figure out some way to handle it without hurting innocent people.

Seeley led the way, heading northeast from the Box B. Cody fell in alongside the cowboy, and after riding in silence for ten minutes or so, until the ranch headquarters were out of sight behind them, the Ranger asked, "You handled chores like this before for Bigelow?"

"Sure," Seeley grunted. He was obviously not a man of many words.

"The small ranchers usually put up much of a fight?"

"Sometimes."

"And it doesn't bother you to run them off?"

Seeley gave him a cold stare. "Why should it? They don't pay my wages—Bigelow does. I punched cows for a long time, Cotton. I froze in the winter and sweated in the summer. This beats that." He spat and looked forward again.

Cody sensed that this was the longest speech he was going to get out of Bart Seeley. Some of the cowboys on the Box B were probably honest hands with no knowledge of Bigelow's schemes. But others, like Seeley, had to have a pretty good idea of what the rancher was up to and just didn't give a damn, as long as they got paid.

There was no point in asking any more questions of Seeley. Cody mulled over his own plans as he rode beside the taciturn puncher.

It took them a while to get off Bigelow's far-flung holdings, but eventually they came in sight of another ranch house, much smaller and plainer than the one at the Box B. This structure was made of rough, unpeeled planks and was built in the old Texas style with an open, covered dogtrot in the center. Out back were a barn and a pole corral, and as they drew closer, Cody saw a woman emerging from the barn, a metal bucket in each hand. White liquid sloshed out of the buckets. The woman, the rancher's wife probably, had apparently been doing the milking.

"That's Hazlett," Seeley stated, nodding toward a man who was sitting on a stool and mending harness just inside the barn door. Two young boys were standing close by, watching him. The rancher glanced up as Cody and Seeley approached and quickly got to his feet. He said something to the boys—Cody couldn't make out the words at this distance—and sent them running toward the house, where the woman had disappeared a moment earlier.

Hazlett stayed where he was in the entrance to the barn while Cody and Seeley rode up. He was standing stiffly, and his expression was decidedly hostile. As far as Cody could tell, the rancher wasn't armed.

"Howdy," Seeley called as he reined up in front of the barn. "Mr. Bigelow sent us over to pay a call on you, Hazlett."

"If you need water, you're welcome to it," the

rancher said coolly. "Never turned away a thirsty man or horse yet. Other than that, you Box B men aren't welcome on my place."

With his lined face and gray hair, Hazlett probably looked older than he really was, Cody judged. Life on the frontier could drain the juices out of a man in a hurry, and it was even harder on women.

"No call to be unfriendly," Seeley drawled, leaning forward in his saddle. "We're here on business. Mr. Bigelow was wondering if you'd like to reconsider sellin' out to him."

"I told him no before," Hazlett snapped.

"We heard you had some trouble, lost a few hosses to the Comanches."

The rancher nodded. "That's true." He rubbed his jaw, frowning in thought. "Seems like there's nothing but trouble now. Maybe a thousand dollars wouldn't be so bad—"

"Offer ain't a thousand," Seeley cut in. "Mr. Bigelow says he won't pay more'n eight hundred."

"Eight hundred! Hell, man, even a thousand was robbery!"

Seeley slipped his revolver from its holster, and Hazlett suddenly fell silent.

Cody tensed. He had planned on keeping quiet, on letting Seeley do the talking until he saw how this hand was going to be played. But he couldn't let the puncher just gun Hazlett down. He moved his own fingers closer to the butt of his Colt.

"I've gone and let my gun get dirty," Seeley announced, seemingly paying no attention to Hazlett now. "Reckon I ought to clean it." The barrel wasn't turned toward the rancher, but it tipped up suddenly, spouting flame and noise. From inside the barn came a bellow of pain.

"Damn!" Seeley exclaimed. "Now how'd that happen? Looks like I've accidentally shot your milk cow, Hazlett."

"My God!" the rancher shouted, stepping forward and clenching his fists. From the house came another cry, and Cody glanced over his shoulder to see Hazlett's wife standing in the doorway, her hand lifted to her mouth. The two wide-eyed youngsters were peeking out from behind her.

"Sorry, Hazlett," Seeley said, obviously not sorry at all. He stepped down from his horse. "Reckon I'd better go see how bad that cow's hurt."

Seeley walked into the barn, striding casually past Hazlett and paying the rancher no attention. A moment later, Cody heard a crash as something was overturned inside the building.

For the next couple of minutes, the noise continued as Seeley went on a rampage, knocking over equipment and smashing everything he could. Hazlett stood just outside the barn like a statue. His mouth worked slightly as he listened to the sounds of destruction, but he said nothing. Once, he looked up at Cody, who forced himself to return the gaze coldly.

Every instinct in the Ranger was prodding him to put a stop to Seeley's wanton harassment. The silver spurs on his boots, the legacy from his father, and his own badge, safely concealed in the pocket watch, seemed to cry out to him to help Hazlett. But he had to sit still and let Seeley carry on. To do anything else would give away his real identity.

Suddenly, an idea occurred to Cody, and while it wouldn't help Hazlett and his family, it might do some good for the other rancher they were supposed to visit. Slipping out of his saddle while Seeley was still in the barn, Cody stepped over to the cowboy's horse, slid his bowie out of its sheath, and swiftly and deftly loosened the shoe on the animal's right rear hoof. Hazlett stared at him in confusion. Finished with the chore, Cody put the big knife away and gave Hazlett a tiny shake of the head, a warning to keep quiet about what he had just seen—not that Hazlett had any reason to do any favors for Seeley.

The cowboy came sauntering out of the barn, quite pleased with himself, and said, "That cow looks like she's in pretty bad shape, Hazlett. Don't know if she'll make it or not. Maybe while you're takin' care of her, you'll think about acceptin' Mr. Bigelow's offer. I'll be back in a couple of days to get your answer."

Seeley mounted up. Hazlett stared down at the ground, and Cody knew that the man's pride had taken an awful beating. The Ranger had a feeling that Seeley would have shot Hazlett had the rancher tried to interfere with him. He was glad things hadn't gone that far.

Cody followed as Seeley turned and rode away from the ranch. When they had put about a hundred yards behind them, Seeley growled, "You could've given me a hand back there."

"Looked like you were doing just fine by yourself," Cody replied. "Besides, I was keeping an eye on that rancher. He could've gone to the house for a gun or something while you were in the barn."

"Not likely." Seeley snorted in contempt. "Hazlett ain't much of a threat. Did you see the man? Comanches hit him last night, and he's sittin' around mendin' harness like nothin' happened! Didn't have a gun on him or a rifle close at hand or anything. You ask me, Hazlett and his family'd be a lot better off if they took the boss's money and got out of this part of the country. They stay on, and the Indians are goin' to get 'em sooner or later."

"Maybe you're right. Maybe Bigelow's just trying to do them a favor by buying them out."

Seeley laughed harshly and said, "Don't you believe it. Bigelow will come out ahead on the deal, you can count on that." He sobered somewhat and added, "When we get to Morton's place, you watch him close while I do my persuadin'. That old goat won't be unarmed, and he's liable to get feisty if he gets the chance."

Cody nodded. "I'll watch your back," he promised.

As they rode along, the Ranger glanced down at the hooves of Seeley's horse. The shoe he had loosened ought to be coming off soon. . . .

Maddeningly, though, the horse's gait didn't change.

After a while, Cody asked, "How far is it to Morton's?"

"We're about halfway there," Seeley answered. "Another hour, maybe—" He broke off suddenly when his mount stumbled. Reining in, he exclaimed, "Son of a bitch!"

Cody pulled his own horse to a stop. "Looks like you've thrown a shoe," he said. Swinging down from the saddle, he stepped over to lift the hoof of the other animal. "Yep, that's what happened, all right."

Seeley turned the air blue with curses as he dismounted and looked at the horse's leg. "I can't ride this damned nag like this!" he complained.

"Maybe you'd better start walking back to Bigelow's while I go on to Morton's," Cody suggested.

"You'd leave me afoot out here?" Seeley was angry at the idea, but Cody faced him down without flinching.

"Bigelow told us to put the fear of God in both ranchers," the Ranger said. "You've known the man longer than I have. What do you think he'll do if we come back and tell him the job's only half-done?"

Seeley glowered at him for a moment, but finally he gave a grudging nod. "Reckon you're right," he said. "The boss wouldn't like it at all. But do you think you can handle Morton?"

"I saw how you handled Hazlett." Cody chuckled unpleasantly. "Besides, these aren't the first men I've put the run on. But I'll remember what you said about being careful around Morton. Everything'll be all right."

Seeley spat fiercely. "I don't like it, but I don't see as we've got much choice. But I ain't gonna walk no farther than that stand of cottonwoods over there. You get me a horse at Morton's spread."

"Good idea," Cody agreed with a nod. "Now, tell me how to find the place."

After Seeley gave him directions to the Rocking M ranch, Cody left him trudging toward the distant stand of trees. Once he had his back turned and was riding away, a broad grin broke out on Cody's face. He hoped Seeley would have sore feet tomorrow, for he deserved every ache and pain the walk would give him.

The Ranger had no trouble finding Morton's ranch. When he rode up to the small adobe house, he wasn't surprised to see a shotgun in the hands of the bearded, leathery individual who stepped out the door.

"Who be ye?" the old-timer demanded, training the muzzle of the greener on Cody. Despite his age, the twin barrels of the weapon didn't waver a bit.

Cody was prepared for that question, but first he asked one of his own. "Are you Mr. Morton?"

"That's right. Ebenezer Morton, the owner of this here spread. And you ain't answered my question, you young galleywampus!"

"Take it easy, Mr. Morton." Moving carefully so as not to spook the old man, Cody raised his right hand and displayed what he was holding. Morton's rheumy eyes widened at the sight of the silver star in its silver circle.

"A Ranger!" Morton said. "Lord, that makes a feller breathe easier, son. When ye rode up, I had ye figgered for one o' Bigelow's gunnies."

"Well, actually, Bigelow sent me here."

"What? The hell ye say! What's goin' on here?"

"If you don't mind me getting down from my horse, I'll tell you all about it."

Morton hesitated, then nodded. "All right. Light an' set. I got a jug inside."

Over homemade whiskey that brought tears to the Ranger's eyes with a single small swig, Cody told Morton what he was doing in the area and why he was pretending to be working for Ben Bigelow. The old rancher seemed somewhat reluctant to believe him at first, but Cody finally convinced him. Revealing his identity was a calculated risk, Cody knew, but he needed more time to discover the full extent of Bigelow's plans, and Morton could help him gain that time.

"What is it ye want me to do?" the old-timer asked

when Cody mentioned that he could use a hand in his plan.

"I'm going to tell Bigelow that you turned down his offer of eight hundred dollars for your ranch, but you said you'd take twelve hundred instead. Bigelow won't agree to that, of course, but at least it'll show that I talked to you and got you to start reconsidering. I'll write up a statement detailing all of this so that you can sign it."

Morton nodded. "Fair enough. Ain't sure what such a thing'll gain ye, but I'm willin' to go along with it. Anythin' else?"

"Bigelow sent another man out with me, but his horse threw a shoe." Grinning, Cody added, "I'd rather see him get good and footsore, but to keep up the story, I could use the loan of a horse."

"One of the Box B punchers, is it?"

"Yeah. Fella named Seeley, Bart Seeley."

"I know him," Morton grunted. "He deserves to have sore feet."

"That's what I figured when I loosened one of his horse's shoes."

Morton returned the Ranger's grin. "You know, son, I like the way you think." He held out the jug. "'Nother snort?"

CHAPTER
11

Tom O'Rourke had awakened with a headache many times, but this was the first time in recent weeks that the throbbing pain in his skull didn't come from too much whiskey the night before. Instead, it was a result of the beating he had taken from Reb Turner and his men.

O'Rourke didn't have to open his eyes as consciousness seeped back into his brain, for he knew it was morning by the light seeping through his eyelids. He was lying on his back on what felt like a hard bunk, and as the events of the previous night filtered back into his memory, he realized he was probably in one of the cells at the jail.

With consciousness came the sound of men talking in low voices. At first O'Rourke couldn't make out the words, but gradually they began to make sense.

". . . had enough," one man was saying. "Reb don't want to wait any longer and chance the Rangers gettin' a whiff of what's goin' on. He said for me to tell you we're hittin' the bank this afternoon and clearin' out."

"About damn time!" another man exclaimed. "When we came to Twin Creeks, I never figured we'd wait this long 'fore makin' a move."

"Well, just between you an' me, I think Reb sort of liked pretendin' to be the sheriff. Gave him a good feelin' to be able to lord it over folks like he done." That was a third voice, and O'Rourke knew he was listening to a conversation among several of Turner's deputies. The man continued, "I'll sure be glad to get out of here—but I bet Bigelow won't be too happy when he finds out about it."

One of the other men laughed. "Folks usually don't think it's funny when somebody double-crosses 'em. Bigelow should've knowed better than to trust Reb."

That comment drew chuckles from the others.

O'Rourke stayed motionless, keeping his face carefully slack in case any of Turner's men were where they could see him. But the wheels of his brain were spinning rapidly, and he forced the pain of his headache into the back of his mind and concentrated on what he had just heard.

So Turner was planning to double-cross Bigelow, to desert the man who had brought him here—but only after the owlhoot and his gang robbed the Twin Creeks bank. O'Rourke was not surprised. The conversation was also proof that Ben Bigelow was indeed behind the trouble that had hit the area, just as a lot of people had suspected. But that knowledge wasn't going to do O'Rourke any good, locked up as he was.

The former sheriff opened his eyes into narrow slits. He shifted slightly, as an unconscious man might, and his head sagged sideways a little, giving him a view of the cell door.

As he had guessed by how clearly he could hear the deputies' conversation, he was in the first cell, next to the open door leading into the office. This was a small cage usually used for special prisoners, such as men who were too violent to be put with other prisoners in the larger cells at the rear of the cellblock. Now that his senses had fully returned, O'Rourke could also hear the murmur of low-voiced conversations from the other direction and knew they were probably coming from the members of the citizens' committee Turner had ordered jailed. It was doubtful that any of those men had overheard the talk among Turner's deputies, for they were too far from the office.

O'Rourke heard a step in the doorway and squeezed his eyes shut again. He didn't want the deputies to suspect that he had been eavesdropping on their plans. The man who came into the cellblock stopped in front of O'Rourke's cage, and a second later a harsh voice said, "Reckon you've had enough beauty sleep, O'Rourke. Time to wake up."

Cold water hit O'Rourke in the face with a shock like the blow of a fist, and he didn't have to fake coming up off the bunk in a snorting, blowing frenzy of surprise. He shook his head from side to side and then wiped water out of his eyes while somebody laughed. When he could see, he focused on one of Turner's men, the one called Harvey, standing just outside the cell with an empty bucket in his hands.

"Sorry about that, O'Rourke," the man said snidely. "Reckon it would've been better to use a bucket of whiskey. You probably don't get near water these days."

O'Rourke's pounding pulse slowed a little, and he slumped back onto the bunk and the now-sodden blanket. He didn't say anything, just letting his head sag forward and his hands droop between his knees, a picture of dejection and defeat.

Harvey guffawed, then scoffed, "Don't see why Reb was ever worried about you, mister. You ain't nothin' but a damn drunk."

O'Rourke still said nothing—but he was sober, stone-cold sober, and the bastard baiting him didn't know what a big mistake he was making. Because sooner or later the tables were going to turn, and then it would be Tom O'Rourke's time to settle the score.

Unless he was just fooling himself. Nothing about this situation was going to change—unless *he* found a way to change it.

But no matter how hard he tried, he could not think of a way to get out of here. He was all too familiar with this jail; it was solidly constructed, and unless Turner's men really slipped up, there would be no chance to escape.

As the morning passed, O'Rourke's mental state slipped further and further into the depression that he had started out faking. Not until he heard the street door open, followed by the sound of female voices, did he look up again from the stone floor of the cell.

"We've brought food for the prisoners," a woman said in the office, and O'Rourke's heart began to pound as he recognized Sally Edwards's voice.

One of the deputies on duty said dubiously, "I don't know about that. Nobody said nothin' to me—"

"You can check with Sheriff Turner," another woman informed him crisply. "He gave us permission. He was going over to the Ace High, if you really want to bother him."

"Well . . . I reckon it'd be all right—but we're goin' to search those baskets first, ladies, just to make sure you're not tryin' to smuggle in guns to those menfolk of yours. They're mighty desperate hombres." The deputy's smug, mocking comment drew laughter from his companions.

Getting to his feet, O'Rourke went to the door of his cell and leaned against the bars. He glanced toward the other cells and saw that the rest of the prisoners were doing the same thing. All the townsmen wore anxious expressions on their faces, but their features tightened in anger, just as O'Rourke's did, when they heard the lewd remarks that the deputies exchanged while searching the food baskets.

When the women were finally allowed into the cellblock, Sally Edwards led the way, blushing furiously and her eyes downcast from the things that had been said in front of her. O'Rourke's hands clenched into fists, and he longed to smash them into the arrogant faces of Turner's men. The other women were clearly equally embarrassed.

Sally stopped at O'Rourke's cell, and in her gingham dress with a bright red ribbon tied in her hair, O'Rourke thought she was the prettiest girl he had ever seen. He wished he'd told her that before all the trouble started.

Keeping her eyes downcast, Sally took the checked cloth off the basket she was carrying. "Hello, Tom," she said softly. "I brought you something to eat." Taking out a sandwich wrapped in brown paper, she passed it through the bars to him. "It's roast beef. And I have some corn fritters and an apple."

"Thanks, Sally." O'Rourke wished she would look at him. "How's your father?"

"He had a bad night. He was restless, didn't get much sleep. But he was dozing when I left the house. Patrick is watching him."

"Sally . . . I'm sorry—"

Finally, she lifted her head and let her eyes meet his. "For what? You tried to help us last night. We should have listened to you and never even had that meeting."

He didn't like the sound of defeat in her voice. Somehow, even though he himself had been wallowing in self-pity and despair for weeks, it seemed wrong that Sally was on the verge of giving up. She had always been so determined to see things set right again.

"Listen to me, Sally," he whispered urgently, reaching through the bars to catch her free hand. "You and your father and the others were right. We have to stand up to Turner, we have to fight back."

"Oh, Tom," she breathed, her eyes beginning to shine again. "Do you mean that?"

"I surely do. The only trouble is, we don't have much time left. I overheard something a short while ago."

Lowering his voice even more, O'Rourke bent closer to the bars and told Sally about the conversation among Turner's cohorts. Her eyes widened as he mentioned the bank robbery planned for that very afternoon.

"Somebody's got to tell Cousin Sam," she said when he had concluded his story.

O'Rourke frowned. "Cotton? I know he's been butting into our business, but why would he want to stop Turner from cleaning out the bank? I got the impression he was just a drifting gunslinger himself."

Sally hesitated for a long moment, then leaned even

closer and whispered so that only he could hear, "He's not really my cousin. He's a Texas Ranger."

It was all O'Rourke could do not to exclaim, "A Ranger!" Instead, he blinked rapidly for a moment, the breath catching in his throat. Finally he asked, "Are you sure?"

Sally nodded. "I'm certain. He showed me his badge."

"That doesn't mean anything. Anybody can carry a badge—"

"No, I'm sure he was telling me the truth, Tom. I can tell. He's out at Mr. Bigelow's ranch now, trying to get to the bottom of everything." A look of determination came over her face. "I've got to ride out there and tell him what Turner's planning."

Tossing the sandwich on the bunk, O'Rourke grasped her hands through the bars. "You can't!" he protested. "It'd be too dangerous."

"It's worth the risk to stop Turner from looting the town," Sally insisted. "He won't stop with the bank, Tom. You know that. He and his gang will lay waste to Twin Creeks. No man—and especially no woman—will be safe."

The truth of those words went into O'Rourke like a knife. Turner had threatened the night before to take what he wanted from Sally; now, leaving town, he would have no reason to wait before carrying out his threat.

Like it or not, Sally was right. If the tall stranger really was a Ranger, he had to be alerted to Turner's plans.

O'Rourke nodded. "All right. But be mighty careful."

"Don't worry," Sally assured him, smiling and slipping her hands out of his. "I will. Now, here, take the rest of this food."

She handed the fritters and the apple through the bars to him, then gave him another smile and left, carrying the empty basket. O'Rourke's pulse hammered painfully in his temples as he watched her go, knowing that he might never see her again.

He sighed, sat down on the bunk, and ate the food she had brought him. He supposed it was good, but he didn't taste a bite of it.

The sun was high overhead when the band of Rangers led by Captain Wallace Vickery topped a rise overlooking a shallow, narrow valley. A small creek ran along the bottom of it, and a ridge dotted with mesquite rose on the other side. Vickery held up a hand to bring the group to an abrupt halt. He stared across the valley for a long moment, leaning forward in his saddle, then turned to the other Rangers and called, "Well, brothers, it looks like the Lord has led us to our enemy."

Mounted on stocky ponies on the opposite ridge, stoically regarding the Rangers, were at least two dozen Comanche warriors. They were painted for war, with red lightning bolts zigzagging across their right shoulders. The tall brave who sat his horse slightly ahead of the others wore his thunderbolt on his face, and it was a scar instead of paint.

"Red Thunder himself," Vickery said quietly to Lieutenant Oliver Whitcomb, who had ridden up beside him. "We can be thankful we finally got the chance to rid Texas of that murderin' heathen."

"I suppose so," Whitcomb said dryly. The lieutenant's voice was cool, his bearded face calm. He might be a stickler for routine and military discipline, but no one had ever questioned his courage under fire. "Why do you suppose Red Thunder is meeting us like this in the open, rather than laying an ambush for us?" he asked.

Vickery pondered the question for a few seconds, then replied, "He prob'ly had scouts out who spotted us trailin' him. When he realized we weren't bein' fooled by that false trail anymore, he figured it'd be best to stand up to us and get it over with. Shoot, he's got to be confident. He's got us outnumbered two to one."

"We have more rifles. Some of those savages aren't armed with anything but tomahawks and lances."

Vickery shook his head. "That don't matter to a Comanch', especially a war chief like Red Thunder. He thinks no white man can hold a candle to an Indian when it comes to fightin', no matter how they're armed." The captain took a deep breath. "God willin', in a few minutes we'll prove him wrong."

Sitting their horses side by side in the column behind Vickery and Whitcomb, both Seth Williams and Alan Northrup were thinking that they sure would have felt a lot better if Sam Cody was here. But Cody was supposed to be in the settlement of Twin Creeks, and that was miles and miles to the south.

"How long are we going to sit here like this?" young Williams asked in a near whisper. "How long are the captain and Red Thunder going to just stare at each other?"

"They can keep it up just as long as they want to, far as I'm concerned," Northrup replied. He licked his lips and moved his hand closer to the stock of his sheathed Winchester.

The answer to Williams's question came sooner than either young man expected. Red Thunder suddenly let out a high-pitched war whoop and sent his pony charging down the hill toward the creek. The other Comanches followed him, shrieking out their defiance of the white men.

"He's insane!" Whitcomb exclaimed with a gasp, sliding his rifle out of the saddle boot. "All we have to do is stay here and cut them to ribbons as they charge up the hill on this side!"

Vickery's gaze darted from side to side. "Red Thunder's mean, but he ain't crazy," the captain retorted. "This's got to be a trap—"

Rifles suddenly barked from the brush to the right and left of the Rangers. Vickery wheeled his horse as lead sang through the air near his head and howled, "Ambush! It's an ambush!"

More riders came out of the mesquite along the trail the Rangers had just ridden, and arrows zipped from the Indians' bows. With that route of retreat cut off, there was only one way for the Rangers to go: down the hill, right into the face of Red Thunder's charge.

Vickery wasted only a second cursing himself as he hauled out his old Paterson Colt and raised it in the air. "Follow me, men!" he commanded, spurring his horse and sending it galloping down the slope. If they could break the back of Red Thunder's charge and maybe bust through the line of Indians, they would have a chance.

The long-barreled Texas Paterson boomed as Vickery released the hammer. One of the braves who had just reached the creek spilled from the back of his pony, throwing silvery drops of water high in the sky as he splashed limply into the stream. Next to Vickery, Whitcomb's rifle barked again and again, as fast as he could work the lever. Behind the captain and the lieutenant the rest of the Rangers rode down the hill, automatically spreading out so that they wouldn't be in each other's line of fire. The rattle of a ragged volley of gunshots echoed through the rolling hills.

Several of the Indians went down, and glancing quickly over his shoulder, Vickery saw that all his men were still in their saddles. They were carrying the fight to the Comanches. Near the forefront of the charge, Williams and Northrup were guiding their horses with their knees and coolly emptying their Winchesters. Vickery felt a surge of pride in the young recruits. This was their first real baptism of fire, and they were proving to be real Rangers.

"They'd charge hell with a bucket of water," Vickery muttered to himself just before he blew a fist-sized hole through another Comanche with his old Colt.

An arrow tore the captain's jacket, and a slug burned along his left forearm. Beside him, Whitcomb's hat was plucked from his head by a bullet. Several of the

Rangers were wounded now, but they kept coming. Two-thirds of the way down the slope, they met the onrushing line of Indians.

The air was filled with dust, gunshots, war whoops, rebel yells, grunts of effort, shrieks of pain . . . and the rattle in the throats of dying men. The battle was largely hand to hand now, a brutal give-and-take with knives, gun butts, and fists. Most of the Rangers managed to stay on their horses, and suddenly, after thirty seconds that seemed like a year, they broke through Red Thunder's men, surging into the creek and then heeling their mounts to fire up the hill.

All of the Indians were in front of them now, instead of surrounding them, and the Rangers didn't have to hold back. For long minutes, it was load and fire, load and fire, and then Red Thunder let out another *ki-yi-yi!* and waved his bow over his head, calling his men to him. He whipped his horse up the slope, then over the crest of the rise, disappearing from sight of the battle below.

"They're pulling out!" Whitcomb shouted excitedly.

"Maybe not. They could just be regroupin'," Vickery warned. He glanced around at his men as the valley became strangely silent, the sounds of battle dying away. Some of the Rangers were still mounted; others had leaped off their horses to take cover behind the rocks along the creek and pepper the retreating Comanches with rifle fire. But the Indians had followed Red Thunder, and now there were no more targets.

At least half a dozen Comanches were sprawled lifelessly on the ground. Only one Ranger was down, an arrow lodged in his throat and his shirtfront horribly flooded with blood. Others among Vickery's men had crimson stains here and there on their clothes, but everyone seemed to be in reasonably good shape.

The captain spotted a Comanche lying on his stomach and reaching for a fallen rifle. Spurring his mount toward the man, Vickery leveled the Paterson at him and said, "I got one ball left in his hogleg, son. I hope for your sake you savvy white man's talk. Leave that rifle alone or I'll splatter your brains all over creation!"

The Indian hesitated, obviously understanding Vickery's threat. He was undersized and darker-skinned than most Comanches, and his calf had been torn through by a Ranger slug. He sighed and rolled over, away from the rifle.

"That's usin' the brain the good Lord gave you, son," Vickery boomed. Not taking his eyes off the Indian, he called, "Somebody take charge of this prisoner! We're gettin' out of here while we got the chance!"

One of the men caught the reins of his dead comrade's horse and led it over. Two more Rangers bound the wounded Comanche's hands, then lifted him into the saddle after relieving him of his knife and tomahawk.

Vickery ordered that the fallen Ranger's body be loaded onto the back of the horse behind the Indian, who looked uncomfortable at the idea of riding with a corpse. However, the captain wasn't about to leave the body of one of his men behind if it was at all possible to take the dead man with them and give him a proper Christian burial later. Vickery's stomach crawled at the thought of what the renegades would do to the body if they got their hands on it.

"Let's go!" he called when everyone was mounted and ready to ride. The minor wounds could be patched up later, when they had put some distance between themselves and Red Thunder's bunch.

By the middle of the afternoon, when Vickery called a break to rest the horses and tend to the injured, the Rangers were somewhere northwest of Twin Creeks. Vickery picked out a couple of men for burial detail and had the captive taken off the horse. "Put him over there under that shade tree," the captain ordered.

Striding over to the prisoner, Vickery paused in front of him. He had already noticed the telescope the Comanche wore on a thong around his neck, which set him apart from the average warrior. Looking into the Indian's dark gaze, the captain also saw unusual intelligence, along with an abiding sorrow. "I know you understand English, son," he remarked. "One of our boys will have a look at that wounded leg of your'n in a few minutes. How you feelin'?"

The Comanche leaned over, the telescope swaying slightly on its thong, and spat next to Vickery's feet. "How would you feel if you were in the hands of your enemies?" he demanded.

"Well, I reckon I'd be a mite scared. Probably be prayin' the Almighty's ears off."

"I am not frightened."

"Maybe you ain't got sense enough to be scared. Ever think of that?" Vickery knelt in front of the brave, who had his back against the trunk of the tree. He slipped out his bowie knife from its fringed sheath and let the Comanche see the sunlight glinting from the blade. "I've seen plenty of white captives who've been worked over by your people. Reckon it'd be a sin to give in to temptation and do a little payin' back on you." A grin broke out on Vickery's seamed face. "But then, the good thing about bein' a Christian is that the Lord'll forgive your sins, happen you ask Him to."

The Indian swallowed. "You would not—"

"Don't try me, son," Vickery said softly. "Just answer a few questions. I can tell by lookin' at you that you ain't the same bloodthirsty sort as Red Thunder. What're you boys doin' in this neck of the woods, anyway?"

For a moment, Vickery thought the Indian wasn't going to answer. But then he said, "We came here because a white man told us he would give us whiskey and guns and horses if we raided the ranches."

Vickery leaned forward. "A white man?"

"Yes. His name was . . . Big . . . Big'low. A foolish name."

Vickery grunted. "What do they call you?"

"I am Three Eyes," the Comanche replied proudly. "My third eye sees farther than the eagle can fly."

"Telescope, eh? Took it off a dead white man, more'n likely." Playing a hunch, Vickery went on, "Did this feller Big Low send you after some men who were bringin' a wagon from Twin Creeks to Del Rio?"

Three Eyes nodded. "I do not know why the white man wished them stopped, but he did. We would have killed both of the men, but a tall Ranger and another man helped them."

"I know about that," Vickery remarked.

The Comanche smiled humorlessly. "But did you know that Red Thunder sent men to kill the tall Ranger later?"

Vickery felt something cold knot in his belly. "He sent braves after Cody?"

"If that is the Ranger's name. The warriors never came back, but our band has been moving a great deal. It could be they simply have not caught up to us yet."

Or maybe Cody had killed them and continued with his mission, Vickery told himself. That was what he wanted to believe. But he had to accept the possibility that Cody might not have reached Twin Creeks.

"Where'll Red Thunder go, now that we got out of his trap?" the captain asked.

"Back to the white man's ranch. Red Thunder said he wanted the payment promised him, and then we will leave this land and go to Mexico. Red Thunder is tired of fighting for now, and so am I. That is the only reason I tell you these things, Ranger."

Vickery nodded, mulling the information over. He knew that even if Cody had escaped from the Comanches who went after him, the big Ranger might still be in trouble. Whoever this Big Low was, Cody would probably be getting close to him by now. If Red Thunder showed up and recognized Cody, that would be the end of him.

"I told that boy he'd get in trouble one of these days,

playin' lone wolf like he does," Vickery muttered to himself. Straightening from his crouch, he turned to the other Rangers. "Get this feller back on his horse," he ordered. "And mount up! We're ridin' for Twin Creeks!"

CHAPTER
██████████████ **12** ██████████████

Ben Bigelow was waiting in front of the ranch house when Cody and Bart Seeley got back to the Box B, with Seeley riding the horse that Cody had borrowed from Morton and leading his own mount. Cody had made it sound as if he had taken the horse from Morton at gunpoint, and Seeley seemed to accept that story easily.

"What happened?" Bigelow asked with a frown as the two men rode up. "What's wrong with your horse, Seeley?"

"Threw a shoe, boss. Got this other nag at Morton's."

"Ah, you saw the old man, then?"

"I did," Cody replied. He reached in the pocket of his shirt for the note he had written up and the old rancher signed. Handing it to Bigelow, the Ranger added, "He wasn't too agreeable, but at least he's thinking in the right direction now."

"Twelve hundred?" Bigelow crumpled the paper after he had scanned it. "Bah! That old bastard'll learn he can't dictate to me. What happened with Hazlett?"

"He's beat," Seeley said. "He just ain't admitted it yet. You don't have to worry about him, boss. When we go back over there in a couple of days, he'll agree to sell."

"I hope so," Bigelow grunted. "Well, get those mounts unsaddled and put them in the corral, then see if there's anything else Garrison wants you to do."

Cody and Seeley nodded and swung down from their saddles. They were leading the horses toward the corral when Cody spotted a rider approaching. Turning back to Bigelow, he sang out, "Rider coming in, boss!"

Bigelow stopped and muttered, "Who the hell is that?"

Cody was asking himself the same thing as he stared toward the horseman. No, he corrected himself, it wasn't a horseman at all, but a horse*woman,* wearing a divided skirt and a brown hat with the strap drawn taut under her chin. In fact, unless Cody missed his guess, it was Sally Edwards.

What the devil was she doing out here?

"Cousin Sam!" Sally called as she rode into the ranch yard. "I'm so glad I found you!"

"What is it?" Cody asked, unsure how to play this and hoping Sally wouldn't say anything to give him away.

Before Sally could reply, Bigelow strode over. Motioning for Seeley to continue putting up the horses, the rancher asked, "What can I do for you, young lady? You're Martin Edwards's girl, aren't you? I believe I met you with your father once."

"That's right, Mr. Bigelow. I've come to see my cousin." She nodded toward Cody.

Cody grimaced and made his voice hard and cold as he said, "Sorry, boss. I didn't invite the gal out here. I'd just as soon the whole bunch would leave me alone."

He saw a flicker of hurt in Sally's eyes, but it lasted only an instant and was replaced by a look of understanding. She had caught on to the act he was putting on for Bigelow's benefit.

"Well, I'd just as soon not have to fetch you," she said tartly. "But my father—" Her voice broke, and she lowered her eyes. After a moment, she forced herself to continue, "My father is dying, and he wants all of his family around him. He . . . he asked me to bring you back to town, Cousin Sam."

Cody put a look of annoyance on his face as he

glanced at Bigelow, then back to Sally. "Are you sure about this?" he asked.

She chewed nervously on her lower lip and nodded.

With a sigh, Cody turned to Bigelow again. "Reckon I ought to ride into town, boss, if that's all right with you. I'm sure sorry about this."

Bigelow waved a negligent hand. "Don't worry about it, Cotton. We all have family responsibilities. And you've already taken care of the chore I had for you today. Go ahead if you want to. Take a fresh horse."

Cody shook his head and patted the shoulder of his big dun. "This old boy's not quite played out yet, are you, son? I'll take him, since he's already saddled and all."

"Fine. Whatever you like. Just be back out here to-night."

"Sure," Cody promised. He put his foot in the stir-rup and mounted. Glancing at Sally, he muttered, "Well, let's get going."

Side by side, they rode away from the ranch house. Cody glanced back once and saw a flicker of motion at one of the windows on the second floor. A curtain had been pulled back, and someone had looked out to watch him ride away. He thought he saw a flash of blond hair. . . .

Gloria. He had hoped to have a chance to see her alone again, to assure her that he was working to get her out of the trap that the Box B had become for her. But something was obviously very wrong in town, or Sally wouldn't have risked coming out here to get him.

When he was sure they were out of earshot of anyone on the ranch, he said, "That was mighty quick of you, the way you played along with me. What's wrong, Sally? What's happened in Twin Creeks?"

"Tom's in jail," she said quickly. "So are a lot of the other men. We had a meeting of the citizens' commit-tee last night, and Turner and his men broke it up and arrested nearly everyone there."

"Damn!" Cody exclaimed. "I was hoping it wouldn't come to that."

"That's not the worst of it," Sally said, her face grim. She told him about the conversation among the deputies that O'Rourke had overheard, and the Ranger's expression became equally bleak.

"If Turner's going to be brought to justice, it'll have to be now," he declared when Sally had finished her story.

"I just hope we're not too late."

"So do I," Cody said, thinking of the showdown that was finally about to happen. "So do I."

Tom O'Rourke leaned against the door of his cell, his left hand tightly gripping one of the bars while his right one—trembling from a bad case of the shakes—wiped away some of the sweat that was beading on his forehead. "Hey, out there!" he cried, ignoring the looks of contempt and disgust the men in the other cells were giving him. "I need a drink!"

One of the deputies appeared in the cellblock door. "What the hell do you think this is, O'Rourke?" he demanded. "It's a jail, not a goddamn saloon! Keep your mouth shut."

"You don't understand," O'Rourke pleaded, his voice quivering as much as his hand. "I *really* need a drink."

"I understand. I just don't give a damn, mister."

Another deputy looked past the first one into the former sheriff's cell. "Aw, you're bein' too hard on O'Rourke," he said. "The poor fella just wants a drink. What's wrong with that?" Grinning, he stepped past the other deputy and lifted the bottle he was holding. "This what you need, O'Rourke?" he taunted.

The big man licked his lips and nodded, never taking his eyes off the bottle. "Please," he whispered.

"Well, hold out your hands."

"I don't know if you should be doin' that, Gilliam," the other deputy warned.

"Hell, what harm's it goin' to do? Hold out your hands, O'Rourke, and I'll give you a drink."

O'Rourke thrust his arms out, cupping his hands together. Gilliam slipped the neck of the bottle between the bars and tipped it down, pouring a couple of ounces of whiskey into O'Rourke's waiting hands. Carefully, so as not to spill a drop, O'Rourke brought them to his mouth and lapped up the liquor like a dog.

Gilliam burst out in laughter. "Hell, this's the funniest thing I ever seen. Want some more?"

O'Rourke licked the last of the whiskey off his palms and nodded eagerly. He glanced at the other prisoners and saw the utter revulsion on their faces as they watched him degrade himself. Let them think whatever they wanted, he told himself. At least he was getting what he needed.

The deputy poured more whiskey into O'Rourke's hands, and O'Rourke sucked it up greedily, twisting away from Gilliam as he did so. This time he wasn't as careful, and some of the whiskey splattered on his shirtfront. That made Gilliam laugh even more.

"Shoot, you need a trough, just like a hog. Ain't that right, boy?"

"Whatever you say," O'Rourke replied obsequiously, wiping the back of his hand across his mouth. "You can say anything . . . I'll do anything . . . just don't let me get thirsty again."

Gilliam shook his head. "Hell, it ain't as much fun to kick a dog that just cringes all the time. Here, boy." He flipped the bottle through the bars.

O'Rourke lunged desperately to catch it before it could fall to the stone floor and shatter. He grabbed the bottle in midair and retreated to his bunk, scuttling across the cell like some sort of giant insect. To all appearances, he was nothing but a feeble, shattered husk of the man he had once been. Keeping his face turned to the wall, he emptied the bottle in a matter of moments, then looked at Gilliam for more.

The deputy shook his head. "If you want more to drink, you got to be more entertainin' than that. I got a full bottle in the office. What're you willin' to do for it?"

"Anything. Anything you say," O'Rourke gasped.

An idea lit up Gilliam's face. "We ain't got a trough, but I seen pigs eat out of buckets." He disappeared into the office, then came back a moment later, carrying a metal bucket and another bottle of whiskey. He pulled the cork with his teeth and upended the bottle, letting the liquor gurgle and splash into the bucket. O'Rourke watched the flow avidly.

Gilliam set the bucket on the floor and then came to the door of the cell, taking a ring of keys from his pocket. As he unlocked the door, he said, "Get down like a pig, boy, if you want that whiskey."

O'Rourke hesitated only a second, then dropped to his hands and knees.

Gilliam swung the door open. "Come on, piggy!" he said, chuckling. "Grunt for me, boy!"

O'Rourke took a deep breath and lowered his head to the floor, grunting and snuffling like a pig as he crawled across the cell. Gilliam backed away from the door, one hand on the butt of his gun. He stood to one side as O'Rourke went across the corridor to the bucket of whiskey.

One of the other prisoners cried out, "For God's sake, Tom, don't do it! Hell, man, remember who you used to be!"

Completely ignoring him, O'Rourke lowered his face to the liquor in the bucket and began drinking again. He had only taken a little when Gilliam said, "That's enough."

O'Rourke glanced up, a stricken look on his face. Gilliam laughed and went on, "Don't worry, boy. You'll get more. I just want the other fellas to see this." He motioned for O'Rourke to back away from the bucket. When the former sheriff had done so, Gilliam picked it up and carried it into the office. Then he turned around and called, "Come on, piggy. Find what you're lookin' for." Signaling to the other deputies, he cackled, "You fellas got to see this. It's the funniest damn thing."

Crouching on the stone floor, O'Rourke pretended to be a pig again. He crawled and grunted, and the other deputies joined in Gilliam's hilarity as O'Rourke came into the office in search of the bucket full of whiskey. Only one of the men wasn't laughing, and he said, "I don't know if it was a good idea to let him out, Gilliam."

"Aw, what the hell harm is it goin' to do? Does he look dangerous to you? Besides, he ain't got no gun, and we're all around him."

O'Rourke reached the bucket again and plunged his face into it, slurping the liquor, and laughter filled the office as the deputies watched his antics. In his haste to lap up the whiskey, O'Rourke tipped the bucket over, grabbing at it desperately as the contents began to spill. A moan of dismay escaped from his throat as he looked down at the spreading puddle on the floor.

"Well, hell, ain't no use cryin' about it!" Gilliam called out. "Just lick it up!"

O'Rourke hesitated only an instant, then went after the spilled whiskey. That was even funnier to the deputies. Gilliam was wiping tears from his eyes when O'Rourke suddenly slumped to the floor, sprawling out full length with his head next to the pool of liquor, his eyes closed.

"Drunk as a skunk," Gilliam said, chuckling.

"Hadn't we better drag him back into the cell?" one of the other men asked.

Gilliam shrugged. "Why waste the energy? He ain't goin' nowhere. Leave him be and let him sleep it off."

"But what if he wakes up?"

Stepping over to O'Rourke, Gilliam drew back his foot and drove the pointed toe of his boot into the former sheriff's side. O'Rourke grunted in pain and shifted slightly on the floor but didn't regain consciousness. "He ain't goin' nowhere for at least an hour," Gilliam asserted. "We'll be gone by then."

As if to prove the deputy's statement, the door of the office opened and Reb Turner stepped inside. He looked around at his men and announced, "Reckon it's time, boys. You ready?"

The deputies nodded. Several of the men took their guns out of their holsters and spun the cylinders, checking the loads.

Frowning, Turner gestured at O'Rourke lying on the floor. "What's he doin' out of his cell?" he demanded. "Is he dead?"

"Naw, he just passed out, stinkin' drunk," Gilliam replied with a grin. "We was just havin' a little fun with him, Reb."

Turner looked down at O'Rourke and sneered. "To think that he was actually sheriff of this stinkin' town. Reckon he's gonna suffer real good, once he finds out what we've done." With a jerk of his head, the owlhoot ordered the deputies, "Let's go. The others are waitin' for us. We'll loot the bank, clean out the tills in the stores, and then hit the trail—after I make one last stop at the Edwards house."

"We takin' that gal Sally with us, Reb?" Gilliam asked, leering.

"Damn right. Just don't get ideas, any of you. You can't have her—until I'm through with her."

Turner stalked out of the sheriff's office, his cohorts close behind him. Their pretense of being lawmen was over.

The street door slammed behind the last man. For long moments, the jail was quiet. There were muttered curses from the cellblock, but the only sound in the office was the harsh breathing of Tom O'Rourke.

Suddenly, O'Rourke stirred. His head lifted slowly, and his eyes blinked open. Shifting his shoulders, he got his hands under him so he could lift himself to his knees and then to his feet. As he stood there, looking around the office, his eyes glittered with a cold, clear, angry light. Despite the fact that he was disheveled and his clothes were soaked with whiskey, he looked like a different man as he strode over to the desk and pulled the center drawer open.

Good, he thought, plucking up the ring of keys he found. At least some things hadn't changed around here.

The last half hour had been the worst of his life as he allowed Gilliam and the other deputies to humiliate him. But the ruse had worked. He had spilled more liquor than he drank, although he had been forced to swallow enough of the fiery stuff to make his head pound slightly. It would have been easy, so easy, to go ahead and wallow in the whiskey the way he had pretended to. Fighting off that urge had been harder than anything else.

Several of the prisoners exclaimed in surprise as O'Rourke walked through the cellblock door, the keys in his hand. "Quiet down," he snapped as he thrust a key into the lock of the first closed cell. "There's guns in the cabinet in the office. One of you bust the lock on it and start passing out the rifles. Shells're in the desk drawer."

"But, Tom," Margulies the storekeeper said, "we thought you were . . . were—"

"Never mind," O'Rourke told him. "I know what all of you thought. But so did Turner's men." He swung the barred door open. "All that matters now is that you're free to fight back." He rubbed the sore, bruised spot on his side where Gilliam had kicked him. "It's time to settle some scores, if you're willing to do more than just talk about it. Turner intends to clean out the town. It's up to us to stop him. Are you with me?"

The men came hurrying out of the cell, and the apothecary, Cole, clapped O'Rourke on the shoulder. "Damn right we're with you," he declared. "Like we should have been right from the start."

"Get those guns, then," O'Rourke said, jerking a thumb over his shoulder toward the office. "I'll unlock the other cells."

In a matter of minutes the prisoners were all freed.

Although there weren't enough rifles in the gun cabinet to go around, most of the men were armed. Hefting the loaded Winchester in his hands, O'Rourke faced them. He saw fear on their features, but he also saw determination, and a cold smile formed on his mouth.

"Let's go take back our town."

"We'd better circle around and come up on the bank from the rear," Cody told Sally Edwards as they reached the outskirts of Twin Creeks. "When we get there, I want you to stay back."

"What are you going to do?" she asked. "Turner and his men have you outnumbered."

"Reckon you could say that," Cody replied dryly. "But I'll have the element of surprise on my side." He paused, then continued, his voice serious, "You've got to stay out of the line of fire, Sally, in case anything happens to me. Captain Vickery and a group of Rangers will be here in a few days at the latest, and I'm counting on you to tell the captain everything I've told you about Bigelow and Turner and the Comanches."

She managed to nod, but her lower lip trembled slightly as she said, "You don't think you'll be coming back out of the bank alive, do you?"

He grinned. "I wouldn't say that. I'm pretty fond of living. Don't worry, I'll be careful."

They were riding their horses at a walk through an alley behind the shops along Main Street when Cody spotted the impressive redbrick bank two blocks away. He signaled Sally to keep her voice down.

Abruptly, a man stepped out of a narrow passage ahead of them, leveling a rifle. Cody's hand flashed to his gun, but he froze, recognizing the man as the local blacksmith. Sally called out softly, "Wait, Mr. Hendryx! It's me, Sally Edwards, and my cousin Sam!"

"Sally!" Joseph Hendryx exclaimed, lowering the rifle. "Tom said you were going for help, but we didn't know if you'd get back in time."

"What's going on here?" Cody asked, seeing more men waiting in the passage behind Hendryx, many of them clutching Winchesters.

Tom O'Rourke pushed his way to the front of the group. He came over to the two riders and asked anxiously, "Are you all right, Sally?"

"I'm fine," she answered, reaching down to touch his shoulder. "But how did all of you get out of jail?"

"It was the neatest trick you ever saw, Sally," Nicholas Cole, the apothecary, said. "Tom fooled Turner's men and got us loose. We're on our way to the bank now to stop those outlaws from robbing it."

"We figured we'd better sneak up on them," O'Rourke explained. "That's why we were cutting through to the alley when we heard the two of you coming." He looked up at Cody. "Sally told me the truth about you, mister. Sorry I gave you trouble."

Cody swung down from the saddle. *"De nada,"* he said with a grin. He slipped his watch from his pocket and flipped it open. "Reckon there's no need to hide this anymore."

He took out the badge, reversed his vest, and pinned the silver star to it.

The townsmen murmured in surprise as they realized that this tall drifter was really a Texas Ranger. From the back of the crowd, a voice piped up, "Ah, I knew it all along!"

"Patrick!" Sally declared.

The boy slipped through the crowd to emerge, grinning. "Hi, Sally. Hi, Cousin Sam."

"You're supposed to be watching Dad," Sally admonished.

"He's the one who told me to come down here and keep an eye on things," Patrick replied. "I've been watching the jail and the bank. Turner and his men are all inside the bank now, except for one fella they left standing guard at the front door." The youngster looked up at Tom O'Rourke and remarked, "I heard Mr. Cole say you rescued all of the prisoners, Tom. That's really something!"

"Thanks, Patrick," O'Rourke said with a smile, patting the boy on the shoulder. "But we've got to stop Turner, or it's all for nothing." He turned to Cody. "We're lucky they're all in the bank. With them gathered in one place like that, we've got a chance to get the drop on them."

The Ranger nodded. "We need some sort of diversion, though, something to get them off guard so we can take them by surprise. Otherwise, a lot of folks could get killed."

"That's what I was thinking." O'Rourke's smile widened. "And I've got an idea what to do. . . ."

Within minutes after Tom O'Rourke had detailed his plan to Cody, the Ranger and the former sheriff had their small force of townspeople in position. Cody and O'Rourke were standing at the rear corner of the bank building, along with Sally and Patrick Edwards.

"Good luck," Cody said to O'Rourke, clasping his hand.

"You'll need it more than I will," O'Rourke replied with a grin. He turned to Sally. "You and Patrick be sure to stay back," he cautioned. "After everything we've all gone through, I wouldn't want anything to happen—" He broke off with a shake of his head.

"We'll be fine," Sally assured him. Impulsively, she leaned closer and kissed him on the cheek, and they looked intently into each other's eyes for a moment.

Cody turned his head and grinned. Those two were starting to see some things he had noticed right off—like how they were probably in love with each other.

Patrick put a hand on O'Rourke's arm. "Be careful, Tom," he pleaded.

O'Rourke ruffled the boy's hair. "Take care of your sister, son. Make sure she stays back. I'm counting on you, now."

"Sure." Patrick swallowed hard.

"This's mighty touching," Cody drawled, "but

we've got us some owlhoots to take care of. You ready, Tom?"

O'Rourke nodded, his expression one of fierce determination. "I'm ready."

Inside the bank Reb Turner and his men were just about ready to leave. Several of the outlaws were holding guns on the customers and the bank employees, while others were loading money from the vault and the tellers' drawers into canvas bags. Turner himself stood in the center of the big room, legs spread, thumbs hooked in his belt, and a cocky grin on his face as he watched.

Suddenly, a strange, wailing noise came from the street outside. Turner frowned as the mournful cry continued, and he turned to the guard at the door and demanded, "What the hell is that?"

The wailing turned into singing that was nearly incomprehensible and definitely off-key. The deputy at the door stepped outside, then returned a few seconds later, grinning broadly. "It's that drunken fool O'Rourke," he announced. "He must've woke up and come outside lookin' for more to drink. He's stumblin' down the street now."

"Well, get out there and shut him up," Turner ordered. "The rest of the town don't know what we're doin', and I don't want 'em findin' out just yet."

"Sure, Reb," the guard responded. He stepped onto the porch of the bank again just as O'Rourke staggered up to the railing. Leaning heavily on it, the former sheriff managed to pull himself up the single step onto the porch.

"Who're you?" he demanded, blinking owlishly at the deputy.

The man put his hand on the butt of his gun. "Get out of here, you damn fool! Go on—or I'll shoot you if I have to, to stop that cacklin'!"

O'Rourke put both hands on his head, groaned, and

stumbled a step closer to the guard. The outlaw cursed and started to slide his gun out.

With blinding speed, O'Rourke lunged forward. His right fist smashed into the guard's face while the fingers of his left hand closed over the cylinder of the man's gun, tearing the pistol free. At the top of his lungs, O'Rourke gave a rebel yell.

Waiting at the back door of the bank, Cody heard O'Rourke's signal and acted instantly. The heel of his boot drove against the lock with all the power of his strong body behind it. The facing of the door splintered, and Cody charged through the opening as the door slammed back against the inside wall.

At the same moment other members of the citizens' committee leaped up from the positions they had crawled to along the walls of the bank. Smashing the windows with the barrels of their rifles, they trained the weapons on the startled outlaws inside.

Cody saw Turner whirling toward him in surprise. The bank employees and customers were diving for the floor and hugging it for dear life—except for one young clerk who stood between the Ranger and the gang leader. He froze in horror.

"Dammit!" Cody growled as Turner raced toward the clerk with the obvious intent of using him. The outlaw had his gun out, and its barrel was coming up rapidly. The revolver roared and belched flame, sending a slug whistling past Cody's head.

The petrified clerk finally unfroze, leaping to one side with a hoarse yell. But in his blind panic he jumped in front of Cody as the gang leader triggered another shot. The bullet caught the clerk in the side, sending him spinning off his feet with a scream of pain. That left Turner without a hostage or a shield.

"You won't take me!" the gang leader yelled and fired again.

The slug whipped past Cody as the Ranger dropped the hammer on his Colt. Turner's head jerked back as the bullet struck him an inch above his left eyebrow and bored on into his brain. The gun in the outlaw's hand blasted one more time as his finger clenched spasmodically on the trigger, but the shot went into the floor. Turner crumpled lifelessly.

All over the bank, guns began hitting the floor and outlaw hands were thrust frantically into the air as Turner's men surrendered.

From the doorway, with the pistol he had taken from the guard clutched firmly in his hand, Tom O'Rourke said in a clear, strong voice, "You're all under arrest."

Cody stalked over to Turner's body as the members of the citizens' committee poured in the front and back doors of the bank to cover the defeated outlaws. Bending, the Ranger grasped the sheriff's badge that was still pinned to the dead man's shirt. He ripped it free, straightened, and tossed the symbol of authority toward O'Rourke, who caught it effortlessly. Wearing the broadest grin Cody had ever seen on the man, O'Rourke pinned on the badge.

"You heard the sheriff," Cody told the townsmen with a slight smile. "You'd better get these men over to the jail and lock them up."

"We would be most happy to, *mon ami*," a familiar voice responded.

Cody looked around. Andre Duval, the owner of the Ace High, was standing with the other townsmen. "Didn't notice you in the bunch before, Duval," the Ranger remarked.

"I was not with them," Duval said with a shrug. "I did not have the courage to be part of their group. But when I saw what was happening over here, I was shamed. I . . . I would like to help now."

Cody shrugged. "That's up to the other folks."

"Duval got here before the shooting started," Richard Margulies pointed out. "He brought a gun and was right with us when we threw down on Turner's men. I reckon he took his chances then, just like the rest of us." The merchant nodded to the saloonkeeper. "I'd be proud to have you help us get these polecats behind bars, Andre."

Beaming, the Frenchman joined the others in gathering up the outlaws' weapons and marching them out of the bank.

Cody knelt beside the injured clerk and checked the man's wound. It was a fairly shallow graze, producing quite a bit of blood but otherwise not doing a whole lot of damage. "Reckon you'll be all right, son," Cody assured him. "The doc can patch that right up for you, and you'll be good as new."

The sound of rapid footsteps made Cody look around as he stood up, and he saw that Sally and Patrick had entered the bank. Sally flew into O'Rourke's arms, and O'Rourke kissed her with a passion that he had obviously been storing up for a long while.

It was good to see things put right, Cody thought. But this wasn't over—not by a long shot. Ranger justice had caught up to Reb Turner, but the man responsible for Turner's evil was still free.

Now it was Ben Bigelow's turn.

CHAPTER
13

"**S**orry to break up the celebration," Cody told Tom O'Rourke and Sally and Patrick Edwards as he stepped up to them. "But we've still got to deal with Bigelow."

"Then he *is* behind it, just as we all thought," O'Rourke said.

Cody nodded. "He brought Turner in to make life miserable for you folks here in town, and he's been using Comanche renegades to scare the smaller ranchers into selling out to him."

"Can you prove that?"

"Bigelow admitted hiring Turner, and I've got a witness who'll testify about his connection with the Indians," Cody replied. "It'll stand up in court, if it ever gets that far. But I've got to arrest Bigelow before he finds out what happened here in town, or he's liable to take off for the tall and uncut. I was planning to string him along and find out all I could about his operation before I made a move, but Turner has sort of forced our hand with this bank robbery."

"I'll ride out to the Box B with you," O'Rourke quickly offered. "And I'm sure some of the other men would be willing to go along, too."

Cody shook his head. "If Bigelow or his men spot us riding up in force, there'll be too much gunplay. It'd be better if I went back out there by myself. Bigelow's not suspicious of me yet, so I'll get him alone and then arrest him. Tell you what, though. You deputize a

posse and follow along half an hour behind me. When
you get to the ranch, there's a band of chaparral you
can use for cover. I'll bring Bigelow out the back way
and meet up with you. Even if Bigelow's ranch hands
catch on to what's going on, they won't be able to do
much as long as I've got a gun in their boss's back."

"Sounds like a good plan," O'Rourke admitted. He
stuck out his hand. "We'll be there. You can count on
it."

"Hell, I know that," Cody said, grasping the sheriff's hand firmly. Tom O'Rourke was a changed man.
Somewhere he had found the will to knit together the
shattered remnants of his pride, and now he was
stronger than he had been before Reb Turner ever came
to Twin Creeks.

Sally smiled up at the Ranger. "It seems like I'm
always telling you to be careful, Cousin Sam. I hope
you don't mind me calling you that. I'll always think of
you that way."

"Don't mind a bit," Cody assured her. "A fella can
always use some extra kinfolks." He leaned forward,
brushed her forehead with his lips, and then looked
around for Patrick. The boy would probably be upset if
Cody left without saying good-bye.

However, the youngster was nowhere in sight, and
Cody supposed he had followed the townspeople over
to the jail to watch the prisoners being locked up. The
shooting had brought people out all over Twin Creeks,
and Main Street was hectic at the moment.

He couldn't take the time to look for Patrick now
when everything depended on his reaching the Box B
before Bigelow found out that his whole scheme was
falling apart. Murmuring to Sally, "Tell Patrick so long
for me," the Ranger went out the back door of the
bank.

The big dun was waiting for him, hitched to a mesquite about a block away. Stowing away his Ranger
badge in its hiding place, Cody turned his vest around
again, then mounted up and headed west toward the

Box B, his mind on Bigelow and the task in front of him.

And so he didn't see the figure following on horse-back behind him—a twelve-year-old boy who was wor-ried about his friend the Texas Ranger. . . .

By the time Cody reached the Box B, he had thought through the plan he had worked out with Tom O'Rourke and was convinced that it was a good one, the best chance of getting Bigelow away from the ranch without a lot of innocent men getting killed. The sun was lowering toward the western horizon when he came within sight of the ranch house, and as he ap-proached, his keen eyes spotted Bigelow standing at the front door.

The rancher must have been waiting for him, be-cause Bigelow waved and then motioned for him to come straight to the house. Cody rode into the yard, and as he dropped from the saddle and tied his horse at the hitchrack, he saw the big grin on Bigelow's face. Bigelow certainly looked pleased about something.

"I'm glad you got back when you did, Cotton," the rancher said as Cody stepped onto the porch. "Come on into the study. We've got some things to talk about."

Following Bigelow down the hall toward the study, Cody frowned, wondering what these new develop-ments were. Maybe some of the smaller ranchers were giving Bigelow trouble, in which case he might want Cody to visit them and try to intimidate them. The Ranger was fairly certain that Bigelow didn't know yet about the botched bank robbery and Turner's death. Cody had acted too quickly for word to have reached the Box B.

Reaching the study, the rancher grasped the knob and turned it, opening the door. Cody stepped into the room behind him—and froze.

Several ranch hands—Bart Seeley among them—

were waiting inside the study, all of them with guns drawn and aimed directly at him. Cody's instincts almost sent his hand darting toward the gun on his hip, but reason made him stop the gesture before it started. The odds were too high against him at the moment. Shad Garrison wasn't here, and Cody guessed that the crusty old foreman wasn't quite corrupt enough to be in on whatever Bigelow was planning. But Seeley and the others would kill him without blinking, if the rancher ordered it.

Bigelow went behind the desk and motioned curtly to his men. The smile was gone from his face, replaced by a look of cold hatred as he regarded Cody. A couple of the cowboys stepped up to the Ranger and took his Colt and bowie knife, then roughly shoved him into a chair in front of the desk.

"So, Cotton—or whatever the hell your real name is—you're a Texas Ranger," Bigelow began. "I'm not fond of admitting it, but you had me fooled into thinking that you were just another drifting hardcase. I don't like being made a fool of, mister."

"Name's Cody," the Ranger said coolly. "Don't reckon it'll hurt to tell you now."

"No, it won't," Bigelow replied with a shake of his head. "Because you're not leaving this ranch alive, Mr. Cody. I can promise you that."

Cody felt his heart thudding in his chest. He was as close to death as he had ever been. Knowing he had to stall for time, he kept himself outwardly calm as he remarked, "Seeing as how I've done some confessing, how about you, Bigelow?"

The rancher smirked and spread his hands. "What do you want to know?"

"How'd you manage to get Red Thunder and his band of renegades to work for you?"

Bigelow raised his eyebrows. "Oh, you know about that, do you? Well, it was easy enough. I simply promised the good chief and his men enough arms and ammunition to go on a rampage the likes of which this part of Texas hasn't seen in years. And whiskey, too, of course, to make sure Red Thunder and his men stay in the proper frame of mind."

Cody clenched his jaw. "You son of a bitch," he breathed, unable to contain the revulsion he felt for the man facing him across the desk.

Bigelow's face hardened, but only for a moment. Then he eased back in his chair and mocked, "Call me whatever you want, Cody. I've won this game, and you've lost. I suppose I can afford to be gracious— before you die."

"Who told you I'm a Ranger?"

Bigelow lifted a hand, and one of his men opened a side door. Cody tensed as a tall Comanche warrior strode proudly into the room. The jagged scar on his face told the Ranger who he was. "Red Thunder," Cody muttered.

"That is right, white man," the Comanche war chief said with a sneer. "I am Red Thunder, and I am your death."

Leaning forward and clasping his hands on the desk, Bigelow asked, "What about it, chief? Is this man the Ranger your braves were sent to kill?"

"He is," Red Thunder declared. "I have not seen him until now, but I was told of him by my friend and scout, Three Eyes." Fingering the tomahawk that was thrust behind the sash around his waist, the Comanche stepped closer to Cody. "Three Eyes is either dead or a prisoner now, taken by the other Rangers in battle earlier today. I wish he could be here to watch this white man die."

"You say you fought the Rangers today?" Cody asked, not knowing whether or not Red Thunder would answer.

The war chief nodded. "We slew many of them," he said proudly. "Then we came here and discovered that our friend Bigelow had a rattlesnake in his blankets." Red Thunder spat on the floor. "That rattlesnake is you, Ranger."

Bigelow glanced distastefully at the spot where the Indian's spittle had landed, then said, "Red Thunder and his men were thinking about leaving Texas and going to Mexico, but I persuaded them to stay awhile longer. I have another . . . present for them."

Red Thunder grinned, and Cody didn't like the menace in that cruel, wanton expression. The Ranger waited, knowing that Bigelow couldn't resist explaining. The rancher's arrogance had grown even greater, now that he was convinced Cody couldn't hurt him.

"Did you notice those boxes in the cabin where you bunked last night?" Bigelow asked after a moment. "You didn't by any chance take a look in them, did you?"

Cody shook his head. "I figured they were just supplies."

"Oh, they're supplies, all right. Those boxes are full of dynamite."

Catching his breath, the Ranger couldn't keep from revealing his shock and surprise. "Dynamite!" he exclaimed. "You're not planning to give it to—"

"To Red Thunder and his men," Bigelow finished. "That should make things rather interesting around these parts, don't you think?"

Interesting wasn't the word for it, Cody thought. With a large supply of the newfangled explosive in their hands, Red Thunder and his renegades could lay waste to a large part of the Texas frontier. Bigelow had no idea what a devil he was unleashing.

"By the time the Comanches are through, small ranchers won't dare set foot in this part of the country again," Bigelow continued. "The grazing lands will all belong to me. And from there"—he took out a cigar and stuck it in his mouth—"well, from there it's just a short step to the rest of the state, let's say."

Bigelow was crazy, Cody realized, insane with the lust for power. And that made him even more dangerous.

The rancher pushed back his chair and stood up. "There's been enough talking," he growled. "Chief, if you want this Ranger, he's yours to deal with any way you like."

Red Thunder grunted his appreciation. "His death will provide much enjoyment for my men," the Comanche said. "Many of my braves have met their own deaths at the hands of his friends. Our vengeance will be great."

A chill as cold as any blue norther went through Cody. It would be better to try to grab a gun and force them to kill him quickly, he thought, than to let the Indians get their hands on him. He tensed, trying to pick out one of the cowboys to lunge toward—

Cody's head jerked around when the door from the hall opened just then, and one of the Box B hands stepped into the study. He was dragging a young boy by the arm.

"Cousin Sam!" the terrified captive exclaimed wretchedly.

Seeing Patrick Edwards, Cody's blood froze.

The ranch hand holding the boy said, "Look what we found snoopin' around outside, boss. Looks like he's worried about his *cousin*."

"That's too bad," Bigelow muttered. "Too bad for the boy." He grinned mirthlessly at the Ranger. "It seems there'll be one more person to watch you die, Cody. In fact, we'll all watch, won't we, boys? Even my wife will be on hand." He turned to Seeley. "Fetch her for me, Bart."

"Sure, boss," Seeley said with a grin.

As Bigelow turned his cold gaze back to Cody, the Ranger was certain that the rancher had found out somehow about Gloria's visit to Cody's cabin the night before. That was one more reason he would want Cody to die.

"Take him," Bigelow snapped, and strong hands fastened on Cody's arms, dragging him out of the chair before he had a chance to make a move.

"Cousin Sam!" Patrick screamed. "No!"

Bigelow stepped over to the youngster and cruelly yanked his arm. "Come along, boy," he said. "You wouldn't want to miss this."

Cody struggled futilely against the grip of the hands

holding him as he was pulled out of the study and down the hall toward the front door. Bigelow's men kept a tight grasp on him as they led him across the porch and into the yard.

Red Thunder emerged from the house and stood on the porch beside Bigelow. Then the war chief let out a shrill cry, and a moment later, more than a dozen Comanche braves rode out from behind the barn and dismounted.

Sagging in the hold of Bigelow's punchers, Cody felt them tense at the sight of the Indians. The ingrained hostility between Comanche and white man could be felt in the air, but both sides were honoring an uneasy truce.

Bart Seeley came out of the house, pulling an unwilling Gloria Bigelow with him. She let out a cry when she saw Cody. "I'm sorry, Sam!" she cried. "I don't know how he found out—"

"Never mind, Gloria," Bigelow snapped. "It doesn't matter. I would have had your friend killed anyway. He's a Texas Ranger." Without warning, the rancher's free hand flashed up and cracked across his wife's face in a vicious slap. Gloria would have fallen if Seeley hadn't been holding her. Bigelow grated, "But if you ever cheat on me again, I'll give you to the Comanches. Remember that, woman!"

Sobs racking her, Gloria managed to nod.

Red Thunder stepped down from the porch and told the men holding Cody, "Tie him to a corral post and remove his shirt. I intend to skin him alive—very slowly."

The Box B hands hesitated, unsure whether to obey the Indian's orders, but when they glanced at Bigelow, he flipped his hand in a curt gesture that told them to go along with whatever Red Thunder wanted. They hauled Cody over to the corral, where another man stepped up to the Ranger and ripped the shirt and vest from his body.

Shoved up against a post, Cody felt his arms wrenched behind him, and rawhide thongs were bound around his wrists. The Ranger's teeth clenched tightly together as he looked at Patrick and Gloria and wondered what would happen to them if he didn't find a way out of this mess.

How much time had passed since his arrival at the ranch? Tom O'Rourke and the posse were supposed to be half an hour behind him. If they took up their positions in the chaparral the way he had told them, they would be able to see what was going on when they arrived. O'Rourke wouldn't stand by and let him be tortured to death, and he certainly wouldn't allow Patrick and Gloria to come to harm without a fight. Cody wasn't sure, but he had a feeling the half hour hadn't gone by yet. Somehow he had to keep stalling.

"That boy can't hurt you, Bigelow," he called to the rancher. "Why don't you just let him go?"

Bigelow smiled. "You know better than that, Cody. He's seen and heard too much already. But don't worry. After he's watched what the chief has in store for you, I'll see that he gets a quick, painless death."

Cody's pulse throbbed in his temples. He had never hated anyone more than he hated Ben Bigelow at that moment. He could have killed him with no more hesitation or remorse than if he were about to step on a scorpion.

"This is all for nothing, Bigelow," he declared, controlling his anger and trying a new tack. "Your plans have fallen apart. Everybody in Twin Creeks knows what you've been up to."

"I'm not worried about Twin Creeks," Bigelow called back, chuckling. "Reb Turner will keep it under control."

"Turner's dead," Cody snapped.

Bigelow frowned slightly. "What?"

"You hired me in the first place because you were afraid Turner might try to double-cross you. Well, that's exactly what he did. He and his men held up the bank earlier this afternoon—they were going to clean it out and then leave town. Tom O'Rourke and the citizens' committee stopped them. And Turner stopped a bullet."

"You're lying to buy yourself a few more minutes of life," Bigelow retorted with a sneer. "But you're crazy if you expect me to believe that a drunken fool like O'Rourke could ever stand up to Turner's gang."

"He did!" Patrick exclaimed, trying to tug away from Bigelow's grasp. Angrily, the boy continued, "Tom and Cousin Sam captured all those outlaws!"

Cody could see the indecision on Bigelow's face. The rancher didn't know whether to believe him and Patrick or not. But then Bigelow's face hardened again, and he said, "It doesn't matter either way. Turner was just a pawn. The town can't do anything to stop me now, not with the Indians and the men I have here on the ranch."

"Not all your hands are going to go along with you, Bigelow," the Ranger pressed. "Running roughshod over smaller ranchers is one thing; giving dynamite to the Comanches is another!"

Bigelow turned and pointed his cigar at Seeley. "What about you, Bart?" he demanded. "Are you willing to follow my orders?"

"As long as you're payin' the freight, boss, I'm with you," Seeley replied.

Bigelow stepped to the edge of the porch and raised his voice, addressing the eight or ten Box B hands scattered around the ranch yard. "What about the rest of you? Are you with me, too?"

A few of the men looked a bit uneasy, but all of them finally nodded their heads.

"Never underestimate the power of money, Cody," Bigelow mocked. "Now, if you're through stalling, let's get on with this. It'll be sundown soon."

Cody threw all the strength in his arms and shoulders against the thongs around his wrist. The bonds held tight. He glanced over and saw Red Thunder walking slowly toward him, slipping a sharp hunting knife from his belt.

Looking at the other Indians, Cody spat contemptuously and called, "Cowards! There's not one of you who's brave enough to face me alone. You've got to let your chief do your killing for you!"

Several of the Comanches frowned and stirred. They might not understand all of Cody's words, but they got the drift of his challenge easily enough.

"Do not waste your breath, white man," Red Thunder taunted. "You will not trick us into freeing you."

"I'm not trying to trick anybody," Cody stated. "I'll say it straight out: None of you is man enough to fight me."

"He's just spouting words, Red Thunder," Bigelow shouted from the porch. "Go ahead and finish him off."

The war chief was hesitating now. He had to be constantly aware of how he appeared to his men, Cody knew, and it might not look too good if he let this white man get away with challenging them. The warriors might think that their chief was starting to lack confidence in them.

That was the way Cody hoped it would seem. He nodded and said, "Yes, go ahead and kill me, Red Thunder. That way there won't be any chance of your braves finding out that I'm right."

"Silence!" Red Thunder growled, slashing the air in front of Cody's face with the blade, which glittered red in the glow of the setting sun. Cody didn't flinch, knowing his life depended on his show of courage, for the Comanches' pride would goad them to match that bravery.

"I'll make a wager," Cody said, staring directly at the war chief. "I'll fight your strongest man—for the life of the boy."

"If you win, the boy goes free?"

Cody nodded.

"But you stay here, win or lose, for us to do with as we will?"

Again the Ranger nodded.

"No!" Bigelow screamed. "I tell you, it's a trick, Red Thunder. This man can't be trusted."

The Comanche looked from Cody to Bigelow and back to the Ranger. Abruptly, he stepped up to Cody and thrust out the knife. The sharp blade reached behind the prisoner and parted the rawhide thongs around his wrists. "I think he can be," Red Thunder announced. "We accept the challenge."

Cody took a step away from the post, rubbing some feeling back into his numbed hands. Suppressing a grin, he saw that Bigelow was beside himself, almost bouncing up and down in anger and frustration. But the Indians had his men outnumbered, so there wasn't much he could do about the situation.

"Wolf Moon," Red Thunder called to one of his braves. "Come forward."

A warrior swung down off his pony and stalked toward Cody and the chief. Cody scowled slightly. Wolf Moon was even taller than Red Thunder, almost the same height as the Ranger, and muscles corded on his arms and shoulders. He was going to be a formidable opponent, no doubt about that.

Red Thunder turned to Bigelow's men, who were standing nervously nearby, and demanded, "Return the Ranger's knife."

One of the ranch hands held out the bowie to Cody, who took it gratefully. Fitting it into his palm, he decided that the smooth wooden hilt of the weapon had never felt quite so good.

From the porch Patrick cried, "Run for it, Cody! Cut your way out of here and get away!"

The Ranger shook his head and smiled. "I can't do that, Patrick," he said simply, then turned to face Wolf Moon. "I'm ready."

Red Thunder motioned for everyone else to get back. Cody cast one last glance at Bigelow and saw that the land baron was still seething.

Ranger and Comanche faced each other in the open space in front of the corral. Wolf Moon took a step toward Cody, the blade in his hand weaving slowly back and forth, but Cody didn't fall for the trick, didn't let his eyes stray to the weapon. He watched his opponent instead, and he saw the muscles of the Indian's belly tense as Wolf Moon got ready to leap forward.

Cody threw himself to the side, avoiding the lunge and the upward swipe of the knife. Twisting frantically, he slashed at Wolf Moon with the bowie. The Comanche darted away just in time. No first blood yet.

But it was just a matter of time.

Wolf Moon feinted with the knife, then launched a kick at Cody's groin. Cody recognized the ploy and tried to get out of the way, but he was only partially successful. The Comanche's foot caught him on the thigh, staggering him. In a flash, Wolf Moon was after him, trying to press the momentary advantage.

Cody felt his balance deserting him as he retreated, dodging some of the Indian's thrusts and blocking others with his own knife. He was about to fall, and there was nothing he could do to stop himself.

Might as well use it then, he thought in the part of his brain that was still in control of his actions. For the most part he was operating on instinct now, but he knew he was going to have to start thinking if he hoped to win this battle. He let himself go down, but as he fell, he snapped a kick at Wolf Moon's legs.

The heel of his boot caught the Indian just below the right knee. Wolf Moon grunted in pain and his leg buckled. Cody rolled desperately and lunged upward, moving under a sweeping slash of the Comanche's knife. He crashed into Wolf Moon's thighs, and the already off-balance warrior went down.

Cody felt a tongue of pain lick across his side and knew that the Indian had raked him with the knife. He scrambled away as a cheer went up from the other Comanches. Red Thunder didn't join in the shouts of encouragement; he watched the battle stoically.

Gaining his feet first, Cody saw that Wolf Moon was favoring his right leg. As for himself, he felt warm trickles of blood on his left side, but he forced the pain of the wound into the back of his mind. He could still move, and that was all that mattered at the moment.

Wolf Moon charged at him again, but the Indian was moving more slowly now. Although the fight had not lasted very long, both men were already tired. The sudden explosions of movement, added to the strain of being in a fight to the death, drained a man's reserves quickly.

Cody moved nimbly to the side, but he wasn't fast enough to completely avoid the charge. Throwing up his left hand, he caught Wolf Moon's right wrist as the blade sliced toward his face. The Ranger thrust the bowie at the Comanche's belly, but Wolf Moon countered the blow, catching Cody's wrist. They stood there, arms and hands locked together, swaying slightly, their bodies only inches apart.

Suddenly, Wolf Moon's injured leg gave way again, and he sagged to his right. Cody took a chance and let go of the brave's wrist, then drove his left fist across the Comanche's jaw and at the same instant hooked a foot behind Wolf Moon's left knee and tugged. Wolf Moon went down hard, losing his grip on Cody's knife hand.

The bowie slashed crossways, slicing across the right wrist of the Indian. Wolf Moon couldn't stifle the cry of pain as the blade severed muscles and tendons. His knife fell from nerveless fingers.

A backhanded slash would have sliced the Indian's throat, Cody knew, but instead he grabbed Wolf Moon's long, greasy hair with his free hand and jerked him up, moving behind him to encircle his throat with an arm. Putting the razor-sharp blade against the Comanche's neck, Cody called out, "Enough!"

Wolf Moon stood motionless in his grasp as the observers looked on in stunned silence. Patrick Edwards shattered the quiet by shouting, "You beat him, Cousin Sam!"

Red Thunder's scarred face was taut with rage as he declared, "You have won, Ranger. Kill him!"

Cody shook his head. "Nope. Wolf Moon's coming

with me and the boy and Mrs. Bigelow, and we're getting out of here."

The chief was still gripping his own knife. He lifted his arm suddenly, and with a flicker of movement, the blade flew across the intervening space and thudded into Wolf Moon's chest. The warrior stiffened in Cody's grasp and then sagged lifelessly with the knife penetrating his heart.

"He was dead the moment you defeated him," Red Thunder told the shocked Ranger.

Cody let Wolf Moon's body tumble to the ground. Standing there, bowie in hand, his torso smeared with blood and dust, he waited to see what Red Thunder was going to do next.

"We will honor our bargain," the chief declared. "The boy will be allowed to go free. And you, Ranger, in respect for your bravery, you will be given a quick death."

"No!" Bigelow exclaimed. "Kill Cody any way you like, but the boy can't be allowed to talk!"

Red Thunder ignored him, turning instead to his men and issuing a guttural order. Several of the braves lifted the rifles they held, and Cody knew they were about to shoot him.

A rush of hoofbeats made everyone look around sharply as three of the Box B hands came galloping into the yard on lathered horses. "Trouble, boss!" one of them shouted to Bigelow. "Riders comin'!"

"What the devil! Who is it?"

One of the other men sagged wearily in the saddle and replied, "We spotted a bunch comin' through the chaparral toward the ranch. Looked like they were from Twin Creeks. I swear the man leadin' 'em was Tom O'Rourke!"

"O'Rourke!" Bigelow turned a startled gaze toward Cody. "Then you *were* telling the truth. . . ."

"That ain't the worst of it, Mr. Bigelow," the first outrider said. "There's men comin' from the north, too, and they'll be here pretty quick." He swallowed nervously. "They're wearin' Ranger badge s boss."

Cody felt excitement surge through him as confusion began to spread around the ranch house. O'Rourke's force from town combined with the Rangers led by Captain Vickery would be enough manpower to wipe out the renegades and Bigelow's hired guns. They could put a stop to the rancher's evil, here and now.

The big Ranger acted quickly. Lunging at Red Thunder, he slammed his left fist into the chief's jaw. The other Comanches couldn't shoot, not with him so close to their leader.

At the same moment Patrick tore free of Bigelow's grip, twisting around to drive his clubbed hands into the man's soft stomach. Leaping from the porch, the boy raced toward one of the nearby Indian ponies. Cody saw what the boy was doing and shoved Red Thunder out of the way, sending the stunned warrior staggering toward the other braves.

"Kill them!" Bigelow shrieked. He jerked a small pistol from under his coat and tried to bring it to bear on Cody, but before he could fire, Gloria leaped on his back, making him stumble forward as she clawed at his face with her long fingernails. Bigelow cursed and threw her off, backhanding her savagely and knocking her off her feet.

Guns blasted and Cody felt the wind from a slug on his face. He reached the pony, which was dancing nervously around, and grasped its mane, swinging himself onto its back in one lithe motion. Turning the animal and kicking it into a run, the Ranger reached down to grasp Patrick's upthrust hand and hauled the boy onto the back of the horse behind him.

"Keep your head down!" he shouted at Patrick, and leaning forward, he urged the pony on to greater speed. Flying lead sang around their heads as they raced away from the ranch house in a hail of bullets.

CHAPTER
IIIIIIIIIIIIIIIIIIIIIIIIIIIII **14** IIIIIIIIIIIIIIIIIIIIIIIIIIIII

Cody heard Patrick gasp. "You all right?" he called to the boy as the wind of their passage buffeted his face.

"I'm fine!" Patrick replied. Cody wasn't sure whether or not to believe him, but his voice had sounded strong, and there wasn't really time to slow down and check.

The Ranger kept the Indian pony moving at top speed, and the ranch house was falling behind rapidly, which meant they would soon be out of pistol range. Casting a glance over his shoulder, Cody saw that no one had started out in pursuit yet. He and Patrick might have a chance to escape after all.

Cody felt a pang of guilt at abandoning Gloria Bigelow back there, but he'd had to move quickly, and there hadn't been a chance to grab anyone but Patrick. Maybe Gloria would be all right until reinforcements arrived.

At least Cody tried to tell himself so.

Skirting the fingers of chaparral, he headed north along the open land between the brush and the river. He had already spotted some dust in the air and knew it marked the approaching Rangers. Within minutes, Cody could see the men galloping toward him, could make out the black-suited figure of Captain Wallace Vickery. As usual, the Bible-thumping commander was out in front, where the lead would be the thickest.

Cody hauled back on the pony's mane, slowing its

pace. He held up a hand, palm out, just in case the charging Rangers mistook this bare-chested rider on an Indian pony for a Comanche.

"Cody!" Captain Vickery shouted moments later as he reined his horse to an abrupt halt. "Thank the Lord you're alive, son! You hurt bad?"

Cody glanced down at the gash on his side. It was crusted with dirt and would have to be cleaned out thoroughly later, but right now it wasn't bad enough to slow him down. "I'm fine," he answered. "But you'd better have somebody take a look at my friend here."

He helped Patrick off the horse, and as he did so, Cody saw the bloodstain on the boy's sleeve.

"Aw, it's just a scratch," Patrick muttered as Lieutenant Whitcomb cut away his sleeve to check the wound, but Cody noticed that Patrick was a bit pale.

"The lad's been grazed, that's all," Whitcomb announced. He turned and looked at the other Rangers, who were resting their mounts before resuming the advance on the Box B. "Northrup!" the lieutenant called. "Take charge of this boy!"

"Yes, sir," Alan Northrup replied, dismounting to come over to Patrick. The stocky young Ranger's left arm was in a sling, with a bloody bandage wrapped around the upper arm, but he seemed to be in good spirits. Cody had spotted Seth Williams, who had also come through the battle with Red Thunder's band unscathed.

Vickery rested his hands on his saddle horn and said to Cody, "Make your report short, son. I got a feelin' we ain't got much time."

Cody nodded. "The head skunk's named Bigelow. That's his spread. He and his men are there, and so's what's left of Red Thunder's bunch. They've been working with Bigelow."

"What about Reb Turner?"

"Dead."

Vickery nodded. "Reckon that's all we need to know now. We've got a prisoner who told us about Red Thunder bein' mixed up with Bigelow. We stopped at a ranch owned by a feller named Morton, and he told us how to find the Box B. You feel up to helpin' us clean out that rat's nest, Cody?"

"I'll need a gun."

Northrup handed his six-shooter to Cody. "Be pleased to have you use mine."

"Thanks," Cody responded, grinning. He was still wearing his belt and holster, so he sheathed both Northrup's Colt and the bowie. Turning the pony around to face the ranch, he said, "Let's go."

As the Rangers broke into a gallop again, a crackle of gunfire sounded from the chaparral east of the ranch house. Men on horseback were trying to escape in that direction, only to be met by the force from Twin Creeks. In the forefront of the posse was Tom O'Rourke, who wheeled his horse this way and that while firing the revolver in his hand.

The Comanches broke away from the ranch in another direction. Veering to cut them off, the Rangers closed in on them. Cody guided the pony with his knees as he brought up the Colt in his fist and began to trigger it.

Rangers and Indians came together in a wild melee. In the haze of dust and gun smoke that filled the air, Cody suddenly saw Red Thunder looming up in front of him. The war chief sent his horse straight at Cody's, and he screamed his defiance as he drew back the lance in his hand and flung it toward the Ranger.

Cody swayed to one side as he fired, while the lance cut through the space where his head had been an instant earlier. As the spear fell harmlessly to the ground, Cody's bullet struck Red Thunder in the chest, lifting the war chief from the back of his racing pony and spilling him in a limp heap on the ground.

Seeing that their leader was dead, some of the Indians tried to cut and run, but there was nowhere to go, for they ran into Bigelow's men, who were trying to escape from the Twin Creeks posse. Caught in a cross fire, the Comanches and the Box B punchers had no choice but to surrender or die.

A few threw down their weapons and surrendered. The rest died.

Cody caught Vickery's eye and waved to let the captain know he was all right; then he turned the pony toward the ranch house. Bigelow was still unaccounted for, and the Ranger wanted to find Gloria and make sure she was unharmed.

As Cody dashed into the yard in front of the ranch house, a carriage burst into view around the corner of the building. Cody caught a glimpse of Bigelow's face, contorted with rage and fear, as he whipped the pair of horses pulling the vehicle into a gallop. Beside him on the seat was Gloria.

A thickset figure ran out of the bunkhouse and tried to get in front of the carriage. Cody recognized Shad Garrison. The foreman was trying to stop Bigelow from getting away, and Cody had to give him credit for that, even though Garrison had obviously turned a blind eye toward a lot of wrongdoing. But Bigelow wasn't stopping for anybody or anything, and he sent the carriage thundering past as Garrison leaped frantically out of the way. One of the wheels clipped the foreman's leg, knocking him down.

Cody galloped up as Garrison yanked out his pistol and pointed it at the fleeing carriage. "No!" Cody yelled, almost riding over the foreman. "Gloria's in there with him!"

Garrison cursed and tried to get up, but his injured leg wouldn't support him. "I know I'm probably goin' to jail," he told Cody, "but I don't want to see that son of a bitch escape! Get him, Ranger!"

So, Garrison knew he was a Ranger. Must've heard about it while Bigelow still held the upper hand, Cody thought. Dropping off the pony, he held on to its mane as he let out a shrill whistle. A grin broke out on his face as his dun came running up. He'd figured that the big horse would be somewhere close by.

Letting go of the Indian pony, he swung up into the saddle of his own mount, heeling the dun into a run. It pounded after the carriage.

Bigelow was heading south, away from the fighting. Or rather, the mopping up, Cody thought. The Rangers and the posse had just about put an end to any resistance.

The carriage had a good lead, but Cody knew his horse could catch up as he leaned forward over the animal's neck, urging it on. Bigelow was heading south, and it wouldn't be long before the fleeing rancher reached the Rio Grande. If he made it to the other side of the river, Cody could not legally follow him into Mexican jurisdiction.

Not that a little thing like that was going to stop him, though, the Ranger thought grimly.

Gradually, the magnificent horse under Cody cut the distance between the Ranger and the carriage, and Cody holstered his revolver as he drew even with the vehicle. It would be too dangerous to start throwing lead now; a stray bullet might hit Gloria.

Bigelow obviously wasn't worried about that. Holding the reins with one hand, he fumbled and got his pistol out, then snapped off a shot at Cody. The bullet whined past the Ranger's head. Bigelow tried to fire again, but he was struggling to keep the horses under control, and the carriage was bouncing and careening wildly. Finally he got another shot off, but it went almost straight up as the carriage bounded in the air for a split second.

Cody wasn't going to wait for Bigelow to get lucky, and he kicked his feet free of the stirrups and flung himself into the air, landing on the side of the carriage. Gloria screamed as he grabbed for a handhold and threw a punch at the rancher at the same time.

Bigelow slashed at his head with the gun. The barrel raked along Cody's temple and knocked him backward, and for a few seconds that seemed much longer, he hung on to the side of the swaying vehicle, barely maintaining his grip. Desperately, he managed to hook a leg over the side of the carriage. Then Cody brought a sweeping left hand around and smashed it into

Bigelow's face, using the momentum of the blow to help him tumble into the carriage.

Bigelow's gun went off beside Cody's head, and even the small-caliber explosion was deafening at these close quarters. He felt the sting of burning powder on his cheek, but the bullet missed him. However, it struck one of the horses in the neck, and the animal let out a scream of pain and raced on for a few more feet before it stumbled. As the team piled up, Cody felt the carriage starting to tip over.

Another shot went off as he grabbed Bigelow's gun hand and twisted the barrel away from himself. Bigelow screeched, and Cody saw his eyes widen in pain, but there was no time to notice anything else. Grabbing Gloria, Cody pulled her off the seat and out of the carriage as it crashed, tearing free from the team and tumbling over and over.

Cody and Gloria landed hard, and the breath was knocked from the Ranger's lungs. He rolled several times, finally coming to a stop on his belly. Lifting his head, he saw Gloria sprawled a few feet away. She was moaning and moving around, so at least he knew she was still alive.

The carriage was lying on its side. Not far away, one of the horses was dead and the other was trying to kick itself free from the tangled traces. Bigelow had been thrown out of the carriage. He was lying, unmoving, about twenty feet from Cody.

Forcing himself to stand, Cody discovered that all of his muscles seemed to be working, and no bones were broken. He was lucky—he knew that. His pistol had fallen out of the holster sometime during the struggle, but the bowie was still sheathed on his left hip, and he slipped it out as he approached Bigelow, just in case there was any fight left in the rancher.

There was no fight—or anything else—left. Bigelow was dead, his hands clutched to his belly. His shirt was bloody, and Cody knew that the last shot had struck him.

Turning back to Gloria, Cody knelt beside her,

gently lifting her head into his lap. She opened her eyes as he began probing at her body, trying to determine if she was injured.

"I . . . I don't think this is really the time . . . for that, Sam," she whispered dryly.

Cody grinned. She had some bumps and bruises, but it looked as though she had been lucky, too. "You just lie still and rest," he told her. Glancing up, he saw riders coming, Captain Vickery and Tom O'Rourke at their head. "It's all over now."

"He's . . . dead . . . ?"

Cody didn't have to ask whom she meant. "He's dead."

"Then it *is* over." She sighed and closed her eyes.

"You just rest," Cody repeated, and that advice sounded pretty good to him as well.

Twilight was settling by the time Cody, Gloria, O'Rourke, Vickery, and the others got back to the ranch. Cody and Gloria were riding double on the big dun, and the beautiful young widow rested wearily against the Ranger.

It looked as though every lamp in the big house had been lit, and as Cody reined in, Sally Edwards came out of the house onto the porch. Patrick was with her, his arm bandaged, and his sister's arm was looped protectively around his shoulders. Pulling free from her, the boy ran down the steps to meet the riders.

"Are you all right, Cousin Sam?" Patrick asked anxiously.

"Right as rain," Cody assured him. He'd be stiff and sore for a few days, and the gash on his side would need to be cleaned and maybe stitched up, but overall the Ranger felt pretty good.

"When I discovered Patrick wasn't in town, I knew where he must have gone," Sally said as she came down the steps. She looked up at O'Rourke. "What about you, Tom? Are you all right?"

"Never better," the sheriff of Twin Creeks replied.

Swinging down from the saddle, he gathered both Sally and Patrick into his long arms.

"You got room in your jail for all them prisoners, Sheriff?" Vickery asked as he dismounted.

"We'll make room," O'Rourke promised.

"Reckon you've got a church in Twin Creeks, too."

"Sure. There's a Baptist church."

"Good," Vickery declared. "We'll head into town and get those boys locked up for the time bein', till we figure out what to do with 'em, and then we'll have a prayer meetin'." He turned his head sharply, a bushy-browed glare silencing the groans of protest from his Rangers.

Cody grinned and climbed the porch steps with Gloria. She had recovered from the crash, although she, too, was still moving a bit stiffly. Looking at the house, she said, "I think I hate this place. I'm going to sell the ranch if I can."

"You won't have any trouble finding buyers. It's a mighty nice spread. And I'm sure the Edwardses would let you stay with them in town until you get things settled."

"I think I'd like that," Gloria said softly. "It's been so long since I've lived anything like a normal life. I . . . I hope I remember how."

"It'll come back to you," Cody assured her.

She turned to look at him intently in the fading light. "What about you? What are you going to do?"

He hesitated, then said, "I told you that when the job was over, I'd have to be riding on. Well, it's over."

"So you'll ride away, just like that?"

Cody put his hands on her shoulders and smiled, drawing her closer to him. "Maybe not right away. Hell, I'm wounded, after all. Even a Ranger gets to rest up a mite—"

"Cody!" Captain Vickery bellowed as he pulled himself into the saddle again. "You comin', son?"

"No thanks, Cap'n," Cody called back with a wave and a grin. "I reckon you can go to prayer meeting without me this time."

Epilogue

||||||||||||||||||||||||||||||||||||

"**O**h, *chéri,* that must have hurt like the very devil," Marie Jermaine murmured, her fingertip gently tracing the healing knife wound in Cody's side. "You should soak it in a warm bath."

"That was my idea, too," Cody declared as he finished taking off his shirt.

They were in his room at the Rio Grande Hotel in Del Rio, where Marie had been waiting for him in a silk dressing gown, her long red hair flowing loose and luxurious around her shoulders. The tub full of hot water was behind her, and as Cody reached for his belt, she shrugged out of the gown and let it fall around her feet.

Just for an instant, Cody thought of Gloria Bigelow and the time they had spent together over the last few days. Despite all the blood that had been shed during his mission to Twin Creeks, he would remember Gloria fondly—but they both had their own lives to lead now. He brought his attention back to the lovely nude form of Marie as she stepped daintily into the bath.

Somebody knocked on the door.

"No," Marie groaned, and for a second Cody thought of turning around and putting a bullet into the ceiling to see if that would scare off whoever was knocking. Then he sighed, slipped his arms back into the sleeves of his shirt, and went to answer the summons.

He left the inner room and crossed to the hallway door, throwing it open. Alan Northrup stood there, looking distinctly nervous. The young Ranger gave Cody a weak smile and said, "The captain sent me."

"I figured as much," Cody grunted. "How come he didn't send Seth?"

"Well, actually, he did. Seth matched me for the job, and I lost. So I, uh, have to deliver the message to you."

"What message?" Cody asked warily.

"You remember Diego Alvarez?"

"Of course I remember him!" Cody said impatiently. "It's only been just over a week since I brought him in."

"Well, he sort of . . . escaped."

Cody closed his eyes.

"The day after we all left to chase down those renegades, in fact," Northrup continued. "He said our gringo justice wouldn't hold him, and doggoned if he wasn't right."

Cody opened his eyes again and asked sarcastically, "Why'd the captain wait this long to tell me? I've been back in Del Rio a whole damn half hour!"

The young Ranger shrugged. "Cap'n Vickery said he figured you'd want to know. He wanted you to be rested up good before you started after Alvarez again, though. That's why he didn't send word to Twin Creeks while you were still up there. The rest of us found out about it as soon as we got back to headquarters, three days ago."

"All right," Cody said, nodding. He glanced over his shoulder, and through the partially open door to the other room, he could see Marie waiting in the tub, pouting prettily.

Damned if he was going to let that water get cold again.

"Tell the captain I'll be heading out," Cody said as he closed the hallway door, "first thing in the morning!"

CODY'S LAW: BOOK 2

||||||||||||||||||||||||||||||||||||||||||||||||||||||||||||||||||||||||||||||||||||||||||||||||||||

DIE LONESOME

by Matthew S. Hart

Who has stolen over two hundred repeating rifles from a U.S. Army depot? Where are the stolen weapons? Can the gun smugglers be stopped before they sell the rifles to the Comanche warriors who'll then use them against settlers on the Texas frontier? These are the questions—and the dilemma—facing Texas Ranger Samuel Clayton Woodbine Cody. He's assigned the case after an informant, a saloonkeeper named Halliday, notifies the authorities about the robbery.

Going to San Antonio to question the informant, Cody discovers that Halliday is in fact a beautiful—and mysterious—woman. The seemingly amoral Angela Halliday is disturbingly vague about her motive for helping the Rangers, but Cody's forced to trust this questionable woman when she becomes pivotal to the success of his mission.

Posing as husband and wife, Cody and Angela join a wagon train heading for California, for the Ranger surmises that one of the pilgrims is actually the mastermind of the smuggling ring. He soon finds that he has quite a list of suspects to choose from, Angela among them. The undercover assignment is filled with risks and dangers for Cody—not the least of which is learning the truth about Angela and his growing attachment for her.

Read DIE LONESOME, on sale September 1991 wherever Bantam paperbacks are sold.

CODY THOUGHT the man was bluffing, but he wasn't sure. He was glad this was just a poker game, not life or death. "I'll call," the tall Texas Ranger said, his dark eyes glinting with anticipation as he tossed a few more chips onto the pile in the center of the baize-covered table. He laid down his hand. Two pair, jacks over treys. Not bad.

Not good enough, he saw a moment later as Axel Farnum, the only other player left in this pot, spread out his cards and revealed three sixes. Farnum grinned and reached out to rake in the chips.

"At least it was somebody else got took this time," muttered one of the other players, a drifting cowhand known only as Pierson.

Cody glanced at him, as did the other men around the table, but nobody said anything. Farnum's eyes narrowed and he let out a grunt. That was his only response, and Cody was glad the rancher decided to let the veiled insult pass. A brawl wouldn't serve any purpose right now.

Cody, Farnum, and Pierson, along with three other men, were sitting around one of the tables in the bar of the Rio Grande Hotel. As Del Rio's leading pleasure palace, not to mention being one of the best-known stops for travelers between Brownsville and El Paso, the Rio Grande always did a brisk business.

At the moment the saloon was so busy that Ernest Palmatier, the proprietor of the place along with his wife, was helping out behind the bar, serving the customers his regular bartenders hadn't gotten to yet. Men stood two deep in places along the long hardwood counter, and all of the tables were full too. Waitresses in colorful, spangled, low-cut gowns moved among the tables, serving drinks and generally brightening up the room—when they weren't heading upstairs with one of the customers for a few minutes of passion bought with a gold coin. The piano player tried valiantly to provide a counterpoint to the loud talk and laughter that filled the air, but his tinkling melodies were lost for the most part. A blue haze of smoke from dozens of quirlies hung in the air along with the din.

All in all, the Rio Grande was one of Cody's favorite places in the world, and it was as close to a home as he had these days. One of the rooms upstairs was always reserved for him, no matter how much his Ranger duties kept him away, and he got to enjoy a friendly game of poker, though he wasn't fanatically devoted to the game the way some men were. An evening spent like this one would normally be relaxing for him.

Tonight was different. Tonight he was working.

Axel Farnum still had the deal, and he was shuffling the cards as Cody, thoughtfully stroking his dark mustache, casually watched him from across the table. The rancher was known to him mostly by reputation. Farnum's Box AF spread to the northeast of Del Rio was a growing, thriving operation, and the man's success showed in his clothing. Rather than the range outfits many cattlemen wore whether they were on their ranches or in town, Farnum sported an expensive gray suit, a starched white shirt, a silk tie, and a cream-colored Stetson now pushed to the back of his head. Cody guessed that Farnum was in his early to mid-forties, ten or twelve years older than himself; his brown hair was showing streaks of gray, and his features were a bit heavy and florid. Not enough work and too many nights in town had softened him somewhat from the rugged stockman who had started the Box AF several years earlier. But he was still one of the leading citizens of the area.

The man called Pierson was at the other end of the scale—a cowhand who, judging by the looks of him, had never aspired to anything more than forty-a-month-and-found. His clothes were worn and patched, his boots down at the heel, and his hat stained and battered almost shapeless. About the only items he appeared to take good care of were his gun and holster. Appearances could be deceiving, though. Cody had good reason to know that.

"You gonna shuffle them pasteboards all day, or you gonna deal 'em?" Pierson asked, impatience and frustration putting a jagged edge in his voice.

"No need to get in a huff," Farnum said smoothly. He straightened the cards and set them down on the table for the man beside him to cut. Once that was done, Farnum began dealing the next hand.

Cody glanced at his tablemates. One of the other men was also a rancher, not as successful as Farnum but with a good spread. His name was Bailey, and Cody knew him slightly. The remaining pair of players were both townsmen, a storekeeper called Clements and a livery stable owner known as Moe. Cody wasn't sure of his last name. None of them were all that important at the moment. Pierson was the only reason Cody was at this table.

The Ranger had been keeping an eye on the drifter for the past few days, trading off with some of the other members of Ranger Company C, which was headquartered here in Del Rio. Captain Vickery, the company commander, had been tipped off that Pierson was tied in somehow with a bunch of wide loopers who had been hitting the local ranchers and then running the stolen stock across the border into Mexico. Of course, such things had a tendency to balance out— gringo rustlers rode across the Rio at night and came back with plenty of cows belonging to the Mexican ranchers—but the Rangers had to at least make an effort to see if they could put a stop to the situation. Cody didn't know if the *rurales* across the border went to that much trouble, but he suspected they didn't bother.

Still, orders were orders, and if a fella had to work, this was about as pleasant a chore as he was likely to find.

Cody glanced lazily at his cards. Shit. Ten high. He'd keep the ten and the eight, he decided, and toss the small fish back when the time came.

A slight stir in the saloon noise made him glance over his shoulder. A tall, beautiful, redheaded woman in a green gown was coming toward him. Her ample breasts threatened to spill out of her daring neckline as she reached Cody and bent over to run her arms around his neck. Her lips nuzzled his ear, and her white teeth nipped playfully but a bit painfully at the lobe.

"Are you coming upstairs any time soon, chéri?" she asked in a throaty whisper.

Cody grinned, knowing that probably every man in the room was directing an envious stare at him. Marie Jermaine's beauty was legendary in these parts, and though she was hardly Cody's girl alone—anyone who could pay the high price she commanded could have her, after all—Marie made no secret of the man whose company she preferred . . . with no exchange of money necessary.

"Maybe a little later, darlin'," he said easily. He held up the cards. "I'm a mite occupied at the moment."

She pouted prettily. "With a game? If it is games you want, I can show you much better ones that we can play in private? . . ."

It was a mighty tempting offer, but Cody was supposed to keep an eye on Pierson until he was relieved at midnight. That was still two hours away. He sighed. Marie would just have to wait, and so would he.

She clearly knew from the sound of his sigh what his answer was going to be, for, not waiting to hear it, she stood and started to flounce off angrily. But then she paused and looked back over her shoulder, and Cody saw a hint of a smile on her face that told him it was going to be all right. He and Marie understood each other, and sometimes Cody thought that was more important than the lovemaking they shared.

Farnum's luck continued. He won most of the hands, though Cody or one of the other men would occasionally take a pot. Except Pierson. He lost consistently, and the pile of chips that had been in front of him when the game began shrank steadily. The cowhand glowered across the table at Farnum and muttered something under his breath several times, but the rancher continued to ignore him.

Cody was getting bored. The Rangers had been watching

Pierson in hopes that he would say or do something to lead them to the rest of the rustlers, but that wasn't likely to happen as long as the man was just sitting here playing poker. And Marie was still hanging around near the table, sometimes watching the game, sometimes sipping a drink, but refusing all the offers that came her way. Obviously she intended to wait for Cody tonight, no matter how long that took.

As a new hand began, Pierson tossed one of his few remaining chips into the center of the table for his ante, then said, "Don't know why I'm still playin'. I always thought poker was supposed to be a game of chance. Chance ain't got nothin' to do with this game tonight."

"You've been mouthing off a lot lately, friend," said Moe, the small, wiry stable owner. "You might have better luck if you'd just watch your cards."

"Nobody asked you to stick your nose in it," Pierson snapped, not taking his eyes off Farnum. "I'm talkin' to somebody else."

A muscle twitched in Farnum's cheek. Pierson's complaints were finally getting to him, Cody decided, as he watched with narrowed eyes. Farnum had the deal, as usual. For a second the rancher looked as if he was going to respond to Pierson's taunt, but then he went on with his shuffling.

Just for the hell of it, Cody watched Farnum's hands as he passed out the cards.

A few moments later, as the Ranger riffled out the cards Farnum had dealt him, he saw that he had drawn one of his best hands of the night. He had two pair to start with, sevens and deuces, so even if he didn't get the card he needed for a full house, he would be in good shape.

He was sitting to Pierson's left, and by the time the betting got to him, the stakes had grown considerably, bumped up by the cowhand's raise. Cody stayed, wondering what kind of hand Pierson had drawn.

When Farnum said, "Cards, gentlemen?" Cody threw in the odd jack on his turn and got an eight in its place. He didn't let his disappointment show on his rugged, tanned face. He still had the two pair, after all. Pierson, too, had only taken one card, and the cowboy looked happy for a change. Must've got what he wanted, Cody thought.

Pierson certainly bet as though he was satisfied. By the time play had gone around the table twice more, the pot was one of the biggest of the night, fueled by Pierson's plunging. Cody and Farnum stayed with him, but the other three men gradually dropped out.

The bet was back to Farnum. With a smile, he said, "It had to come down to this sooner or later, I suppose." Carefully, he pushed out exactly the same number of chips as Pierson had left.

Pierson's face flushed. All he could do was call, but if he won, he would more than recoup the money he had lost in the course of the evening. He matched the rancher's bet, saying, "That cleans me out. But you know that, don't you, mister?" He then looked over at Cody.

Cody grimaced. This had gotten out of hand in a hurry. If he raised, he was sure Farnum would match it, and then Pierson would be forced to drop out. He didn't really care if he won or not, but he didn't want Pierson to lose. The cowhand was drawn as taut as a bowstring, and his eyes were hot and shining with anger.

"I call, too," Cody said, throwing in his chips.

Without waiting for Farnum to lay down his hand, Pierson slapped his cards faceup on the table. "Full house," he snarled, "queens over jacks. Beat that if you can!"

Cody shook his head and threw in his two pair. "I can't."

"What about you, mister rancher?" Pierson asked, his voice quivering with hate.

A grin slowly spread across Farnum's face. "There's a lot of royalty staring up from the table, my friend," he said, gesturing toward Pierson's cards. He put his own cards down, one at a time. "All I have are these lowly little hearts. Five of them, to be exact."

Pierson's mouth tightened into a grim line as he stared at the flush. With a laugh, Farnum started to reach for his winnings.

"No!" Pierson cried. Silence fell over the barroom as the patrons turned to look at the commotion.

Cody sat forward slowly, his muscles tense. The other

rancher, Bailey, ventured to say, "No need to get upset, Pierson. Axel beat you fair and square."

That was the worst thing he could have said. Pierson countered, "No, he didn't. The bastard cheated me! He's been cheatin' all night!"

The other three men at the table pushed their chairs back and got up in a hurry. Farnum's face reddened as he leaned forward and said quietly, "I'll give you a chance to take back that rash statement, boy."

"I ain't takin' nothin' back!" Pierson shouted. "You're a low-down card cheat, Farnum!"

The rancher's lip curled in contempt, and his right hand darted across his body toward the Colt Cloverleaf he carried butt forward in a belt holster on his left hip. Even as his fingers closed around the grips of the little .41-caliber pistol, Pierson was coming up out of his chair and grabbing for his own gun.

Cody exploded upward, his hands closing on the edge of the table and heaving. It tipped over, chips, coins, and paper money scattering. The Ranger wanted to separate Farnum and Pierson before they could start shooting, and this was the quickest way.

He was a second too late. Pierson cleared leather and fired from the hip, the detonation of the shot deafening even in the big room. Farnum cried out and was thrown backward by the impact of the slug. Out of the corner of his eye Cody saw the rancher falling from his chair, but there wasn't time to see how badly Farnum was wounded. Cody had to stop Pierson before anybody else got hurt.

The drifter was backing up in a hurry, his eyes darting frantically around the room. He turned and took a step toward the door of the saloon, but one of Farnum's ranch hands who had been drinking at the bar yelled, "He shot the boss! Stop the son of a bitch!"

Several more men moved to block Pierson's path. He jerked around, his features contorted in panic, and it was obvious that he had never intended for anything like this to happen. His temper had run away with him, and now an important man lay bleeding on the floor. Escape was clearly the only thing on Pierson's mind.

He lunged to one side, reaching out with his free hand and grabbing Marie Jermaine's upper left arm. His fingers dug cruelly into the soft flesh as he yanked the redhead in front of him.

"No!" Cody shouted. "Let her go!"

"Ever'body just stay still!" Pierson ordered in a loud hoarse voice. "Me and this gal are walkin' out of here, and nobody better try to stop us!"

Cody's Frontier Colt was in his hand, his fingers tight on the walnut grips. He didn't even remember drawing it. Studying Pierson, he saw the desperation on the cowboy's face. Marie appeared fairly calm, considering the circumstances, but Cody could see the fear in her eyes. *Dammit, Marie,* he said to himself, *why didn't you get out of the way a little quicker?*

No point in thinking about that now. Keeping his voice cool, Cody said, "Just put the gun down, Pierson. Nobody wants this to get any worse than it already is."

Farnum let out a groan from the floor.

"Just stay out of my way, Ranger," Pierson warned. "You think I trust you? Hell, no! I give up, you'll turn me over to Farnum's men for a lynchin' party! The hell with that! I'd rather shoot my way out and die that way!"

That's what it was going to come down to, Cody thought bleakly as he glanced at the Box AF riders. There were a good half dozen of them in the room, and they didn't look as though they were in any mood to make a deal with Pierson, hostage or no hostage.

Cody fastened his gaze on them. "You men clear out," he instructed.

They shook their heads stubbornly. One of them said, "That bastard shot the boss. He's got to pay."

"Goddamn it, this is the Texas Rangers talking!" Cody roared. "Now clear out!"

They hesitated, shuffling around. There wasn't a man among them who didn't respect the authority of the Rangers, but they had been raised to ride for the brand. That meant sticking up for their boss, no matter what.

Marie took the decision out of anyone else's hands. She moaned and lifted a hand toward her face, as if she was on the verge of fainting. Her hand continued up, and from the pile of red curls on top of her head she snatched a long, sharp hairpin, then jabbed it into the back of the hand holding her other arm.

Pierson screeched in pain and automatically let go of her. Marie flung herself to one side, out of the line of fire, and most of the other people in the room hit the floor as Cody shouted, "Drop the gun, Pierson!"

Cursing fervently, Pierson brought up his Colt and triggered it. He fired three times, but the last two shots went into the floor as he staggered backward, his shirtfront turning red where Cody's bullets had hit him. The Ranger extended his arm, the revolver held steady, and squeezed off another shot. Pierson went down, landing with a thud on the sawdust-covered floor.

Cody drew a deep breath and walked over to the fallen man, keeping the gun trained on Pierson until he had kicked the gun out of Pierson's hand. The drifter was dead, not much doubt about that, but a man didn't take chances.

An eerie silence had settled over the room after the thunder of gunshots died away. Cody broke it by turning to Marie and asking, "Are you all right?"

She was picking herself up off the floor, not bothering to wait for anyone to help her. As she brushed the sawdust from her gown she said, "Of course I am all right, chéri. Why would I not be?"

But despite her casual tone, her eyes were wide, and Cody thought she looked like a deer about to bolt. He knew the feeling. There was nothing good about a gunfight, and he could understand why some of the most famous shootists in the West had to find a nice dark alley and puke their guts out after they'd faced down their latest challenger.

One of these days he'd come up on the short end himself. Cody knew it, and so did every other man who lived by the gun. But not tonight. He holstered the revolver, touched Marie lightly on the arm for a second, then turned to see how seriously Axel Farnum was hurt.

The rancher had crawled over to the wall next to the overturned table where he sat with his back against the wall. Now that Pierson was dead, some of the other men in the saloon were getting to their feet, and they hurried over to cluster around Farnum.

Cody waved them away and said, "Give the man some room." He knelt in front of Farnum and pulled the wounded man's coat back. The starched white shirt had a bright red stain on it high on the right side, just under the shoulder. Cody studied the location of the wound for a second, then grunted, "Looks like the slug might've missed the bone. We can hope so, anyway. Best send for a doctor." He looked up at the faces crowding in. "Somebody go fetch Doc Johnston. The rest of you—back off!"

The bystanders muttered among themselves, but they did as Cody had ordered, going back to the bar and the tables and resuming their drinking and talking. With no one standing close around them now, Farnum looked up at Cody and asked, "How . . . how bad is it, Ranger? You think I'll make it?"

Still kneeling beside the rancher, Cody nodded and said in a low, grim voice that couldn't be heard more than a couple of feet away, "I reckon you will, if that bullet hole doesn't fester. But if you ever try anything like that again while I'm around, I might just kill you myself."

Farnum was already pale from loss of blood, but his taut, sweating features seemed to turn even more ashen. "I . . . I don't know what you're talking about," he protested.

"Sure you do," Cody replied in the same soft voice. "You're nothing but a goddamned cheater, just like Pierson said. You're good at it. Pierson spotted you before I did, and I might not have seen that bottom deal even then if I hadn't been looking for it."

Farnum tried to summon up some wounded dignity to match the wound in his carcass. He said stiffly, "You're insane."

"Nope. Reckon you're the one who's a mite crazy, Farnum. You've got plenty of money, enough to buy and sell a gent like Pierson twenty times over, but still your pride makes you cheat at cards just so you can beat him." The Ranger's eyes narrowed in anger. "You could've got Miss Jermaine killed."

"But I didn't mean—"

"Just shut up," Cody snapped. "Sit there and be quiet until the doctor comes." He straightened, hooking his thumbs in his gunbelt and glaring down at Farnum.

He was good and mad, all right, for a couple of reasons. First and most important, as he had told Farnum, Marie had been in danger, and the rancher's cheating had been to blame. Cody wasn't going to be quick to forgive that. And second, he had been forced to kill Pierson—hadn't been time not to—and the Rangers' possible lead to the gang of rustlers had died along with the drifting cowhand.

On top of that, Pierson had been right, despite the fact that he was a proddy son of a bitch and probably an owlhoot. Tonight Pierson had been the victim for a change, and it had gotten him killed.

Cody sighed. He wasn't about to waste any tears on Pierson—but he wished things had worked out differently.

Doc Johnston, a tall, gaunt man with graying bushy eyebrows and bristling mustache, came loping into the saloon, looking more like a farmhand than the skilled medico he was. He crossed the room, knelt beside Farnum without asking any questions or sparing more than a glance for the dead man, and began a swift, efficient examination of the rancher's wound. A few moments later Johnston announced, "He'll live."

Sheriff Christian Burke, Del Rio's local lawman, entered the barroom in time to hear that diagnosis. Burke looked might relieved to hear the news, Cody thought. The sheriff was five or six years older than Cody, a heavyset, stolid individual with a fondness for good whiskey. Bad whiskey would do in a pinch, too, for that matter. Cody was convinced that the sheriff *wanted* to be a good lawman; he just had absolutely no imagination and very little flair for leadership.

"Heard there was a shootin'," Burke said as he came up to Cody. "Should've figured you'd be mixed up in it. Mr. Farnum get clipped by a stray bullet, did he?"

Cody gave Farnum a cold look. "Something like that." The Ranger nodded toward Pierson's sprawled body. "That gent on the floor took exception to the way the cards were being dealt. The argument might not've amounted to much if he hadn't lost his head. He shot Farnum, then grabbed Miss

Jermaine and tried to use her as a shield to get out of here. He didn't make it."

"Can see that," Burke grunted. "Reckon Miss Jermaine and the other folks around here will back up your story, Cody?"

"They saw what happened." Cody looked around when Marie didn't speak up, only to see that she had disappeared. She'd gone on up to her room, he supposed. He couldn't blame her for wanting some privacy after what had almost happened to her.

Marie's testimony wasn't needed, though. At least a dozen men in the room, including Ernest Palmatier, eagerly volunteered to share their versions of the gunfight with the sheriff. Burke listened for several minutes, then nodded his head and waved away the rest of the would-be witnesses. "don't need to hear the whole thing over again," he said. He raised his voice and asked, "Anybody here want to argue with what's already been said?"

Nobody did, and Burke nodded his head emphatically. "That's that, then. The coroner'll probably want to hold an inquest in the mornin', Cody, but I don't reckon it'll amount to much."

"I'll be there if I can, Sheriff."

★ WAGONS WEST ★

This continuing, magnificent saga recounts the adventures of a brave band of settlers, all of different backgrounds, all sharing one dream—to find a new and better life.

☐	26822-8	INDEPENDENCE! #1	$4.95
☐	26162-2	NEBRASKA! #2	$4.50
☐	26242-4	WYOMING! #3	$4.50
☐	26072-3	OREGON! #4	$4.50
☐	26070-7	TEXAS! #5	$4.99
☐	26377-3	CALIFORNIA! #6	$4.99
☐	26546-6	COLORADO! #7	$4.95
☐	26069-3	NEVADA! #8	$4.99
☐	26163-0	WASHINGTON! #9	$4.50
☐	26073-1	MONTANA! #10	$4.50
☐	26184-3	DAKOTA! #11	$4.50
☐	26521-0	UTAH! #12	$4.50
☐	26071-5	IDAHO! #13	$4.50
☐	26367-6	MISSOURI! #14	$4.50
☐	27141-5	MISSISSIPPI! #15	$4.95
☐	25247-X	LOUISIANA! #16	$4.50
☐	25622-X	TENNESSEE! #17	$4.50
☐	26022-7	ILLINOIS! #18	$4.95
☐	26533-4	WISCONSIN! #19	$4.95
☐	26849-X	KENTUCKY! #20	$4.95
☐	27065-6	ARIZONA! #21	$4.50
☐	27458-9	NEW MEXICO! #22	$4.95
☐	27703-0	OKLAHOMA! #23	$4.95
☐	28180-1	CELEBRATION! #24	$4.50

Bantam Books, Dept. LE, 414 East Golf Road, Des Plaines, IL 60016

Please send me the items I have checked above. I am enclosing $_____
(please add $2.50 to cover postage and handling). Send check or money order, no cash or C.O.D.s please.

Mr/Ms _____

Address _____

City/State _____ Zip _____

Please allow four to six weeks for delivery.
Prices and availability subject to change without notice.   LE-6/91

**FROM THE PRODUCER OF WAGONS WEST
AND THE KENT FAMILY CHRONICLES—
A SWEEPING SAGA OF WAR AND HEROISM
AT THE BIRTH OF A NATION**

THE WHITE INDIAN SERIES

This thrilling series tells the compelling story of America's birth against
the equally exciting adventures of an English child raised as a Seneca.

☐	24650	White Indian #1	$4.50
☐	25020	The Renegade #2	$4.50
☐	24751	War Chief #3	$3.95
☐	24476	The Sachem #4	$3.95
☐	25154	Renno #5	$4.50
☐	25039	Tomahawk #6	$4.50
☐	25589	War Cry #7	$3.95
☐	25202	Ambush #8	$3.95
☐	23986	Seneca #9	$3.95
☐	24492	Cherokee #10	$3.95
☐	24950	Choctaw #11	$3.95
☐	25353	Seminole #12	$3.95
☐	25868	War Drums #13	$3.95
☐	26206	Apache #14	$3.95
☐	27161	Spirit Knife #15	$4.50
☐	27264	Manitou #16	$4.50
☐	27841	Seneca Warrior #17	$3.95
☐	28285	Father of Waters #18	$4.50
☐	28474	Fallen Timbers #19	$4.50
☐	28805	Sachem's Son #20	$4.50

Bantam Books, Dept. LE3, 414 East Golf Road, Des Plaines, IL 60016

Please send me the items I have checked above. I am enclosing $_____
(please add $2.50 to cover postage and handling). Send check or money
order, no cash or C.O.D.s please.

Mr/Ms _____

Address_____

City/State_____ Zip _____

LE3 -3/91

Please allow four to six weeks for delivery.
Prices and availability subject to change without notice.